30 Years
of Publishing

1976 - 2006

BEGGING QUESTIONS

Seán Virgo

Exile Editions

30 YEARS OF PUBLISHING

2006

Library and Archives Canada Cataloguing in Publication

Virgo, Seán, 1940 -

  Begging questions / Seán Virgo.

Short stories

ISBN 1-55096-077-6

  I. Title.

PS8593.I72B44 2006   C813'.54   C2006-905007-4

Design and Composition by Homunculus ReproSet
Typeset in Minion and Stone at the Moons of Jupiter Studios
Printed in Canada by Friesens

The publisher would like to acknowledge the financial assistance of
The Canada Council for the Arts and the Ontario Arts Council.

Conseil des Arts
du Canada   Canada Council
               for the Arts

ONTARIO ARTS COUNCIL
CONSEIL DES ARTS DE L'ONTARIO

First published in Canada in 2006 by Exile Editions Ltd.
RR#1 Gen. Del.
144483 Southgate Road 14
Holstein, Ontario, N0G 2A0
info@exileeditions.com
www.ExileEditions.com

Sales Distribution:
McArthur & Company c/o Harper Collins
1995 Markham Road, Toronto, ON M1B 5M8
toll free: 1 800 387 0117   fax: 1 800 668 5788

for
Melanie

ONE

GUARDIANS

Down among the weeds, below the gravel shoulder, the earth was caked and fissured, a miniature livid-grey landscape of slump and erosion. His heels stirred up the surface dust as he jolted down; it rose and drifted back against him, coating his legs below the knees, settling on his shoes when he stopped, fine as talc. This dust, when the next rain fell, would become a potter's slip: a slick clay that would run from itself, exposing another face to be parched and blown and washed away in its turn.

Yet the weeds grew somehow. Their roots fumbled into this subsoil, and changed its nature. The lupins stood high as pines, in their own scale; the purple vetches had launched themselves over the tiny freshet ravines, and stitched an underbrush through them, snaring pockets of gravel washed down from the highway's shoulders, luring insects and seeds, hugging various tatters of human trash.

And in time, perhaps . . . .

The diesel growl of the bus came back down the river, echoing off a rock-cut, the bus itself dwarfed and vanishing round the curve a mile away. The sound lingered, and surged, and was swallowed by the valley. The riffle of the shallow, swift water returned.

He sat among the weeds, above the naked stones of the embankment, and began to go through his pockets. He had planned to scrape a small grave for his things, but pushed them down instead, one by one, through the springy vetch canopy into one of the deeper ravines. He had almost nothing, but he meant to take nothing at all.

His driver's licence, the bus ticket, the pharmacy label; a faded restaurant stub from his breast pocket, perhaps from the last time he wore this jacket, with its smell now of closet and his own ghost-sweat, years ago. *Lepanto's 9/7/84.* Nine years. Two lives. His own archaeology. July 9th? September 7th? *Table 3. 2 Persons.* Who else? *$67.73.* No clues. Not even the name of the town. He made a tent of the papers and reached in his back pocket for his money.

He counted it, despite himself. A twenty, two fives and a two. He smiled at the thought of some drifter or hitchhiker, later that summer, stumbling upon treasure. It was anonymous anyway, why should he burn it? He emptied the plastic vial between his feet and crammed the bills into it. The coins, too. A dollar eighty-two. He snapped back the cap and poked the vial out of sight through the vetches. The pills lay like a drift of candy eggs. He had three matches left in the box.

The sun was fierce on his neck, it glared back at him off the dry bankside, but he was cold through and through. As he knelt, he wrapped the jacket around him – so loose that he could pin it closed with his elbow while he struck the match. A brown worm crept up the side of his driver's licence; the flame in the sunlight was a mere shimmer of air. The printed words stood out for a moment, half of his name, iridescent on the crumpling black tent. A breath from the river scattered it through the lupin forest.

So, then. He got to his feet, breathing hard, and made his way back up to the roadside. But his back was in spasm already, his lungs fluttered against him. Now that he was here, he began to doubt his strength.

Just take your time. He would treat the road as a border – across it was another land, with its own rules, and he would learn them. He fingered the pills, like beads in his side pocket. If he took one now, before he stepped out, it could only help.

He held it under his tongue, trying to make enough saliva to wash it down. It was bitter, beneath its pink shell, crumbling and soaking up the liquid of his mouth. A fragment lodged in his throat; he had to swallow repeatedly. He would need to find water, somewhere, up in the woods. His shadow reached almost to the white median line. And as though he had taken a pleasure-drug, the blacktop seemed brighter, more defined. It seemed to float, inches above the ground.

He stopped, in the sunlight, out on the highway, and lifted his face, breathing in. The bridges were burnt now; he was touched by a kind of unreal gaiety. He raised his left leg, in a prowling slow-motion step, flourished his hands and clapped them. He was an old negro man, doing the cakewalk on this long, shiny stage, laughing back at the world. His face rehearsed the vocabulary of childhood – all the stretching and twisting contortions of monster and clown. He danced to his shadow. His jacket swinging and flapping around him, he yipped and he cackled and he howled. His lungs had come back to life. Bent forward, on tiptoe, he ran and saluted the creature that shared his stage.

The porcupine lay on its side, plump as a stuffed toy animal, its legs pointing stiffly at the forest. Its eyes were half closed, a slip of grey tongue pushed out past its front teeth. He crouched beside it, and reached for its paw. It was more of a hand, or a flipper even, its smooth pads cold against his fingers, its sheaf of blunt claws not meant for flat earth, or for highways. A coarse odour, sweaty and close, came up at his face; he'd the quick sensation of being inside the creature's lair. Then he gripped the front leg, and stood, and set out for the trees, speeding up at the sound of a car rounding the bend. But the car had seen him: it beeped three times and pulled over. He hurried on. A voice cried, "One minute, please. Excuse me, sir. Yes!"

He stood, incredulous, trapped, the porcupine dangling from his hand. He looked up through the forest where he should be climbing. The car door slammed, and feet padded towards him. He waited, there was nothing he could do. And a face peered round, smiling up at him over the porcupine. "Hello, good day," said the face, Japanese and eager: "You have a beaver here, I think." Another door slammed, a cooing girl's voice came running.

"It's a porcupine," he said. "Ahh, *por*-cupye," the face nodded happily, and turned to pass on the knowledge. "Ohhh" – the girl was broad-faced, smiling too, bobbing her head in greeting – "You shoot him?"

"No," he said, "no," not sure of their English. He made a vague semaphore at the road – "Car hit it. Killed it" – and held it up higher, by its hand, for them to see, finding himself making car-and-brake sound effects, nonplussed by this reality.

The absolute happiness of the couple beamed over him. "Please," the man said, taking his shoulder, "please." He turned as directed, towards the river, the man backing off across the black-top, adjusting a yellow camera and waving directions to the girl. Who came laughing to stand beside him. "Okay," the man cried, "Okay, like that," and clicked the shutter. "One more," and he was smiling down at the girl, still holding the porcupine out in front of him. Click.

She tugged a red-and-black notebook from her shorts' pocket. "You write down name, please," she said. "We send you photo." And she handed him a pen, while the man scurried round, taking more pictures. Well, if these were the rules .... The girl watched as he wrote. "Address, too, please, of course." Her feet were doing a little dance by themselves. This was insane. He wrote down Moira's address. On the facing page, in high-school script, the name of an RCMP corporal from the Huntsville detachment.

He succumbed to a little whirlwind of pleasantries. He was nodding and bowing, the notebook went back in her pocket, they laughed and shook hands, and ran back to the car. Then she ran back again, and the notebook came out, and he wrote down *POR-CUPINE* beside his own name. They waved and beeped, as they roared away, and he held up the trophy one more time for them. Then the road was empty, and he turned back to the forest.

It was the next stage, and perhaps he took it too quickly. The hill was not big, he could see the crest already up through the trees, but it was clumsy with moss-covered rockfalls, and he kept stumbling and slipping, losing his breath, uncoordinated. There was a thick feeling in his teeth, his hand was in spasms from the weight it was clutching. He laid the porcupine at the base of a yellow birch, without due attention, almost throwing it down. Its meek, black face stared into the hillside. Exhaustion crowded out everything but the soundscape – the jew's-harp whine of some chickadees below him, the rapid-fire knocking of a woodpecker. And by the time he took his second rest, sliding down with his back to a half-decayed stump, he could hear only the rasp of his breath, and the trundle of his heart at his eardrums. His arms and legs were shuddering with weakness.

He told himself that he had all day. A truck passed below on the highway, gearing down for the bend, and again for the climb up the valley, and he realized how much further he had to go, to get out of that world. But when he stood up, it was so much easier, like a second wind, and his feet found their way up and out of the trees.

He came out to bare rock – a flat, narrow hilltop dividing two valleys. He looked down over young trees to a crescent of water, the arm of a small lake. This was the Shield country he loved: moulded and stunted by winter, but glistening wherever he looked, in its summer skin. There was a place for him down there, waiting. Be calm, and he'd find it. Or it would find him.

He sat on the warm stone, his hands clasped round his knees; forgetting, and watching. The farther hillside, like a landscape jigsaw puzzle, was a shuffle of greens, with splashes of orange and red, premonitions of Fall, and the lances and pennants of mature single trees jutting out of the skyline. Pale, spermy figures drifted across the sky wherever his eyes moved. A solitary bird cried out overhead; a raven drifting fast and high, dipping a wing towards him in recognition. *You'll sit on his white hause-bane And I'll pike out his bonny blue eyen . . . .* He lifted his hand. "*Look for me tomorrow,*" he murmured. And was smiling.

He thought of the place that was waiting, and himself dissolving there. If the mad, suicidal parasite that was eating its way through his ribs and spine were only *something*, itself. Something distinct that could tumble out of his bones when he was finished; like amber, enduring, or ambergris to breathe again on a rich woman's skin. But it was only him. *Or that the Everlasting had not fixed His cannon gainst self-slaughter.* He felt in his pocket for another pill, and squinted at it in the sun, between thumb and forefinger. In defiance of Hamlet's meaning, he had always held on to his first misreading of those lines – of God as a grim-faced gunner, slab-lipped, slouch-hatted, squinting down from a grey battlement into a forest clearing, menacing death with Death. *You take Mary, I'll take Sue. There ain't no difference 'tween the two . . . .* He chewed the pill quickly this time, getting it down before his mouth could dry up, squirming against the bitterness. A man was a sheaf of quotations, haphazardly ordered, to be read by no one.

The porcupine smell was on his tongue now, mingled with the opiate.

He went down towards the water, breasting through spruce and young pines no taller than himself; his feet stirred up a balsamy pitch-aroma, feeling their way around submerged stumps of the trees that were logged off here a generation back. The lake was no more than fifty yards wide, the water clear and warm where the rocks sloped into the shallows. He knelt and scooped water up, one-handed, to his lips, then over his face. Dragonflies crisscrossed, close to the surface; to his right was a thicket of willow-wands, growing from rock-clefts, rooted below the water. Some creature splashed and dived out of sight to his left – the ripples came round to meet him. He dried off his hands on his jacket. He would need water; he must look for something to carry it in.

The rocks were grey, a granite with dense white veins and sills, all smoothed to one surface by time and ice. But the outcrop beyond the willows was almost pink in the sunshine, with mica-flecks winking all over it. He skirted it, seeking the end of the lake, and saw, in the same instant, the yellow canoe and the three half-naked bodies that lounged by the water.

It was too close, and too sudden, to back away. The blond girl lay on her stomach, facing him, her feet in the water. There was a glass by her outstretched hand. Her lazy eyes took him in. "Excuse me," he said, and gestured his surprise.

"It is okay," she said, "you can sit with us if you like. We shall not mind."

"No, no – I was just on my way round the lake. I didn't expect to see anyone."

The other girl was black – or her features, at least, were African: her skin had a reddish tinge, with yellow shadows, it seemed, stealing up from her ribs, beneath her breasts. She leaned on one elbow, against a small boulder, her long legs crossed at the ankles. She took off her sunglasses. "In any case, take a break," she said. "Sit down and describe your business." The blond girl laughed and the boy beside her lifted a dripping wine-bottle in salute.

"You see," he said, "we speak only English while we are in Canada. We conduct some bizarre idioms, maybe!"

The black girl patted the rock beside her: "Sit, sit," she ordered, and turned back to her friends: "So give him some wine."

The boy had a line of red beard along his jawline. Yet the hair which fanned out below his navel, from his skimpy white briefs, was a dense, flaxen scrawl. "We have no more glasses," he said.

The blond girl slid her half-empty glass towards him: "He can use mine, all the same."

It was too strange to question. The rock was warm; the stillness and company, seductive. He found himself savouring the sweetish white wine, while they idly talked and paid him no heed at all. "Are you students?" he asked, at last.

They started to laugh – everything seemed to set them off laughing together, as if the fact of their being here was some deep, shared joke. "Yes, yes," said the boy, "we are all students; but this month we are" – and he held up his forefinger, like a pedantic instructor – "fly-by-night tourists." He had moist, humorous lips, and his eyes were of different colours.

The blond girl skimmed a cigarette package across the rock, without opening her eyes or lifting her head. "Have a Kraut cancer-stick," she growled, "and give one to Ulli."

He passed the cigarettes over and reached the cigar from his inside pocket. "I was saving this for the end of my hike," he told them, "but I think I should smoke it now." His hand still smelled faintly of porcupine.

He struck a match, and reached over to light the black girl's cigarette. Her fingernails dug lightly into his wrist, and when she exhaled, the match went out. Even that set them laughing. He lit the cigar with his last match, and sat watching the blue smoke hover and stretch and then swoop away over the water.

"And where is this 'end of your hike'?" the boy demanded. His left hand rested on the blond girl's calf. She shifted, and propped her chin on her hands.

"Up there, I think." He nodded towards the hillside behind them, across the lake.

"There will be a great view, alright," said the blonde, and laid her cheek back down on the rock. She yawned, her teeth white and even, her tongue strangely pink. "If you can find an outlook."

"In the meantime" – the black girl leaned towards him, with her pale palm outstretched – "you can, perhaps, tell me what is this." The body husk was intact, though the tail was crushed, and the miniature lobster-claws, bluish-grey with their smooth, tooth-like serrations, gaped on her slender fingers.

"It's a crawfish," he said, "or what's left of one." They stared at the creature together.

The blond girl sat up abruptly, curling one leg beneath her. Her breasts were full and golden, the nipples dusky. "I will tell you what I think," she announced. "I think that every man, women and child in your country must be given one square kilometre of this wilderness, to be responsible for."

"Why do you say that?" he asked, through the others' laughter.

She sniffed contemptuously. "Because," she said, and lay down again on her stomach, "and because I think so."

The cigar had gone out. He shook the empty matchbox. The boy stood, and came up from the water's edge, pulling a lighter from the waistband of his briefs and stooping to light the cigar. "Now," he said, "I will ask you a question," and turned back to face the lake. The shallow ply of his ribs showed through the skin. His arm sketched in the whole landscape: "Can you tell me what is the oldest thing in this place?"

"The oldest thing?"

The boy did not move. The black girl's eyes were teasing.

"Alright," he said. "Well, I guess these rocks would be the oldest things."

"No," said the boy, "you are wrong. Try again."

The blond girl's laughter was deeper, less kindly than her friend's. Her green eyes were fixed on his, crinkling against the sun's glare. She reminded him of a tiger. "Try," she said.

He puffed twice at his cigar, and brushed it against the rock between his feet. The featherweight ash-nub began trickling, intact, towards the black girl's legs. She bent forward and blew at it gently; it swerved around her and rolled on down to the water. "Try again," she repeated.

It was easier not to resist. "Then the water, I guess."

She leaned back happily on her elbows. "Try again."

"Very well," said the boy, "I will give you a clue." He was jiggling the lighter from hand to hand. "It is the oldest thing in this place, *and*" – and he lowered his voice theatrically – "it is the youngest thing too. Now you tell me."

"You call that a clue?" he laughed.

"An *excellent* clue." The black girl's voice was deep and affected, mimicking someone. Was it him? Or somebody they all knew, at home perhaps? Their laughter broke over him.

"Oh I don't know," he said. "The air? The wind? . . . I give up."

Three grave expressions mocked him. Three heads shook slowly together.

"No. It is the *Echo* – watch . . . listen." The boy stretched out his arms towards the water and barked, "Hell-OH!" *Lo, lo,* came back at once from the opposite shore, and a moment later, *Lo-lo-lohh,* from somewhere up on the hillside. High behind him, out of the sun's glare, the raven cried down in response.

"Now it is your turn," the blonde said. "You must pay your penalty."

"No, no – wait a minute. How could there be an echo before the rocks?"

"It was waiting, of course," she drawled. "Is this not obvious?"

He was stung by her insolence. "It's not obvious to *me*."

"Okay," said the black girl, "then answer me this: which came first, the echo or the rock?"

"No, no," he said, "that doesn't work. The rock may create the echo, but how can the echo create the rock?"

Her chin lifted, she aimed a finger at his chest. "Suppose you were lost in the fog?" Her breasts were shivering with laughter.

"In the fog? You mean, if I were out in a boat, perhaps?"

"Very good," said the boy, "*Excellent*." He tossed the lighter, glittering, high in the air, and as soon as he caught it, lobbed it over to the black girl. She flipped it at once to the blonde, who snatched it one-handed out of the air and in the same movement, almost, sent it flying towards his face. He barely held onto it and then, with childish ferocity, he hurled it back. Their laughter went up, his mingled with theirs, and echoed across the lake. The third time around, the lighter went wild and he and the black girl scrambled to catch it. He got to it first. "End of game," the boy called. "It is yours to have for a keepsake."

"No, no," he said, and, "Always you say 'No, no'," the blonde chided. "You must begin to say 'Yes, yes.'"

"No, *no*," he laughed, and held up the dead, half-smoked cigar. "I've had my smoke for the day. I won't be needing it." He made to throw the cigar off, into the willows.

"I will take it," she said, kneeling up. "I will smoke your cigar, and I will be Chancellor of our party." She came over on hands and knees, her full lips pouting to be fed the cigar, and her comical wink made innocence out of his eyes upon her body. Her skin gave off a light, peppery scent. She drew at the lighter flame and then sat back on her heels, face to the sky, loosing the smoke from her lips in a lazy purl.

He reached for the glass beside him, and toasted her clowning. The black girl began clapping, slowly and rhythmically, hands together, then hands upon knees. He realized that for the first time in six weeks he did not feel cold. He set the glass down, and clambered to his feet.

The boy was draining the wine bottle. He gestured with it: "One moment," and wiped his mouth. "There is one thing more that you can do for us." He rummaged among the clothes in the canoe's prow, and brought out a small camera. "If you please," he said, holding it out. "Come Ulli, come Katya." They slithered into a kneeling group, practised and automatic as musicians mugging for a film crew. The boy's arm lay upon the blond girl's shoulder; his other hand brandished the bottle. The girls' hands. rested together on the black girl's thigh. Their heads tilted, their eyes were huge. The blonde let out a perfect smoke-ring as the shutter clicked.

He was half in love with them all. He wished he could carry that picture away with him, and the thought, somehow, was not bitter.

He set down the camera by the glass and the lighter and the empty matchbox. "May I have the bottle?" he asked. "I want to take some water with me."

The boy's mismatched eyes were shrewd and gentle as the bottle changed hands. In the warm shallows the bubbles came gulping to the surface. The label began to lift from the glass. The water was clear, several feet out; a fish belly flashed for a moment, the stones of the lakebed swam into focus.

When he looked up, they were back as they had been when he arrived. The black girl had her sunglasses on, the other two lay together, face down. He walked past them, unacknowledged, and to the end of the rocks. "Well, goodbye," he said, "and thank you."

"You are welcome," the black girl spoke without looking up. "Safe journey," the blond yawned, settling her cheek more comfortably on her arm. The boy raised a casual hand.

A moment later he had passed out of sight; the valley might have been empty.

And he was not cold. It was as though he'd become acclimatized. Above the treeline a cinder moon, a shade past the full, clung to the pale sky. He rounded the end of the lake, and began to climb. The wine lingered on his tongue. His breathing was warm, and regular; his back was supple; the odours of sap and bark, of dry moss and wild-currant flowers, breathed over him. When he stopped, it was to get his bearings, not from exhaustion. The slender lake was blue and unruffled below; there was no sign of the yellow canoe. The raven came back down the sky, planing under the moon's dead face. *O'er his white banes when they are bare The wind sall blaw for evermair* . . . .

His grave was waiting for him, somewhere up there. Like the spot you drift towards in the woods, to make love in, it would find him.

He drank a little water from the bottle, and moved on.

If there was nothing, so be it. He would at least be one with the elements. And now that fate and outrage had dispelled themselves, and he had left all other calls behind – across the highway, at the end of a bus ride, in the brief, uncluttered letter on his desk . . . . It was really too easy.

Once there had been forest, green upon grey, with the punctuations of ice and fire, and then forest again till the short, catastrophic ellipsis of the machines, and perhaps, again, forest. It was starting around him. And that echo? Waiting? He found himself laughing again, crying out like a child to the hillside. His *Ha* resounded, repeating itself, flocking out over the valley. There was no response this time, from the raven or down by the lake. The echoes retired themselves.

He veered to his left, towards the highest point of the ridge, following a dry stream bed like a path through the trees. It ended in a tumble of stones, dark-shagged with moss: a ruined culvert. Above it a flat shelf of ground, a clearing aslant in the hillside. He climbed up and found an old logging road, grassed over, with saplings of alder and willow in procession between the faded ruts. The air moved, up here, threading the young forest, smelling of pine resin. Almost at once he heard voices.

He'd come to the wilderness, and kept meeting people. The couple were just a few yards away, arm in arm on the trail. He felt dizzy; panic was close at hand. They wore shorts and hiking boots but drifted like Sunday strollers, so absorbed in each other that they nearly collided with him.

Their eyes focussed slowly, like dreamers wakened. He could find nothing to say. He stepped to the left, to make way, and the girl did the same. They dodged right and left together till she laughed, and put her hands on her hips. "It's like trying to get in an elevator," she said. "I'm not moving till you've passed!"

He chose to go round on the boy's side of the trail. He could sense the hostility; he had to say something. "Does this road lead anywhere?" As though mocking himself. No challenge, no edge. It would have to do.

The boy glared in distrust. His eyes lingered on the wine bottle, the city clothes. "Well, the map says it used to go right round the hill." At a glance from the girl, his wariness faded: "We're supposed to wind up where we started, down at the old rail trestle." His hand reached out again for the girl's shoulder.

Her hair was trimmed close to her skull. Her skin looked as though it had never known makeup. "Which way are you going?"

He gestured: "I came from down there."

Her eyes were so clear, and healthy. "Are you lost?"

"No, no. Just tell me where you're heading, and I'll stay out of your way." For there was sex in the air between them; he had blundered in.

How young they were. But kind, as the young can be kind.

"Have you seen the red cliff?" she said. "Have you seen the caves?"

"There are Indian pictures," the boy said, "right down by the waterline."

"I've just been wandering, so far," he told them. And smiled, stepping shyly back off the trail, to let them go.

"Just wait till you've seen the red cliff!" And she ducked in under her lover's arm as they moved off, throwing a bright glance back through the leaves to say their laughter wasn't aimed at him.

He went on, uphill from the trail. There were some old trees now, pines and maples, disfigured by wind or lightning, spared by the loggers, their bark smudged to eye-level by traces of fire. There was no true wilderness here; he would never find solitude. He couldn't go back, he could never recross that highway, yet the horror of being *found* was upon him now – the image of his dead face, a livid, dissolute bruise heaving up into the light at some hiker's eyes. And the carrying off of "the remains," the autopsies, enquiries, dental records, newspapers – worse, even, than what he had turned his back on, refusing the treatments.

And why this, now, this train of thoughts? It belonged in the other world.

The faces, too. And the names that came with them, and spelled their entitlement. Andrea, Moira, Robbie. He tried to banish them as they came – *I must be cruel only to be kind* – he had left them behind, he told them, at the end of a bus ride. Sparing them and himself. It was all in the letter on his desk. With perhaps a small postscript from Japan.

He was blundering towards the ridge, his eyes blurred with tears, shudders of cold in his chest. He could feel the cancer, a brain-like slug, a lamprey, flexing in his spine.

He was not strong enough, after all. Fate dogged him through the trees, rage clawed off all dignity. He collapsed against a low outcrop of stone. An old dog, rotting inside, panting his heart out. He could hear the sick air in his lungs, as if it surrounded him – a swamp full of creaking frog-calls and whistling birds. What would he do, stumble back to the trail? cry out to the quavering echo? Or call for the two young lovers to come for him, and carry him down to Hell?

Beyond the stone was a shallow ravine, choked with creepers and dense young trees. He raised the bottle to his lips, his wrist ashiver, and felt the water spill through him as if he were glass, or metal.

The grave was watching, waiting for him to see.

An overhang of split rock, just below him, cloaked by the saplings. And when he slid down to it, a space beneath, like an animal's lair. Even the raven could not see into this place. It smelled of ferns, and darkness. The weight of his body helped him over the edge. The fall jarred his bones; a patter of earth followed after. The young pines sprang upright again, as he edged back under the rock.

The dark slash of stone; the sky beneath it, a thin, flat line; and the needle-fret of young branches, backlit and luminous from the day outside.

There was the sound of water running, somewhere, as if the little ravine were an ear for the hillside. And voices faintly, too; murmuring, laughing.

The reprieve from terror.

He wedged himself back against the rock wall, mocking the tumour. And spilled the pills out beside him, the fake-coloured candies, in a curving line.

He took them one at a time. A pill, a draught of water.

Was there a song line, *I'll die with a bottle in my hand,* or had he just made it up?

If there was nothing, so be it: he had always said that. But he'd lived with the vision since childhood – from a picture? a dream? – of the long valley which followed Death: a road curving at dusk along a riverside, towards a stone gorge, and the rush of a waterfall. And somewhere along that road, unvisualized but waiting nevertheless, the Guardians.

There would be riddles to answer, prescriptions to recite, before the gorge was reached. And an animal helper, perhaps, running on before.

He was warm again. The bottle rolled off, into the shadows. He lay in his green tent, hearing those young voices filter back from somewhere below. The rock was wonderfully gentle against his spine.

The green faded out. A girl's voice was crying out to Jesus.

He watched for the Guardians. They might bear cameras. They might be lazy, and naked.

TELEGONY

for Niamh

It was strange to come down from the valley, not into brighter day but to this vaporous lowland. With the late, diffused sun in their faces, the land flowed away from them, in blurred striations of grey and dull blue and indeterminate browns which merged at the milky horizon.

"It's like entering a water colour," she said, "one of those moody landscapes that are just tricks of the brush when you look closely. There's nothing there really – you have to make it up for yourself."

Martin's hand dropped from the wheel, stroking the inside of her leg for a moment. "The sea's just down there," he said, "it's real enough, you'll see. If it weren't for the mists, we'd have seen it already."

She rolled the window down further; the wind riffling her hair against her neck. "I can smell it," she said, "I can, really. You're right." And it was a thrill to have it confirmed this way, like an animal questing by scent. The opaque, hollow taint of the ocean. But to pass through a whole country, she was thinking, in less than a day – it was almost incredible. And the different land-scapes. Just half an hour back it had been narrow bridges, and twisting lanes, the flitter and dapple of cramped, sunlit trees over tumbling streams. And before that the bare flanks of the foothills; the sheep and the stones. Yet they had eaten lunch in England, in an upland Shropshire pasture where the horizon was only three meadows away . . . . Whole, separate worlds, but scaled down. At home they would scarcely have crossed half the province in the time they'd been driving today. She felt, in her passenger seat, an inverse sort of jet lag.

The weather, too. "The weathers," as Martin's grandmother had said, and she was right – you could see them coming, entire, as if weather systems were creatures of valleys, or hillsides, instead of continents. Even now a slow rift of blue was dividing the clouds, just below where the sky was most luminous. She watched without speaking, as the car geared down and turned onto a wider road, and then there were slanting pillars of light, like rays through church windows, gilding the rent in the cloud-wrack, pouring colour, and shadow, back into the world; and then the sun itself, and the wet roofs of the town ahead, and the bright swathe of the sea.

The little town, scarcely three streets deep, curved off above the grey sands. Slate rooftops gleamed in the watery light of the sky. They crept left, between narrow houses and stores, the hiss of the car's tires suddenly magnified, the smell of wet dust and tarmac as strong as the breath of the sea. "There," Martin said, and swung into a lane, barely wide enough for the little English car. *Parking for Taliesin Arms* said the board up ahead.

They parked by the hotel's back steps. Martin let out a breath and stretched back in his seat, smiling into her face. "Duty's done," he said, "we've got two whole weeks to ourselves." "But it wasn't so bad," she murmured, and leaned up against him, "was it?"

"Could have been worse." The laugh lines crinkled about his eyes: "To reassure you one more time, you were wonderful, I was proud of you – they did like you." She kissed him, softly: "They're easy to like, your family. It's nice to know where you came from." "Ah," he said, and swung open the car door, "but I've come a long way." He got out, and went back to open the trunk. "Let's get settled," he called. "Let's get out for a walk before sunset."

It was plain, but exotic: the couple at the desk quiet and friendly, casually switching from Welsh to English and back. There were carved wooden chairs in the lobby, and a spinning wheel, splay-legged and ancient, stood by the low brick fireplace. It was clean, and dark; and somewhere close by sweet bread was baking. The girl who led them upstairs must have been seventeen, but her clothes and complexion, her straight dark-brown hair were a child's. She went ahead into their room, threw open a window looking out on the bay, and bent to turn back their bed on her way to the door, handing Martin the key with a little bob of her shoulders that was almost a curtsy. They heard her singing her way down the stairs.

The billowing curtains relaxed as he closed the door. The sea was a long way out, the slope of wet sands a glaze in the late sunlight, full of scattered clouds. There were only two, distant figures on the beach – a man, perhaps, with his dog. She turned from the window: "Can I take a bath first, before we go out? Would you mind? I've got cramps starting up in my leg."

"You okay?" He looked up from the case he was unzipping: "Did it just begin now?"

"Yes, it's nothing – really." She smiled at the awkward concern in his eyes. "Just sitting too long on the way, I guess. I'll relax in the tub."

"I'll run it for you."

"No, Martin – *relax*. I'm just fine." Her fingers pressed on his shoulder as she stepped around him: "Why don't you phone your kids, while I'm in there?"

He had set their bags down at the foot of the bed. She knelt to pull out her wash-bag, and then leaned heavily forward on her hands, almost falling, as nausea uncoiled below her ribs. She held still for a moment, the bile coming up in her throat, her temples suddenly cold, and wet.

He leaned back against the bed. "No," he said. "I want this to be just for us." His eyes were closed, he was smiling. "Anyway, it's only one in the afternoon back there."

She breathed in, and out, and in, and felt the blood surge and drain in her cheeks as she straightened up. She smiled at him, hastily. "Come visit me, then," she said, "anytime you want," and ten minutes later he did come, and sat on the edge of the bath, trailing his hand in the water beside her.

"Feeling okay now?"

"Mmm." She slipped further down, till the water covered her shoulders. Her hand reached for his. "Just too long in the car," she said, "I'm getting wimpy! But oh, this feels good."

She lapped the water across herself, and reached for the soap, toying with it, tracing it over her breasts. "They're getting huge," she grumbled, half proud, half mortified. "They're going to be ruined, aren't they?"

He laid his palm on her belly. The steam from the bath had misted his glasses; he squinted over them: "A mother's breasts, her nipples, have got far more personality."

"Well, thank you," she said. "So I don't measure up to Monique's!"

He drew back his hand, and reached for a towel from the door-rail. With his glasses off, frowning down as he tried to dry the lenses, he looked older and younger at once, vaguely helpless. "I don't think that way, 'Stina, you know I don't."

"Well I do," she flashed. And after a moment, with a mock pout at her own petulance:"I can't help it!"

He put back his glasses, and stared at her. His eyes pleaded, and twinkled, and then roamed down across her body. They were friends again.

Now *her* hands embraced her stomach. Her navel had opened out and was flush with her belly already, like a pale vaccination mark. "Do women always get stretch marks?" She reached for his hand again: "Don't be cross with me – did Monique get them?"

"Yes," he said, and looked at her gravely with that strange courtly loyalty he kept for his wife, despite everything; as if any sharing of the old, lost privacies was close to betrayal. "She got them suddenly, in the fifth month, with Dezzie. She's always felt disfigured."

She did not speak. She must not intrude on this.

His eyes held hers for a moment. "They're only damage if the love is damaged," he said, and looked down sadly, speaking to his hands. "When I think of her now, the things she would least expect, the signs of the children, the signs of her aging: they're what I feel the most . . . tenderness for."

She lay almost torpid for a minute. "Okay," she said suddenly, with one of those shifts of energy that alarmed and delighted him, "I'll be out in five minutes. Let's hit the beach!"

There was one low star in the West as they walked, hand-in-hand, down from the street outside the hotel, through ankle-deep sand, and onto the hard-packed strand. There were no other lights ahead, except for one pulsing shaft far off on the headland, but their shadows preceded them, cast by the meagre green street lamps, almost to the water's edge. The sea was a dark, sleeping emptiness; white hems of foam came whispering towards their feet, though every so often a sound, like a breaking plank in the darkness, warned of the energy there, just a few yards out.

They stood together, shivering already but entranced, their lips cold as they touched. The little town was a fairyland from here, the beach like a mirror, with tide-marks of sea-coal and shell-dust etched into it, while the actual lights in the buildings beckoned warmth and haven. She looked down, and clutched his arm: "I can feel the sea pulling the sand out from under me." "It's true," he said, "you can even see it – look. 'Sands running out!'"

Safe on the edge of the world, they held hands again and walked back, heads down in the shore wind, retracing their footprints through the maze of reflected colours. Night and the ocean soughed at their backs, as though a high cave were releasing them.

Out of the wind, they strolled down the front street, gazing in shop windows, spying on customers in the one open restaurant. Themselves, they chose to buy whelks and chips from a kiosk, and eat as they walked. "You'll love them," he said, "I haven't had whelks in twenty years." The vendor gave them huge portions. "It's too early in the year," she said, "I should have waited till May

Day to open – there's no one in town at all, just you Americans."
"We're Canadian," 'Stina told her. "Ah, *sheedan*," the woman
smiled fondly as she drizzled vinegar into the cardboard cones,
"isn't that what they all say!"

He showed her, in a shop doorway, how to winkle her shellfish out with the wooden pick, at the same time clutching the
wax-paper chip bag. "Go on," he laughed, "be bold! They're
chock-full of vitamins for you both!" The sensation, after her
first doubtful taste, was almost narcotic. So little meat for such
dense-shelled creatures, yet the secret, explosive juices spread
over her palate. She could visualize minerals and deep ocean
serums thronging into her blood. She could hardly get enough;
she kept pilfering the narrow sea-snails from Martin's package.
"I'm in love with Wales," she announced. "Do we *have* to move
on?"

The window-bay facing her was crowded with souvenirs: little costume dolls, with high-hats and brooms, like hallowe'en
witches; and scallop-shells painted with sea gulls and blue sky;
and thick sticks of candy with the town's name running through
them. "We agreed to go somewhere that was new to us both," he
said. 'No echoes, 'Stina, remember?"

There were mugs and T-shirts and plaques in the window,
too – generic trash for the tourists, with arch, corny slogans. "But
it's up to you," he added. "We can do whatever we like." And then,
"Look," he said, "love-spoons – they must have come back into
fashion." At the foot of the showcase they'd been leaning against,
set off by a runner of scarlet serge, were wooden spoons in a row,
polished and blond, their flat handles fretted with hearts and
nostril-like swirls. "My grandmother had two," he said, "hanging
up in her kitchen." He squatted, to look more closely. "They're
engagement tokens. One was from her fiancé who died in the
war; the other was carved by my grandad."

Above the spoons were two jewellery displays, their moss-
green cushions studded with lockets and rings, all openwork
gold, in the style of the love-spoons below. She bent to look

closely: "They're beautiful, Martin; they're really lovely things." And, turning away, "This store is so schizophrenic. One window of junk, and then this . . . . Like a bookstore staying in business by selling skin-mags."

She drew him away by his arm, and on down the sidewalk. The street was empty, the sea completely invisible. The glimpses she caught, between curtains, of people's lives could have been from another century. She could feel a strange energy building in her, as if she had stumbled into a place that recognized her. "Oh if I were Welsh," she exclaimed. "Why do you never say that you're Welsh? This place is enchanted!"

He looked down at her face, a little distrustful of this shift in mood. "I'm Canadian, sweetheart," he said, with a gravity that made her want to giggle. "I chose what I am. And besides," he shook his head, yielding to the mockery in her eyes, "it was only my mother's family – somewhere we came in the summer, as kids. It didn't mean much; just a few songs: '*Land of our Fathers,*' '*Hob y deri dando.*'"

At the end of the street were dark, narrow steps going down to the sands. They crossed over instead, and turned back towards the hotel.

"I never heard them speak Welsh," he told her, "except to the farmers . . . . Stop laughing at me!"

"But 'Hobby derry down?'" she cried. "Is that what you said?"

"'*Dando.' Hob y deri dando.*" He sang out two lines, in a nasal, cracked tenor, and broke into laughter himself. But she danced away, onto the street, fitting the words to the tune of *O Canada*: "Hobb-y -Der-y-*Down*, Oh Hobby, Derry, Down . . . . What does it mean, anyway?"

"Buggered if I know ," he shrugged. "*Go home loudmouth yankee*?" He looked so proud of her, as he always did when she lured him into frivolity. "Anyway," he challenged, "listen who's talking – you don't know a word of your parents' language."

"That was different," she said, coming back to his side. "They were immigrants, they wanted me to belong."

Across the street was the souvenir store again. "We have to go back there tomorrow," she told him, "and buy something repulsive for my sister." And she was off once more, strutting towards the hotel, her walk on the wild side: "And the coloured girls sing *Hobb-yderr – yderr-yderrydown, Hobb-yderr-yderr-yderrydown—*"

"Cut it out, 'Stina, they'll think we're pissed."

"I am," she said, "I'm intoxicated. With Wales, and the sea, and you, my love, and freedom, and, oh God, Martin, nothing can get at us here." She opened her coat, and thrust out her stomach at the hotel steps. "I'm a Welsh pumpkin," she told the deserted street, "and my advice to you all is 'HOBBY DERRY DOWN!'"

"It's *dando*, for Christ's sake, not *down!*"

She grabbed at his arm, and headed for the hotel door: "Oh Jesus, I need to pee."

She was always having to pee these days. When she'd finished, she washed and undressed, and rinsed out her tights and panties in the sink, hanging them up on the shower-head. Halfway through brushing her teeth, she felt the taste of shellfish and vinegar at war on her tongue with the toothpaste and stopped, staring back at herself in the mirror, the toothbrush still at her lips. She had stood like this from her childhood, in the same pose, watching herself change, but now the changes had overtaken her. It was almost as though she'd hit puberty in a day, and been conscious of it. This new body – her eyes drifted down in the mirror – the new person it was making of her. She started to brush again, slowly, still watching herself.

When she left the bathroom, she wasn't sure quite how long she'd been in there.

He was lying, stretched out on the bed, and shaking with laughter. "Shh," he said, shifting to let her crawl in between the sheets. "Listen."

Behind the headboard, through the wall, someone was making love. A bed was squeaking, fast and regular, almost mechanical. She could hear no human sounds.

He took off his glasses and set them beside the lamp. "I'll leave the best part for *your* ears," he whispered, and leaned across the bed, to grin down at her. He touched his lips to her cheekbone, and his hand slipped gently to her breast. "I won't be long."

She lay there, listening to water run in the bathroom, and the unrelenting bedsprings through the wall. She wanted nothing but the curtain's whisper and the sea beyond. She pulled out a pillow and buried her face beneath it. And there she returned to the face in the mirror, the body that owned it. "Who am I, now?"

She'd fought for this for three years; she'd endured and she'd won, and who was she?

When he got in beside her, she peeped up from under her pillow and reached out for him. Her ritual gesture, pressing her palm there, against his breastbone. It was one of the places she cherished most in his body, that she visualized when they were apart.

"They're still at it?" His head thumped down on the pillow. "It's incredible!"

She didn't speak. The sounds in the next room went on. She turned away, pulling the sheet up over her face.

His fingers played at her neck, and moved on to touch her lips. "Don't you find it kind of exciting?"

"No I don't." She looked back at him over her shoulder. "Do you?"

"It doesn't turn you on, just a little?"

She settled on her back. "Actually," she said, "it's like finding someone else's turds in the toilet."

He snorted with laughter, and for a moment the sounds through the wall ceased. They began to snicker together, into the pillows, uncontrollably. Then *jeek-jeek-jeek*, the bedsprings started in again.

He hugged her against him: "Do you want to compete?"

"I just want to lie here like this and listen to the sea."

"If those sex fiends ever let up!"

"I love you, Martin." "I love you, too." This was his bed face, his eyes free of glasses, completely focussed on hers. But in less than a minute they closed, and his breathing changed. It amazed her, always, that he could fall into sleep like that, when he was relaxed. And she thought of the other times, his tortured insomnias in the last two years; how she'd wake from a dream in the early hours to find him watching her. They had gone through so much together.

A cry made its way through the wall; it sounded suspiciously stagey. Maybe grateful, she thought. In the sense of 'relieved!' But the bedsprings, at least, after two or three lengthy groans, were at peace.

And she *could* hear the curtain, brushing their casement, and a distant pouring that must be the sound of the sea.

The lamp was on his bedside table. When she reached across to it, her right breast leaned upon his cheek. He was so still, his breath almost undetectable. She drew back for a moment; this must have been the face his mother had known, bending over him, asleep in his narrow bed.

She turned off the light, and carefully moved his arm from the pillow before she lay back, open-eyed in the silence as the window reinvented the room. The back of her hand lay against Martin's ribs; if she closed her left eye, his profile loomed on the pale twitching curtain.

His beloved face. He has been so good, she thought, all of this week. Indulging her. Sharing the novelty. Never condescending. Never embarrassed. "He *is* a good person," she thought. "He is innocent and unselfish, and I don't deserve him." She felt for his hand, soft and unguarded in sleep. All of those times he had watched *her* like this, guarding her dreams, he said.

She was happy! "I am," she murmured, "that's what it is – I'm happy." And felt no superstitious dread speaking those words to the room.

He was dressed, as usual, before he woke her: "See you in half an hour?" he said. "Downstairs, for breakfast? I'm going to get a paper and taste the air – it's beautiful out. Sit up and take a look."

The room was full of light. As soon as he'd left, she sat up and pulled the coverlet round her shoulders. Not a whisper of nausea. She slithered across the bed and went to the window. He was crossing the street, with his characteristic short strides. "This is the man I love," she thought, watching the sparse, vulnerable hair at his crown. He'd put on the beloved Siwash sweater that was almost as old as she was, its spreadeagle pattern dark between his shoulders. And he went straight to the souvenir shop.

She was humming a TV jingle. What would it be – one of those spoons? No, it would be a locket, or a ring. Yes, a ring. She hugged the coverlet to her, and felt again that love and gratitude for this place, as though they had won through at last to the Principality of Love and could feel truly married.

He was still out when she came downstairs. She sat at a table for two in the small, low-ceilinged dining room, and the young girl from last night brought coffee in a pewter jug and hot rolls wrapped in a napkin. "Did you sleep well, Miss?"

"Wonderfully," 'Stina told her. "This place is enchanted."

The girl smiled. There was a clear simplicity about her face and movements. "We like it," she said.

"Were you born here?"

"I was, yes. I come back to help out in the summers."

A young man called out, in Welsh, from the kitchen half-door, and the girl answered briskly, with mockery in her voice, so that they both laughed aloud. 'Stina felt no exclusion; she was charmed, in fact. So different from how her parents had used Romansch, to keep secrets from the children, to work out their griefs and quarrels.

"Do you think in Welsh or English?" she asked.

"Either one, Miss. Just now we're learning to think in Swahili."

"Swahili!"

"We're away for a year this September, to Kenya. Volunteers." She gestured across the room: "My boyfriend and I."

'Stina lifted her cup to her lips. It was better coffee than any they'd had in England. "What will you do in Africa?"

"We'll be starting a clinic, in a hill village." She watched 'Stina's expression with a gentle triumph. "We've just finished medical school."

"But you don't look much more than sixteen."

"I'll be glad of that when I'm forty, my boyfriend tells me."

Martin was standing by the table. "The strangest thing just happened," he said.

But she didn't really hear him. "Can you believe that girl is a doctor?" she said, watching the slender figure head back to the kitchen. "I thought she was in high school. Thank Christ she didn't ask me what *I* do!" And then, "Sorry," she said. "What happened, did you say?"

"The strangest thing," he repeated, and sat across from her, pulling his chair in to the table. "I saw a girl."

"Oh la," she said. "So fickle so soon!"

But he frowned through her words. "She was 12 or 13, Dezzie's age, in a store down the street." He reached for the coffee pot but did not lift it. "I'm sure I knew her mother," he said, "the identical face." He looked up: "God, 'Stina, if I hadn't been alone – I mean if you'd been with me – I'd have asked her: 'Is your mother's name Myra?' It *had* to be. But why here?"

"So who's Myra?"

He poured his coffee and topped up her cup. "It's uncanny," he said. "She was a girl I spent a month with at my grandmother's place. Years ago, I mean. The summer before I came to Canada."

"Sounds romantic."

"Oh, it was that." His mouth, with that little grin pulling at it, looked rather silly. His thumbs broke into the crust of a bread roll and tore it in two. "We were young," he said, "Young and free – and horny!" The crow's feet stretched with his smile.

"Charming!"

"Yes, well. But what a weird coincidence. And you can't just walk up and accost a 12-year-old girl."

She felt irritation pinching her brow. She tried to speak lev-elly. "Where was this magic interlude?"

"My grandparents' cottage. They'd moved to England by then." She wanted to say *Don't talk with your mouth full.* "It's only about twenty miles from here, actually."

"They still own it?"

"No, sold it years ago. Too much upkeep." He helped himself to another roll.

"Maybe she bought it. Your 'Myra.'"

He laughed. "Oh no. You don't understand the Brits, sweet-heart. I gave her a holiday, that's all – time out from her real life."

"You're looking smug, Martin."

"You jealous?"

"I won't stoop to answer that, as you would say. Did you keep in touch?"

"No. A postcard came; I didn't get it for months." His hand reached over for hers. "It was a simpler world, 'Stina. We were very clear about things."

The waitress moved in, as though she'd been waiting for a break in their talk. "My mother asked, would you be staying tonight, and will you want dinner?"

"No, we're driving on to Angelsey," Martin said. "We'll be get-ting the night ferry."

"It's an overdue honeymoon," 'Stina told her.

The girl bobbed her head, and spoke a few rapid words, as if rehearsed.

"Is that a Welsh blessing?"

"It's Swahili, Miss. *May the scorpions fly from your footsteps.*"

"No scorpions round here, I hope," Martin laughed.

"We'll take no chances," the girl said. The wink that she flashed to 'Stina was so swift and incongruous, it might not have happened at all.

On the way up the stairs, where the landing turned, 'Stina ran her hand up Martin's back, under the thick wool sweater. "Was she beautiful?"

"Oh, *you*," he said, and stopped, and held her to him. "I thought so, of course. But what did I know – I hadn't met *you* yet."

"Or Monique," she said tartly, "or Wendy, or Susan."

"You've an evil mind." He touched a finger to her nose. "You hoard up things I don't even remember telling you."

And in their room, when he'd set their cases on the bed, she said, "Why don't you take me there, to the cottage? Revisit the old ghosts."

"Cerig 'las?" he said. "I don't know if I could find it. The scale of everything seems to have changed."

"What did you call it?"

"*Rhyd y cerig 'las.* The ford of the blue stones. There's a stream there full of amethysts from an old lead mine."

"Riddy kerry glass, Hobby derry down – does everything in Welsh go to the same tune?"

As he folded yesterday's clothes into his suitcase he started to tell her about the little valley, and the grey farmhouse with its high barn perched by the streamside. But she scarcely heard him, wondering that her desire should return like this, wanting him now, and through him, somehow, the boy she had never known, carefree and wanton, younger even than she was now.

She pulled him, astonished and eager, down onto her, pushing the cases off the bed. The fumbling and tugging at clothes was an old, neglected excitement. She clutched at the back of his neck, lifting her mouth to his, with her eyes open. It was almost a challenge as if they were boys together, roughhousing eye to eye. Could he sense this – he must – that she was this stronger creature, that she had changed, was truly becoming herself? There. But how she loved him, and he was hers now. And it had been a week, no, more than that – not once since they'd crossed the Atlantic. Impossible!

Then something close to terror froze her beneath him. She could feel, while the joy-ripples threaded her stomach, the butterfly tremors of their child. "Oh, be still, Martin," she moaned, and started pushing at his chest. "Are you all right?" he breathed. "I think so yes, but, oh, did you feel it?" And realized it *was* all right.

"The baby," she said, and found his eyes again: "We were making too much commotion," and a giggle came out that rode the last spasms through her belly. "He was banging on the ceiling for us to keep it down!"

"Huh," he said. "*He!*" and rolled away. "Why be so sure of that? Sounds like a girl, to me." He teased the hair off her temple, laughter worming its way through his lover's gaze. "Territorial," he whispered, "jealous, conniving – bossy," and lunged at her ear, fastening his lips on it, making cavernous growls that might have been *A girl, I'm a girl,* and which made her squirm and cry out like a happy teenager. When had he last done that? They *were* on holiday.

"I bet I *could* find it," he said. "I should."

"Should what?"

"Find Cerig 'las. Let's go look, today. You'd love it."

She wasn't sure, now. She'd got all she wanted from that memory, but . . . .

"We'll stay one more night," he said, sitting up. And,

"Okay," she said. "Give me 'ten'."

There were mountains, this time – alpine peaks and snow-lined corries rising before them, higher past every ridge, from this pocket-sized land. Yet the road they travelled was almost a forest trail. "That's what it is," Martin said, as though chiming in with her thoughts, "—all these trees: they're growing them everywhere. That's why the things I've been looking for aren't there. They're all buried in plantations."

They drove on, singing to the tapes she'd prepared back home. *R.E.M.*, and *Rush* and Melissa Etheridge. Tunes he had learned from her; that Monique, he told her, had jeered at: "*Variations on a mid-life crisis.*" The car was a capsule of their times, winding through forest and tiny farm hamlets into the hills.

Then, "Yes," he cried, "look!" They had passed a small church on a hillock above a crossroad.

"What is it?"

"That shiny slate rock," he said. "We kids used to slide down it." He turned right and then right again, up the narrowest of lanes. And there was a sign, blue celtic lettering upon brown: *Rhyd y cerig 'las. Open May to September.* "And that's how you spell it," he said. "Must be a bed and breakfast."

The lane climbed and dipped for a straight half mile and then swerved below a gap in the hills through which, for a moment, she saw the mountains again, clear in the sunlight, almost unnatural.

"God, this is fun," he said. "That's the ford, just down there."

They bumped through the narrow stream, and parked. He went at once down to the water and squatted beside it, rolling his sleeve up. "This must be what Switzerland smells like," she thought, watching the sedges shake in the light wind, all down the stream side. She reached in the car for her camera, and shot him twice as he came back towards her.

"There," he held out his hand, "—*Cerig 'las.*"

The purple, translucent stones were like chunks of candy, full of veins, strangely heavy. She held them as talismans, and turned a slow, full circle, drinking the valley in.

He was fidgeting, eager. "Let's see what they've done to the house."

The track gave out at the next rise. There was a small gravelled place for parking, and below them a footbridge over a smaller stream; and the house. He took her hand, as they crossed the bridge. "Nothing's changed, very much. Here's where we used to swim."

"You and 'Myra'?"

"That, too," he grinned. "Come on."

There were standard roses in pots, all blooming, on the flag-stone patio. Other plants thronged at the panes of a small con-servatory, beside the dutch door. "That's new," he said, "and so are those fruit trees."

The top of the door was ajar. A woman's face appeared: "I'm afraid we're not open," she called, "not till this weekend."

She came out to the patio, removing her glasses: "I suppose I could manage a simple tea, since you're here." The glasses hung at her breast from their necklace. Her smile wavered.

"Martin?" she said.

They stood staring at each other, and 'Stina seemed to have stepped into Limbo. This patio with its roses was a floating stage which she could watch from the shadows, but never step onto.

For a bitter instant she thought, "He planned this. He knew." For this was certainly his 'Myra.'

But the look on his face was unfeigned. His hands went fishing for words in the air.

"This is Christina, my wife. My young wife," he added absurdly.

"Hello, Christina." The woman held out her hand. She had wonderful hands, strong and refined at once. Through Martin's eyes, 'Stina acknowledged their beauty. Her own short fingers were, she knew, her one blemish for him.

"You're lovely," the woman said, as though she both meant it and somehow didn't really care.

Martin was talking too fast. "So it *was* your daughter I saw this morning. You know, that's why we came. I was sure she was yours, and that got me talking about Cerig 'las, and – here we are."

"Yes., that would be Olwen," the woman nodded. Her eyes were alert to 'Stina's discomfort. "They should be back any time."

It seemed to 'Stina that she must establish herself. And give Martin the chance to calm down, as well. Their eyes had not met through all this. She cupped one of the yellow tea roses, and bent to smell it. "Lovely," she smiled, and, "Have you got other kids, then, Myra? It is 'Myra' isn't it?"

The woman's eyes were deep brown; for a moment, haunted. Her chin lifted slightly: "I had a son. A little boy. He died."

"How awful." Instinctively, 'Stina's arms cradled her stomach.

"Yes it is," said the woman. "Well, you'd better come in, now you're here."

Like a child dismissed, 'Stina stood there, quite still. What response had she expected? *Oh, it's all right? It was a long time ago? Life goes on?* She bowed her face again to the yellow rose.

And heard Martin, inside the house: "'Stina's having our baby, in September."

"Ah, September." Almost as though there were some foolishness in that month.

She marched up to the door. Where a huge dog met her, its piebald shaggy face at the height of her breast. It stared up with queer amber eyes. Its yawn was a deep, toothed funnel.

"Well, what have you made of yourself, Martin?" This Myra, standing beside a pine dresser across the room, was impressive, all right. Her elegant, loose-fitting pantsuit, the austere features, the subtly generous mouth. And Martin, lolling in a rocking chair, as though he were visiting alone.

He threw back his head, with that merry, self-deprecating laugh that had first singled him out for her, from the herd. Yet his answer was so predictable, she could have recited it for him. "I'm a traffic controller." He laughed again. "I make sure every red light in Burlington will turn against you!"

All at once, as though a cyclone were sucking the air from around them, the valley tensed, and filled up with sound. The windows trembled, the dog let out a low moan that sustained itself eerily, and an aircraft came over the house, screaming, it seemed, by the rooftop, and was gone again. The dog's keening fell to a whimper. Its great head pushed against 'Stina's breast. The backwash of jet engines eddied round the house, and subsided.

"Here, Telegony. Let her through." The dog turned and padded back into the house, thumping down with a deep sigh in the corner.

"He won't hurt," Myra said. "Come on in."

"What did you call him?"

"Telegony."

"Never mind the dog," Martin said. "What the hell was that plane about?"

"R.A.F. Fighter planes. We're a practice range two days a week." Myra felt behind her and rummaged a cigarette from a wooden box on the dresser. She lit it with a slim malachite lighter. Close up, the skin at her neck betrayed her age; her upper lip, 'Stina guessed, had been shaved.

"So much for rural peace!"

"It's been worse. Most of the planes are still in Iraq, on patrol."

"You've got visitors," 'Stina said. "There's a truck across the bridge."

"That's Brion and Olwen." Myra came past, to the door, and her hand rested on 'Stina's wrist for a moment as though, off guard, such gestures were natural to her.

Martin got out of his chair and came to the doorway. His eyes skimmed from hers, he patted her arm like a stranger.

The girl, it was true, was her mother's young image, though there was something about her, too, like the girl at the hotel. She was shy, and polite, and direct.

"This is Martin Herrick," Myra said. "Iris Williams' grandson. He knew this house as a young boy." She took two shopping bags from her daughter. "And this is his young wife, Christina."

Myra's husband came up, with a quick, ducking motion, to shake their hands. He was shorter than Martin, but he dwarfed him with his energy. Each weaving movement was part of a dance. Like a boxer, she thought, or a sailor. From beneath his black brows, his glance was a quick, grey bird's. His body spoke through the rough woven tunic, with its wide smock pockets. Beside him, Martin was flat-footed, pallid, repressed – until he turned to the girl.

"I wonder," he said, "if that spring is still there on the holt, up in the hazels. Where the gravel dances in the white pool?"

"It's there," she said, "yes." And looked up at him frankly, with eyes almost dark as her mother's. "It's my favourite place."

"Ah," he dropped his voice. "Then I'll tell you *my* name for it, if you'll tell me yours." And, in a whisper, "When no one's listening."

She laughed with pleasure. They were watching a girl, on the brink of young womanhood, being lured back to innocence. "I put my two goldfish there, every Spring. They went in last week."

"So you bring them inside, for the Winter."

"Yes, I do."

"Then they must have names."

She looked around, and back to him. "Dan and Una."

"*Rewards and Fairies.*"

That young laugh again. "You *know.*"

"Shall we help your Dad? Looks like your truck's full of groceries." And they were off at once, towards the footbridge.

"He's good with young people," Myra said.

"Oh, he misses his own kids."

"And here we go," she thought, "'Stina the homebreaker."

"Come inside. Will you help me make tea?"

But 'Stina just watched, in the marvellous, gas-fired kitchen, with its raku pots and Dalmatian tiles, and answered questions.

"His youngest, Desirée – Dezzie – is the same age as Olwen."

"And how do they treat you?"

She wanted to like this woman. She wanted to be liked.

"They tolerate me, I guess. I tried too hard at first."

Myra was slicing cucumber, mushrooms, tomatoes into a bowl. An expensive knife; sure, elegant movements. "It can't be easy," she said.

"It's been a terrible year, a terrible two years for us.

"Most of all for Martin, of course," she felt she must add.

But she wanted to say: "I'm a grown up, too, you know, not a selfish kid." Myra was just too calm, in the silence, just neutral. And stern, perhaps, with her glasses back on.

The great dog looked in at the kitchen door. 'Stina called out, "Teleggeni, here," grateful for the distraction. It came straight to her, pressing against her thigh. "He's got such eyes," she said, rubbing the rough head gently between its ears, "and I love these Welsh names – like our hotel, *The Taliesin Arms*, and Olwen, and Hobby Derry Down and Kerry Glass and Teleggeni."

Myra was smiling but not, as Martin would say, 'at full throttle.' She reached for some plates from a cupboard, so that 'Stina had to move over.

"It could sound like Welsh, I suppose," Myra said, "now you mention it. But no, Telegony means . . . well, that an earlier father leaves something in the womb, I suppose. That he influences later children by another man."

"Is that true?"

"Well, Telegony's mother was a pure-bred Gelert, and so was his father, no question. Solid grey. But look at those colours, and the plumy tail." She laughed at 'Stina's glance: "And no, no gay-blade mongrel slipped over the wall. Not a chance. If one had tried, I imagine he would have got eaten, not romanced!"

"So?"

"Some breeders like to put first-time bitches to a smaller dog, a mongrel, most often. Cerridwen – that's the dam – had a litter by a farm collie."

"And that's where his colours come from?"

But Myra had turned already to the door, where Martin and her daughter stood laden with shopping, and as she efficiently, cheerfully unpacked and organized, 'Stina felt useless, excluded again. She crouched like a child, with her arm across Telegony's shoulders, hiding herself in the coarse mane of his neck, the damp odour, as if she were absorbed in their friendship. Resentment blazed in her towards all of them. Martin was all cheer and unnoticing eyes.

"You've made the house seem twice as big," he gushed. "It's really marvellous." And, turning at last to 'Stina, but as if she were just some outsider: "They've made it a restaurant – *Fine Dining*, imagine. A three-star rating. People come from all over." He was caught up in his own enthusiasm. She wanted to hit him.

"You can make a living that way?" she asked.

"We manage." Myra was packing jars into a cupboard, and did not trouble to turn her head. "I do fabric designs, too, and there's everything Brion makes, and my paintings, of course." She took a last package from Martin. Her "thank you" seemed like a caress.

"You're an artist?"

She did turn this time, her fine-boned face all attention. Her glasses were poised in her right hand. Was that mockery, in the carefully made-up eyes? "Martin didn't tell you that?"

"I'd never heard of you till this morning."

Martin flashed one of his *don't make a scene* looks, but now she refused to catch *his* eyes.

"He gave you a holiday, he said. From your real life."

The woman's face was calm as glass. "The holiday became my life," she said.

Martin cleared his throat. "Olwen," he said, "when I was last here I went up past the Falls and cut a staff from a rowan tree. I've still got it. Christina's seen it." Reproof spoke through every word. "Shall we go and look – see if we can find the axe-marks?"

The girl's eyes looked up for permission. Her mother nodded.

The husband, Brion, was standing behind. He made room for them and then leaned in to the kitchen, his hands up on the door-jambs. He looked massive, dangerous even. And then he slipped 'Stina a wink, like the waitress's this morning. Quick, expressionless. And she thought, "This is the most sexual person I've ever met."

Myra was covering her impeccable salad with a cloth. She turned and leaned back against the counter. "I'll show Christina the rest of the house," she said.

Was he watching, to keep the peace?

And 'Stina thought, "Right. I'll go along with this, but I'm a spy in your house, and my eyes will steal everything." She planted a farewell kiss on Telegony's brow.

Brion moved out of their way. She brushed his sleeve as they passed. "He hasn't said one word," she realized.

She followed Myra through the small dining room, past six or seven round oak tables, and windsor chairs with muted, brocade cushions, and then up a narrow creaking staircase, onto a wide landing. And here the private smell of the house stole into her, the breath of the family.

The doors all stood open, and through each there was a window-vignette of the valley. There were dark wooden beams, and the floors were dark too, but the walls caught the light from outside and lavished the carpets and bedspreads, all mediterranean weaves and colours.

"Oh that bed," she exclaimed. A massive, wide bedstead stood under the window of the front room, its posts and headboards carved deeply, like church-work.

"Yes, Brion made that. He's very good with his hands." Myra went to the bed and stroked the figures on one of the posts. "They're Breton motifs, fantasy animals."

The room smelled of wood, of rush matting, of polish; all blended with the light, elusive essence that was Myra's perfume.

"Breton, did you say?"

"He's from Brittany – they're almost the same as the Welsh. He came visiting just before my son died."

"And stayed!"

"He saved my life."

'Stina stared at the bed. She saw the two of them, Brion and Myra, embracing there, making love. And imagined herself, with that strong, dancer's body pressing down on *her*. That pirate's face at her throat. It was a small triumph.

Myra was watching her. Their eyes met, and said nothing in any language.

Then, "That must be your son." The painting hung on the inner wall, over the mother's shoulder. Myra said nothing, nor did she move.

It was a child's face at a window, looking in from a tangle of branches. It was almost a face she knew. Maybe five or six years old. The smile in the young eyes were like a prayer for happiness.

Her own eyes were wet. "You needn't have shown me this."

"I hadn't planned to."

"You're very good, aren't you. Can I see some more?"

"I think we should go and make tea, don't you?" The woman's voice was richer somehow in this room. She closed the door behind her as they left.

And once downstairs, they were back as they'd been. 'Stina standing there, getting in the way, while Myra gathered plates, and woven mats from the pine dresser, and Brion – appearing from nowhere – carried a table out to the patio. The sun was quite warm now, the valley was gilded by it, the trees on the hillside a net of light and shadow. *"Lovely, Dark and Deep"* 'Stina heard in her mind. She could hear, too, the noise of a waterfall, somewhere.

The meal was set out – salad, and cold lamb, and coarse home-baked bread – and Brion, silent and smiling, was uncorking a bottle of wine, when Martin and the girl came round the house side. "We found it," Martin shouted. His face was clear and elated. He jumped up on the patio: "Here's some of last year's berries, off the very tree I cut my staff from." He beamed round at all of them. "We'll plant them in our garden, Babe. When we *have* a garden!"

Babe! Oh she'd taunt him with that. Babe! Like a redneck crooner, dated and foolish. She felt shame for his earnest face, and his Siwash sweater.

He was oblivious. "And I've learned more Welsh than I ever knew before!" He turned to Myra, with a strange formality: "May I give your daughter a present?"

She raised her eyebrows. "Of course you may," she said. "Though I think you've done so already."

He reached in his sweater's side pocket, and turned to the girl: "For my fellow explorer."

"Mummy, look!"

It was a locket. Golden, with openwork carving, swinging on its chain from the young hand. The girl's face was ecstatic.

She bowed her head, and slipped the chain over her neck. Her mother's eyes were upon her. "Oh, thank you, Martin. I'll wear it for ever!"

'Stina turned away. And found herself stumbling across the rough field, towards the stream. She was shaking with rage and humiliation, cursing *fuck, fuck, fuck,* as she broke into a half-run, blindly. She heard Martin's cry:"'Stina, come back, come back right now!"

Bad girl, oh bad, bad girl. All the days of her life.

There was a shadow at her shoulder, and then Telegony went past, like the wind, galloping ahead of her, his lean body stretched into unbelievable strides, his head lifted – too huge and free for this place, though he belonged here. She slowed down, gasping, and the deerhound circled behind the barn and came back at her again, like an arrow over the grass, hunting her down.

"Telegony" she screamed, in terror, but he vaulted aside, higher than her head. She faced the arc of his body, the pale, naked belly and his maleness there, before he touched earth and sprang backwards, like a puppy, begging her to follow.

She would follow, and he would lead her, up through the passes, back to Canada or that Alpine place in her mind, among the Heidi mountains, where she would know the language and belong, like these bloody people belonged here.

Martin grabbed her by the shoulders as she was falling. The ground crawled, like the sands last night on the beach.

"What the hell's wrong with you?"

"Let me go."

"You've made a complete fool of yourself."

"*I* have?"

"I didn't need one of your moods, your selfish bloody moods, not today." He held her wrists now, too tightly.

"You're so stupid," she started, pulling to free herself. The dog began to growl, deep and ominous. Martin loosed her wrists and stepped back. But the growl became a soft, quavering whine, and 'Stina saw, over Martin's shoulder, a dart coming down from the hills, even as the valley tensed again, and the air began trembling. The warplane was down, and upon them and past, in five seconds, its scream drowning everything out except the convulsion in her belly. She threw herself against Martin, clinging to him.

The aircraft's soundwaves came rumbling back and eddied around them. They saw the plane bank to the west, in the distance already, a dark arrowhead in the sky.

"Are you okay?"

"My baby was frightened."

"Come on, let's go back. Walk carefully."

The dog loped before them. Three figures watched, from the side of the house.

"What got into you?"

The terror had pushed her anger aside. She reached back for it.

"Oh – you and your impulses." Her voice came out low, and bitter. It would seem so petty now.

"What d'you mean?"

"Oh, forget it. No – don't. You're so caught up in your magic past, and Lady Myra, and you're 'so good with young people,' and all that, and I'm nothing, am I? And then you go and give that kid my locket."

"That's crazy."

"No, it's not. I saw you this morning, go into that shop, and I was so happy, and watching you with such love and – oh, forget it."

They were close to the house. The mother and daughter watched still, but the man's figure turned away.

"'Stina, listen. I bought that locket for Dezzie. And I'm not ashamed of my impulses; I'll find her something in Ireland."

Bad girl. Bad, bad girl.

"That bloody plane gave Christina a fright," he said, when they reached the patio. "Forgive us, but I think we should get back to the hotel."

Myra's face expressed proper concern, but her eyes were not kind. The bottle of wine stood open upon the table. Brion beckoned to his daughter, and whispered in her ear.

"Well," said Myra. "It was good to see you both, and catch up on things."

'Stina gripped Martin's hand, and took a breath. "I'm sorry," she said.

Myra gave a little smile. Then stepped to Martin, and took his free hand in both of hers. "God speed," she murmured, and kissed him on the cheek.

"This is for you, Christina." Olwen was standing there, holding her hand out, doubtfully. Her young eyes asked questions, but seemed to expect no answers.

It was a love-spoon, in dark wood, carved through and through. It had two bowls, slender and almost touching.

"My father made it."

"It's beautiful." It was. She looked towards Brion, sure that he understood more than the others could. "Thank you," she mouthed, more than spoke.

"He's very good with his hands," Myra said.

He winked, again. That fleeting, unreadable signal. Then he took up the wine bottle and a glass, filled the one from the other, and toasted them – Martin, 'Stina, Olwen and Myra – silently, one at a time.

"Goodbye, Martin," the girl called. "Goodbye."

The dog came with them, as far as the footbridge, and turned back indifferently to its home.

"We didn't have to leave like that, Martin."

He let go of her hand.

There was silence between them as they got into the car. His hands were rigid on the wheel, the water at the ford splashed over the windshield, he shifted gears with a barely contained violence. The scenery was a lifeless screen for them both.

When they came down to the crossroad, and turned by the little church, she pushed one of her tapes into the stereo. The last, fading chords of "Gloria" and then, abruptly, "Nothing Compares to You." She turned it up, and sang along under her breath with the high Irish voice, as it dipped and stretched. Defiant. This was her world. He sighed heavily, and cleared his throat. He was staring straight ahead. She clutched the love-spoon tightly in her lap. As she sang, Brion came and put his strong hand on her belly: "You will have a good baby." The voice she had never heard.

Martin sighed again. "Do you have to play that stuff?"

"You mean, will I turn it off?"

"That's right."

"Well, sure, *Babe*." But she ratched it up louder, touching the wrong button, and for a moment the car was shot through with frenzied vibration.

He braked so hard that the seatbelt flattened her breasts. She cried out, and he swung the wheel over, hitting the grass verge, halting the car by an open farm gate.

"God damn you," he said, before she could speak. "Your self-centred, spoiled little world. Must you poison everything!"

"I didn't mean it, Martin." But he stormed right over her.

"Other people, other feelings – they mean *nothing* to you."

"Listen," she said, controlling the shake in her voice, "You've got all that life, all those people, your kids, your past, your precious past – your secrets. I've got nothing." She gazed down at her hands.

"You've got *our* life. And time for yourself when I'm gone."

"What good's that to me? I'm left out, either way."

His face was mottled around the eyes, he was glaring right into her face. "You got what you wanted."

"What's that mean?"

"You got what you wanted."

She shrank away from him. His eyes were so desperate. The only times she had heard him like this, his voice high and frantic, were during phone calls from Monique, and how she had hated the woman for doing this to him.

"You got what you wanted," he raged. "You got me to yourself, you got me away from my children – you got yourself pregnant. Everything *you* wanted!"

She sat very still, her cheek against the window. A few feet away, a snail was moving across the gatepost. Behind it, a random, spermy trail gleamed on the stone. She watched the shell hump and turn, the stalk-eyes searching.

"And now you don't want it," she said, dully.

He rested on the wheel, his head in his hands. "Of course I do," he whispered. "I'm sorry, 'Stina. I'm sorry. I'm sorry."

She kept her eyes on the snail. "Let's go home," she said. "Back to the hotel." The heartbreaking face of Myra's son smiled in at her out of Limbo. She knew his face. She knew it.

After a minute, he turned back onto the road. They drove on in silence. She held the love-spoon like a talisman to her belly. She stared at the windshield.

All at once, though, she turned and grabbed at his shoulder. "Don't you dare go and die before me," she cried, staring wildly into his face as he flinched in alarm and wonder, his eyes checking back and forth at the twisting road. "Don't you dare," she repeated, loudly, demanding his eyes. Behind his glasses they were mild, and afraid.

She gripped the loose wool of his sleeve, burying her face into the smell of it, and him. "Don't you dare, don't you dare," she was muttering, as if to herself, and as the little car snaked between fields and plantations, bearing the three of them down to the sea, she did not look up, or open her eyes, even once.

CIAO, FATHER TIME

When J.J. looked in at the office door, Mr Dyce was standing by the window, gazing down at the yard and the wet streets beyond and so absorbed by his thoughts that the room lay in slumber behind him.

J.J. rapped, triple-time, on the door jamb. "We're logging off, now, Chief. It's all yours."

Mr Dyce gave no acknowledgement. He had his quirks and foibles, which his two young assistants laughed at but never questioned. J.J. sauntered through to the desk with the ledger and cash tray, still talking: "I'm heading north, Boss Man, out on the road." He twirled the ledger on the polished desk top. "We got that gig up in Lindsay I was telling you about. Hallowe'en bash in an aircraft hangar. Eight until three, nonstop – should be wild!"

He turned and leaned back on the desk. "So think of me, Wise One, out there losing my religion, breaking hearts, tearing the stars down because yes, yes, we only come out at night and the night is long." His words spilling out for their own glad sake, hands conjuring the strings of a mighty guitar. He snapped upright again.

"Anyway, Maestro, I brought you a toy. This old girl came in to see if we could fix it; I thought you should check it out. It's really a neat device."

He launched himself back towards the door. "I'll see you Monday, Sensei, early if not bright. Carla will open up in the morning." He turned in the doorway and clicked his heels. "Ciao, Father Time."

"Thank you, Justin. Enjoy your weekend." The murmur scarcely reached the boy's ears, for Mr Dyce was still fixed on the world beyond the glass.

Instead of comprising the usual drab screen upon which his thoughts, with their private images, moved, the street below had come into focus: the shops and the trees and the rooftops. People walked and hurried through the rain, cars turned, lights shed their colours on the wet pavement and sidewalks. Only the sounds remained vague, unreal. He had watched a long time, without moving his eyes, as you'd enter the general world of a Flemish painting, till at last he had fixed on one detail, in the foreground, close to his face through the rain-mottled panes.

Two telephone lines slanted down, from the eaves just above his window, towards the low embankment beside the park, and along each wire raindrops were on the move, coalescing and falling.

The simple, mesmeric play of those winking beads held him rapt as a child. They shuttled, as though on a ghost-handled abacus, and as he searched for some law or pattern in their motions he understood, with sudden and quiet certainty, that his own death would come, like this, in the aftermath of rain and in just this season of the year.

He felt no dread, or disappointment. He knew, simply. As he had known one April day long ago, walking back through the college grounds in the green light of spring, with exams behind him and summer to dream of: looking up at the pink and white candles of the chestnut blossoms, the great billows and flounces of greenery arching above him, and understanding, absolutely, that his father would die, some year in the future, when the chestnuts were in bloom.

When the call had come from his sister, five time zones away and thirty years later, that had been his first question. It was Easter week, and he could not be sure if the trees in old England were further along than the one that he passed each evening; for the glossy, recurving buds above the park gates were still straining upwards, with here and there, in the last day or so, a limp and miniature cluster of five-fingered leaves.

There had been a moment's silence on the line before she put down the phone. He could visualize the room in the old house exactly; he could smell the shadows beside the oak bureau and hear the dull rote of the Dutch clock on the mantel. His sister, he knew, was leaning upon the window seat, craning her neck to look out down the garden. She'd come back to the phone to say yes, that the candle blossoms were out on the trees across the lane.

Yes, a day such as this, with raindrops slipping down the wires. He looked out, as a ghost might look in, knowing all, with a fond, detached sadness.

In the yard below, young J.J. had wheeled his motorcycle out from the shelter of the fire escape. He stood astride it, fastening the strap of his helmet. The black leather "gear," the jacket and jackboots and pants, did little to bulk out his lanky frame, yet no one watching him thrust down now with his heel, till the engine snarled into life and savaged the quiet enclosure, would guess at the sensitive hands, the intuitive patience, the anachronistic instinct for train and escapement which governed his days.

The boy's wrist jerked at the throttle, and Mr Dyce winced. With braggart crescendos, the machine steered its way through the yard gates and into the lane, the wake of its treadmarks fading on the wet asphalt. A moment later it roared out into the street and J.J. stormed off, visible for a moment past the lights, hair whipping below his helmet.

Mr Dyce winced again, and turned from the window.

There was dusk in the room, by contrast, and when he switched on the standard lamp by the desk, the outdoors receded in turn.

Mr Dyce pursed his lips in a silent prayer against wet roads, blind lights and hurtling machines, and turned his attention to the ledger which J.J. had set, upright and ajar, upon the cash tray: a precarious sculpture, capped by the small wooden box.

It was English without a doubt, but there was something too unsevere, too workaday, in its Regency style. A Victorian copy, perhaps, from some sleepy borough where time crept along country roads and yesterday's fashions might linger for 50 years.

The veneer was fine burlwood – a cloudy tortoiseshell grain that seemed to be walnut but was, he suspected, elm. There came to him, then, in a low breath of sawdust and gluepot and damp country air, an image of the maker. A village joiner, the day's work over at coffins and wainscottings, intent by the evening light at his window on this more frivolous challenge. A pattern book from his far-off apprentice days outspread on his bench. The doubt and desire in those blunt hands; a journeyman daring refinement.

Was it a whim of the local squire, or his guest? A gift for a lady? A "toy?" Mr Dyce reached for the box and felt at once the weight of the sleeping machinery within. There was a nub of brass for a catch; he turned back the lid and brought the box up to his face. It was his habit to put his nose to things, as a booklover sniffs at the life of a new acquisition.

It was a music box. Within was a shelf of clear glass, with a foliate key lying on it; the brass cylinder and rust-speckled comb in clear view beneath. Framed by a narrow rim over which the lid fitted, the glass was recessed enough to have held cigarettes, cigars even, but no ghost of tobacco lingered there.

Mr Dyce held the box in both hands, at his fingertips. He noted two base-metal studs on the face, flanking the brass catch, and a round key-socket in the mattwood base; but beyond them, as though from a window bay, were a terrace and steps in warm sandstone, and parkland going down to a river, with scattered chestnuts and lindens round-trodden and browsed by the roan-spotted cattle.

Mr Dyce had diviner's hands, though he was scarcely aware of them. In the mind's light and air of the 1840's he watched the shadows lengthening in that park, heard a woman's voice, laughing, as though in the room behind him, and caught the brief fragrance of orris and dried roses, before he came back to his own hands, in lamplight, turning the little box.

The village craftsman had done wonderfully well. The bevels and joining of the beechwood interior were faultless, almost invisible, with a chaste thumbnail lunette just under the rim the single clue that all was not solid and finished. Mr Dyce set the box down on his desk, and turned on the small, brighter lamp. He was sure now that the box was a copy, or a replacement at least, for the botched or damaged case which had first held this tiny clockwork spinet.

He weighed the ornate, not too ornate, key on his palm: its fluted gunmetal shank had been filed at some point; it was not the original. Someone, at the century's turn, had borrowed it from an American travel-clock. For a moment, he was on a stairway, below decks, with the millstone thud of paddlewheels shivering through him, and the reek of molasses; but he shook those ghosts off, as distractions, and peered down through the glass again at the waiting mechanism.

The rim in the box's right side lifted out, and he was able to slide the glass free and set it aside, under the lamp, with the key.

The spring had been overwound, that was all. Dry and neglected though the workings were, furred with a dust that had long since leeched any oil from the metal, and spotted on every steel surface with cankers of rust, there was nothing that would not restore, nothing broken or missing.

There was a mystery, though. A narrow spindle, vertical from the mainspring's core, with twin vanes mounted upon it – delicate blades shaped like nothing so much as a propeller – stood out beside the brass drum. It had no conceivable function.

Mr Dyce's hands went unconsciously to work at such times. As he seated himself at the desk, his left hand pulled open the central drawer and reached for the tube of compressed air, while the right hand drew out the pocket probe from his fob. The war upon dust began, but his eyes went beyond that work, focussed on the emerging, precise little engine, as the jet of air whistled and squalled through the box and his probe traced the steel tines, the cylinder's countersunk mountings, the slack disarray of the mainspring.

He held up the box, inverted over his desk, and continued to blow air into it. A shower of flecks and grey streamers came down in the dust cloud, smelling of attics and cobwebbed rafters; and as though set free by the scouring blast, a tiny grumble of notes jarred to life. The beechwood shell was such a sounding board: Mr Dyce felt, through his fingers, the dissonant shards of music, little waifs crying out for their home.

The mainspring was not past repair, though he would replace it. His right hand chose tweezers from the pen tray in the drawer. His left hand fumbled for the jeweller's loupe in his jacket pocket and squeezed it free from its chamois bag. Mr Dyce fixed the loupe to his eye and, with even breaths, seized the loose end of the mainspring and tweezed it back round its post till it notched into place. The cylinder lurched forward; three minor notes rang, clear and sweet, in response.

With a sudden intimation of what was in store, Mr Dyce raised the box again, his eyes still fixed on the workings, and felt for the key. How long, he wondered, since it had turned in the socket? He gave it enough pressure only to make half a circle, three ratchet-clicks. A light whirring sound preceded the notes:

Exquisite. But it was the spindle, the blur of the tiny vanes, which had his attention. It was hair-triggered. It went whispering on for a second or two once the music had stopped.

The delicate, frivolous whirligig, like a spendthrift Ariel, flaunted the last leak of energy from the motive force. Useless, light-hearted – *"self-delighting,"* he thought – it mocked the reined-in, functional crawl of the studded drum which actually plucked the steel tines into song. It was a kind of signature from the maker. A signature and a disclaimer.

Mr Dyce gave a little sniff of delight. He understood now why Justin had left this for him.

He would save it for the evening. He would go out among the citizens of the town, with this secret to come home to. Walk up through the park, buy food at the Trichilos, have a quiet supper by the fire, and then work into the night till he was finished. He set the box down and left it there in the lamplight.

When had he last felt this luxury of anticipation? He went through into his study, chose a bottle of Melini from the armoire, and opened it to breathe while he was gone.

It was the heart of rush hour when he stepped out into the street. People crowded the sidewalks, sidestepping each other brusquely, focussed on their destinations. The drivers in stalled traffic stared tensely ahead. The only open faces belonged to streetcar passengers, staring idly out through the dusk as they drifted past. The rain had ceased, but the air was clammy, laced with the blend of exhaust fumes and frying food which beset the city every day at this hour.

He walked briskly against the tide. In his childhood an evening like this would have smelled of leaves burning, of coal smoke. Away from the street the clip of his shoes on the park walkway was distinct above the traffic-hum. The lamps which he passed every fifty paces wore misty blue haloes, sending his shadow ahead of him then reeling it back. He passed no one. The five-acre island of grass, where dogs ran all afternoon and children played, was shifting its mood into shrouded menace.

But emerging again, from the northern gate, was to enter Europe. Here, where in summer whole families crowded the evening porches and conversations were street-wide, the October dusk seemed half-hearted, diluted by the self-contained life of a village. The energy expressed itself everywhere: in the Mary-shrines and painted stone follies on the tiny front lawns, in the crude-coloured porch railings, in the pendant miscellanies at the windshields of parked cars. The distaste he'd once felt for all this vulgarity had long since changed to affection. Through every shop window and doorway he saw intimate portraits – shopkeepers and customers lifting their faces to each other, warm chiaroscuros of human contact, soft Caravaggios – and the breath of fish, fruit and oven-warm bread seemed a timeless denial of the city.

Carla's father was serving an old man, wrapping his meagre purchase in mulberry-hued paper, tying it up with string from the long roll on the counter. He lifted his chin in welcome. "You come a day early," he said. "You have guests to feed tonight, Mr Dyce?"

"No, no," Mr Dyce smiled. "No guests. I thought I would treat myself this evening – I shall be working late."

"Work, work!" Carla's mother came through from the back room, scolding with her finger. "Always *work* with you, Mr Dyce. Why you have the young people if not for the work – my Carla and that rock-a star J.J.?" She leaned over the counter, shouldering up to her husband: "A man alone like you, Mr Dyce, a gentleman, like I always tell you, you should take it easy at your age – put up your feet in the evening, have someone take care of you. Eh, Beppi?" she appealed to the old man, who just grunted and shuffled away with his package. "Hah!" Signora Trichilo slapped down her hand on the counter, then folded her arms and nodded, with a firm and sat- isfied smile. Mr Dyce had such fondness for her that nothing she said ever jarred his sense of decorum. And whether she knew it or not, he divined her courage. One day last spring he had watched her dash some domestic grief from her face as she bustled out to serve him, and the line had come into his mind: *And loved the sor- rows of her changing face.* He hoped – he believed – that her hus- band saw her that way.

Signor Trichilo had escorted the old man to the door, and called out now, "Enough of the bossy-talk, Gianna – you want we should scare away our best customer!" He patted Mr Dyce's arm as he came back around the counter, but there was a whisper of defeat in his pale features, the hint of a stoop at his shoulders. Yet he too had the manners of his tribe, the cheerful address that made life seem carefree and companionable.

This was the sensuous coda to Mr Dyce's week. He would stand at the counter, usually at midday on Saturday, absorbing the orchestral scents of cheeses, olives, pine nuts, herbs, the fresh bread and sausage, with the undertone of ironed sheets which made up the Trichilo world. Mr Dyce looked forward to the leisure of these visits with the same half-serious intensity that J.J. expressed, yearn- ing for Friday nights, his rehearsals or "gigs."

And there was always a treat of some kind, held to the last; something new to the store, or a batch of outstanding quality. It was the Signora, for once, who unveiled the surprise today. "See, Mr Dyce – is Asiago, *real* Asiago from Italia. Is the young Asiago, like you never get see in America." She held out the cheese on a knife point, a thin yellow wafer. It was soft, mild, almost melting – a different creation altogether from the usual hard, alkaline flesh to which, God knows, he was partial enough.

"Oh yes," said Mr Dyce, "yes indeed." The pleasure on their faces reflected his, and it was troubling to see Signora Trichilo stiffen, her warm brown eyes come on guard, as Carla appeared at the far end of the counter. She was wearing a housecoat, with her just-washed hair twisted up in a towel.

"Hey, Padrone," she smiled, quite at ease in her déshabille, "you almost beat me home."

"And you, I see, couldn't wait to wash off the smell of the workplace." With her hair drawn back from her face, and no makeup at all, she had her mother's strong bones, though her skin and her softer flesh surely came from her father's side.

"*Padrone!*" her mother sniffed, and would not look up. But Mr Dyce laughed; it was, of course, one of young Justin's honorifics. Carla never spoke Italian at work, she answered her mother in English on the telephone, and feigned ignorance if a customer ever wanted to use the language.

He touched the mother's hand before he took his change. "Carla is a good girl" he said, "though I shouldn't say so in front of her, I suppose. She is level-headed, and wonderful with our customers. I rely on her absolutely." He could sense Signor Trichilo's gratitude, but the mother's eyes looked into him with unfathomable disappointment. It was as if he were guilty of something vaguely dishonourable.

But the moment passed. And "Ciao," they both called, lingering on the vowels as he turned at the door. "Bye-bye," Carla chirped. "See you in the morning, Kapitan."

Through the window, by the tawny interior light, the family was caught, as though by a Vermeer or de Hooch. The father's hands raised in appeal, the mother's stern, highlit features, the indifferent girl in her bathrobe. Mr Dyce stared in as he passed, with compassion and envy.

The shops for the most part were closing up now, and young people gathered outside cafés and pool halls. Even they, in their gaudy indolence, might have been in a village square. They stood in the brightly lit doorways, boys and girls facing each other, making casual, jesting overtures across the narrow divide. Just so, he thought, you might group the actors for a *Romeo and Juliet*, as the curtain went up on the "public place" in Verona, before the thumb-biting started.

Little Italy, now, Little Portugal five blocks away; but to parents like Lucca and Gianna Trichilo the new country surely must seem to be swallowing them up.

Beneath his thoughts, *What is life to me without thee?* gave way to *I cover the waterfront*. So often his breathing chose music to move through: unbidden songs whose words some part of his mind, like the chamber where poetry slumbered, offered up as commentary. His feet took him on, away from the stores, along quiet residential streets where old maples and elm trees stood over the houses.

Was it peculiar to this season, or this hour – or perhaps to this stage of life – that you could blink your eyes, and find the world utterly changed? Ahead of him the downtown hotels and office blocks stood out like costume jewellery, cancelling and intensifying the night.

Mr Dyce had strayed with his thoughts, several blocks east of his destination. Now, in another eye-blink, the city, as he turned south towards Queen Street, changed its nature again. The traffic was in a lull, the wet sidewalks close to empty, yet he could sense Friday evening, like a nocturnal creature waking and stretching behind the house fronts, almost ready to come into its own. By then he'd be home, though, in lamplight, with the little box that was waiting on his desk. His steps quickened as he turned onto the old thoroughfare.

Each month, it seemed, prosperity, or its trappings, moved a stage further west along Queen. Buildings which had endured twenty years of short ground-floor leases – improbable clothing and junk stores, used furniture, fly-by-night discount records, the windows above ghostly with rags of old curtains – were suddenly whole again, as though somebody really owned them. The old woodwork had been restored and painted. There were glimpses of home-life, even, in the bright upper-floor interiors.

Mr Dyce found himself in the light from a restaurant window, reading the blackboard menu with its flamboyant chalk lettering. A young man in dress shirt and trousers stood smoking by the doorway. "The partridge are good," he said casually, "fresh from the stubbles of Manitoba." Mr Dyce looked up. The young man's head was shaven, a ring gleamed in his left ear. Yet he'd an open face, and a most engaging smile. "Myself, though, I'd go for the brook trout: '*lemon-grilled over cubebs and wild chanterelles.*' They're sensational."

"Fresh trout," Mr Dyce said. "Well, I might be tempted . . . ."

The young man raised an eyebrow: "Ah, but will you fall?"

Mr Dyce was charmed. "Unfortunately," he said, and he held up his shopping bag, "I have my dinner here at hand."

"*Tant pis,*" the other shrugged. He stepped out to the curb, and dropped his cigarette into the gutter. He smiled again, cool, humorous eyes: "We shall be here tomorrow!" and turned back towards the doorway.

"Though perhaps," Mr Dyce wondered, "you could keep my groceries in a refrigerator?"

The young man held out his hand for the bag and gestured, with simple courtesy, to the restaurant door. *Le Chasseur Gai* was painted, in cursive script, above the green lintel. Mr Dyce felt the heady indulgence of impulse.

Two waiters stood by the half-moon bar to his left. The room was long and otherwise empty, but it felt warm despite the plain brick walls, and was fragrant with herbs. They hung in garlands by every table and over the bar. The music of flute and tabla played quietly overhead.

A small table close to the bar was suggested, and he chose to sit facing outwards. His escort went off with his coat and the shopping bag, while another waiter brought bread and water to the table.

"Maurice will serve you," he murmured. And in less than a minute the young man from the street was back, bending to light the candle-lamp on the table. The lights dimmed perceptibly through the room as he did so. "But first," he said, "the music. Let me guess: Segovia? Satie? or perhaps Dinah Washington?"

There was conspiracy in his eyes, light hearted and teasing. "That is remarkable," Mr Dyce said. "How could you have guessed my tastes?" And getting only the slightest of shrugs in response, "But really," he said, "what you are playing now is delightful."

"Mere ambience." The young man, Maurice, laid a narrow menu beside Mr Dyce's napkin. "For our first customer of the night, we offer choice. So – Dinah Washington?"

Mr Dyce smiled up, and surrendered: "I am in your hands!"

And along with the music, wine. They settled on a glass of Montrachet, for Mr Dyce – as he confided – had a serious evening's work ahead of him and must keep a clear head. But as the first piano notes stole into the room – the spare, unmistakable Teddy Wilson proem to "Broken Promises" – he leaned back in his chair and breathed out in utter contentment. The evening seemed to be finding its perfect shape. Some angel – for he'd a firm, though ironic, trust in angelic designs – was at work on his behalf.

He broke a crust from the Calabrese loaf and, as he buttered it, examined the menu: a folded parchment with black, calligraphic text. Almost every dish was wild game – boar, venison, salmon, partridge – the in-season entrées tagged with a star.

Delicious, the light bread, the herb-tinged butter. Mr Dyce sipped his wine and reached out to the brickwork beside him. He could feel the sheen of some sealant, restraining the flakes of mortar he had expected. He found himself talking to J.J. "Now that is clever, don't you think? To ward off our enemy, dust, without seeming antiseptic or varnished . . ."

He chose the crayfish and butternut bisque, with the *Truite Broceliande* to follow. "They were swimming in the Rocky Saugeen this morning," Maurice confided. "My partner caught them himself – out at dawn in his hip-waders, three hours from the city, up with the birdbrains," and he folded the napkin back over the bread loaf, straightening the basket as though for Mr Dyce's convenience.

"It seems very quiet," Mr Dyce observed. "I should have thought Friday was your busiest evening."

Maurice retrieved the menu. "Just you wait," he said.

And in fact by the time the bisque arrived, fragrant and grainy, with an islet of cream and a moist wrinkle of provolone at its centre, three other tables had filled up and the waiters were on the move. Mr Dyce was watching the young trio across from his table, the girl in a light linen suit, cream-coloured, the jacket thrown open upon her green, diaphanous blouse. He was as puzzled by the bodies of these young women as he was by their thoughts, their style, the unaccountable space they had made for themselves. Could people really have changed so much?

The light cream flared out behind Mr Dyce's spoon, folding itself into the orange textures of the soup, and he was lost, even as he took the first tentative sip, to his childhood kitchen, dissolving as slowly as might be his aunt's clotted cream and the drifts of brown sugar into his morning porridge. The sheer remote innocence of that time came over him; the old world with its unspoken values and expectations. His heart was still in that world, the ancestral aromas, his grandfather's fob-watch ticking below his own heart. His left hand reached for it now, as a touchstone, and he looked over again at the girl – animated, confident, with her two companions.

He could not guess at her life. There was some boundary between him and the young these days, as there was, he thought sadly, between the dear Trichilos and their daughter.

Young Carla, spending her evenings with a fellow who at 22 had abandoned a wife and two small children. Yet Carla – and somehow she and the girl at that table were of a kind – was a good girl, not innocent perhaps but with another kind of unspoiled goodness.

Mr Dyce remembered that evening last month, coming down to the shop just after closing time and finding Justin and Carla still there, dancing by the counter to some radio station – J.J. angular, all arms and legs, but Carla abrim with delight and energy, her clear eyes and child-smile discounting altogether the lascivious motions of her hips, the bare young flesh at her midriff.

When they'd seen him they'd laughed, as though welcoming him into their dance. "Why here's Father Time," said J.J., the first time he'd used that title, and Mr Dyce heard himself calling back over the music, "Then you must be Justin Time," disarmed by his own lightheartedness. Almost loving them.

Their laughter came back to him now and the girl with the see-through blouse returned his smile, as though meant for him, and one of her friends raised his glass in casual acknowledgement.

Mr Dyce responded, shyly, but they were absorbed in themselves already. He had finished his soup, and could scarcely remember tasting it.

The room was alive all at once. Customers had been drifting in from the street – all members, it seemed to him, of one carefree, familiar tribe – and their table talk, with the background kitchen excursions and the chatter of glass and cutlery, blended in with the music to a warm conversational drone. The waiters weaved through it, and with them streamed currents of wine and light, saucy aromas, the breath of the place.

"Oh my," said Mr Dyce. Just as the music box started whispering from his study, here was the trout, life-plump on a crescent of chanterelle fans, a watercress sprig at each head and tail. He leaned forward, his glasses misting slightly as Maurice set the plate down before him. A finger tapped the near-empty wine glass – "Shall we have another?"

Mr Dyce smiled up at the smooth, humorous face. "I must restrain myself."

Maurice raised one eyebrow, then inclined his head. "The elegant sufficiencies."

"Exactly so," said Mr Dyce.

"Bon appetit."

Holding the fish knife as one would a pen, slicing along the stipple-line of the trout and exposing, extracting the pliant skeleton whole, was to eat once again beneath his mother's eye: *The elegant way is always the most effective. That is why we have manners.* Who was it that said reading poetry was to break bread with the dead? Mr Dyce dedicated the first dissolving mouthful to his mother's shade. Fleetingly, the tea-dark pools of the unknown Rocky Saugeen gleamed within him, catching light from the dawn, and he wished, as he savoured the blending of river and woodroot, that Justin might carry some wisdom from *him* into the future, something that might come back, surfacing to the occasion, when the boy was in need.

But really – and the trout was superb, with just a hint of marsala, perhaps, elevating its flavour – really Justin was no more in debt to him than he was to Justin. Certainly he had opened up what was latent in the boy, those intuitive skills, but Justin had brought humour with him, a deadpan way with authority which no longer felt disconcerting, and a genuine care for the craft, though the craft was dying and the future was only a blank. The future held no terrors for the young, Mr Dyce had concluded, but they owned no past to sustain them when it arrived. They scarcely believed in a past.

Carla and J.J. laughed fondly at his warnings. And when he was with them, he had to admit, they forced him to laugh at himself. "Dr Doomby," "Woemeister," "I know, I know," he'd protest, "but I'm right all the same."

That rash confidence of theirs. "*It is the common moth,*" he chided J.J. now, "*that eats on wits and arts, and oft destroys them both.*" And he could hear the response: "*Take her easy, bossman, relaxez vous.*" Like Gianna Trichilo's refrain, with her thwarted sense of propriety: "*Take it easy, Mr Dyce. Leave the work to the young people."* To her he should answer, *"Knowledge that sleeps doth die."* But to Justin?

"Now that music box you left with me," he told him. "You were right, 'a neat device' it certainly is. And you knew I would derive pleasure from it. While you are in Lindsay, damaging your eardrums and everyone else's, I shall be breaking bread with a brother craftsman from the last century." He smiled. "But," and he wagged his finger, not altogether humorously, in Justin's face, "the lesson you should take with you from this is, as I've said so often, that neglect is our adversary. We are at war, yes you know what I'm going to say, at war with dust."

Yes, dust. The dust that cocooned and smothered the workings of the little spinet. The dust that awaits us all. The spouse of oblivion, he thought, or should that be bride – the bride of oblivion? He was pleased with that. Mr Dyce was a storehouse, he knew, of quotations from others, but this he had made himself, and might use again . . . . Yes dust, *This quiet dust . . . .* "We have to address it, Justin – there are lessons to be learned from our enemy: if we pierce its armour we find that it has preserved what it seemed to destroy. Yes, it's true. *The old knights are dust, Their swords are rust, Their souls are with the saints we trust* – if we can restore the brightness of those swords, those lovely, wicked blades, then the souls of the dead reawaken to live in us—"

The air, all at once, had turned hollow. Mr Dyce was in pain. He stared at the plate in front of him, the ruined bodies of the trout. The music played alone, and the people at the next table were staring at him, others were sniggering. "I have humiliated myself," he thought.

He left the table, enduring the gauntlet of pity as he made for the bar. "This will cover my bill, I think." He did not look up: he could see himself as they'd seen him, a deluded old man who mouthed and gestured across an empty table. "Where is the cloakroom, please?"

He walked out with a dignity that made him, he knew, look still more ridiculous, and walked a few yards down the street before stopping to put on his coat. Mr Dyce was a stranger to shame. A nerve was at work in his eyelid, his heart felt shrunken and cold. But, *"Steady, the Buffs,"* he told himself, "all is not lost."

Though it felt so. He had fled to the street and now its phantasms assailed him. The street lights and cars and store windows, all glaring light in the darkness that was no darkness. The bodies that passed and approached or were overtaking him. And the smells: the starved, hell-corridor air with its almost visible net of motor fumes and fried food and garish perfumes, eddying over the pavement, waist-high. Sometimes Mr Dyce did have a sense of Hell – that the Old Adversary was a squalid inch or instant away from breaking in with his plagues. Someone jostled his arm, without apology; then another, muttering angrily. A streetcar passed, a thundering barge bearing, it seemed, lost souls in its vague interior. He started to walk, and the people coming towards him were creatures of Edvard Munch, or the Belgian painter – who was it? The name would not surface, but as he searched for it, summoning the carnival mob-tide of that frenzied painting, his mind became clear again. The street was Queen Street, and home just three blocks away.

In that instant, as he passed a bus shelter, a youth lurched shouting into his path. Mr Dyce took in the stained green jacket, the stiff drunken motions, and stepped back to avoid a collision. The boy sensed his presence and swung around, staring into his face with a hopeless snarl before blundering back towards the shelter. Mr Dyce watched in dismay: the group of youths by the shelter drew apart and the boy started beating his fists on the glass wall, while they stood indifferently by. The noise, the crudeness, the ignorance in their faces was unbearable. And then the boy whirled about, leaning back against the shelter, and held up his hands, beckoning. His knuckles were blotched with tattoos. A girl stepped towards him and he drew her close, his cheek upon her shoulder. He was weeping.

Mr Dyce stood, confused and guilty. The girl's brittle features grew softened and strong, drawing upon some instinct of consolation. She held the boy, rocking him quietly, and cared not at all who saw them.

Someone else was watching. Maurice, from the restaurant, was standing there, holding out Mr Dyce's shopping bag. He looked back from the young couple. "All God's chillun got wings," he said. His eyes were shrewd and gentle, more telling than words.

"You are very kind," Mr Dyce said. And was sustained by that kindness as he made his way, by darker side streets, back to his home and workplace.

He stood before the shop for a moment, keys in hand, imagining J.J. four years ago, lingering for the first time by this window. Now, as then, the light of the little aquarium claimed a half-circle of sidewalk, and through the bars the swordtails and angel fish drifted around the Rolex *Oyster* watch above the sunken galleon. The tank would need cleaning next week, he reminded himself; he must speak to Carla.

Below the aquarium the perpetual-motion clock changed over, catching the fish light as he bent to unlock the doorway grating. A window groaned open upstairs, in the house next door. The bronze bead rolled, as it had now for thirty three years, retracing its zigzag channel across the brass platen . . . .

"Mr Dyce, are you there?"

Mr Dyce stepped back.

"Mr Dyce, Mr Dyce why you not shut up your gates in the back?" It was Mr Salukjian, his neighbour since last spring, leaning out over the window sill, his white sleeves billowing. "I call your telephone, but no answer."

Mr Dyce looked up into the agitated face. "Why, what on earth is the matter, Mr Salukjian?"

"Are two men down there – bad peoples come in from the lane, under the stairs."

"Have you called the police?"

"I – no." The man dropped his voice. "Not wanting trouble. What use I call them: only they come after bad peoples smash into house, cut all our throat. Police not come."

"I don't see why they wouldn't," Mr Dyce said. "But I'll go round and look."

His neighbour started to protest, but stopped himself with a hand gesture. "Should lock up gate, Mr Dyce," he said, "always lock up gate." The head withdrew and the window slammed down.

Mr Dyce walked down to the corner and around, under the street lights, to the mouth of the back lane. His neighbour was right, of course – these days it was foolish to leave anything unlocked – but too much suspicion was surely a sign of defeat. Yet entering the lane, still rain-damp and musty between the high back walls, he fell prey to the tense romance of the labyrinth. It was a world of stray cats and raccoons, of garbage cans and sagging electric wires, but of wild trees too – ailanthus and maples – seeding out of the dirt against the garage walls. Such light as there was seeped down from the city sky or was stolen from negligent lives beyond the walls. The child in Mr Dyce was, for a moment, in fearful league with the outlaws.

He shifted his shopping bag to his left hand and stepped in through the gate. It was hard to see anything clearly: the house back itself rose overhead in the city's light, but the space before him was a muffle of shadows, except for one pool of water. Reflected there was his office window, the lamplight on wall and ceiling. *The honey lights of home* came to him, though the poet had been thinking of wife and child . . . .

"I'm going to close these gates now," he called. "If there's anyone here, you had better leave before you get locked in."

There was no sound. His eyes were adjusting, and he walked across to the fire escape where the shadows were deepest. He felt glass crunch underfoot. "I must warn Justin," he thought, "he could get a flat tire."

Then came a scuffling of feet across the yard, and he did not turn around till they had faded down the lane. As he drew the gates closed he saw a curtain fall back in one of Mr Salukjian's unlit windows. His smile was not wholly charitable.

From the back door he made his way through the shop, among the dreaming timepieces, and up the stairs towards the light from his office. He carried the little box across the landing, to his study, and set it down on the table, under his jeweller's lamp. But first he must recork that bottle of Melini; the evening had not worked out at all as he'd envisioned it. Too much stimulation, he thought, too much random and chance. But now to work.

And this was his favourite work. The first time J.J. had watched him unroll the red baize and set out his instruments, with the jars of solvent and oil, in their precise half-circle he'd said, "You look like a heart surgeon, gearing up for a transplant." And was still prone to chime in with, "Scalpel, Doctore? Clamp? Hatchet?" But for Mr Dyce the task most resembled that of a picture restorer, inching through time, he supposed, to enter the mind and hands of the artist, catching glimpses of his heart.

He sat down and adjusted his chair, and thought with a rueful smile of the spectacle he had made in the restaurant, wondering when he had got in this habit of talking aloud, and what it meant. But there was Maurice as well, ironic, intuitive; and the weeping lout by the bus shelter. He bent to his task.

Dust and rust. They were easily dealt with here. Three miniature screws released the whole mechanism and it sat under the lamp, skeletal and obscurely innocent. Piece by piece, section by section, Mr Dyce pursued it, his breathing as steady as his hands.

The circle of light was a cockpit where time could dissolve.

Justin might share in this. That utterly unschooled boy, with his fondness for loud music and louder machines, was in spirit at home with the workshops of Rouen and Wurttemberg; he could work, like this, with their quiet, demanding spirits watching over his shoulder, approving . . . .

Mr Dyce blew upon the curious Ariel vanes, and wondered again at their function. He reached for a Fyffe brush and dabbed it into the jar of sapphire gin, his own specific for tired or neglected metal. The brush caressed the whirligig and its shaft. Perhaps this was, after all, just a joke, a sport; the kind of gay signature he could imagine Justin adopting if there were any future in the craft . . . .

But Justin was a restorer too, not a maker. His Douglas Dragon-fly bike – that oil-streaming, side-valve eccentric to which he had given his heart: wrestled and coerced back to life out of three or four cannibalized carcasses – calling to something unknown inside him till then, as the perpetual motion clock had lured him, gradually, into Mr Dyce's world.

The contrasts in the boy. His measured cursing when he worked on the bike those summer evenings, down in the yard, his radio blaring, cigarette in his lips, his arms black with grease, the beer bottles parked among wrenches and scattered parts; but then the spellbound patience with which he engaged a French carriage-clock or Edwardian hunter, neglecting his coffee or smoke breaks, working till six or seven . . . .

Sometimes Mr Dyce thought of naming Justin as his heir, but where would that lead? The future, alas, seemed hell bent to wizardry and the unkind machines . . . .

He leant back and sighed, as though he'd been holding his breath for a long time. The mainspring was replaced, and only the peculiar, floating mount for the comb prevented him from winding the little instrument and testing it. He would have to reseat it first. He drew the box closer.

One of the base-metal studs, he noted, was crusted, flaking away. "Well, well now," he said, "see what we have here, Justin." He caught himself at it this time, but shrugged it away. Present or not, the boy was his only audience. "What we're looking at here," he explained, "is mosaic gold. A cheap zinc and copper alloy from the 1860s. Not durable, as you can see. The right hand stud is disintegrating. Interesting, that. Why only the one?"

He filed the stud as smooth as was possible without creating more damage.

"So we have a fourth hand, at least, at work on this little creation – a very inferior craftsman. But you know," and he took up the varnish bottle, shaking it gently, end over end, "while many restorers would make up a replica of the other stud or possibly replace them both, by guesswork, with something more 'authentic,'

I actually find this botchwork quite charming, quite resonant. So we shall keep it. It is part of the character." He swabbed each stud with the varnish, and blew upon them. "Just a touch of the Sifton; it's the best we can do."

But even as he spoke he saw why that pinchbeck stud was so worn: it was a moving part. Inside the box, pressed flat against the front wall was a strip of metal. The stud moved it horizontally, back and forth. And that lever, Mr Dyce could now see, had a terminal, decurved pin. "How could I have missed it," he said, "the one vital secret?" For this explained why the music box had stopped working, how long ago one could only guess. And this was why the steel comb floated. "There are two songs, Justin – one drum, one comb, but two tunes."

He hastened now to set the machine back in place and tighten the screws. To ease the lever out from the wall was simplicity itself. And its tip, of course, fitted that unexplained slot in the base of the comb. Fitted, and fitted tightly. It had not come loose on its own – some child or meddler had done this, years and years back.

Mr Dyce slid the glass sheet back into the box, and the wooden leaf after it, and saw himself, as he turned off the jeweller's lamp and swung it away, reflected in the glass of the armoire. He looked almost insubstantial. The books and decanters were visible through his body; the window behind him was at once night sky and a second, still ghostlier mirror. He drew out his watch. Twenty minutes to two. How long was it since he'd felt quite so consciously happy?

"We shall drink to the makers, and the menders, and to all the listeners," he said – talking now not to J.J. but to his own reflection, and through that to the ghosts themselves. He crossed to the armoire and poured himself a sufficient measure of Millésimé, in a stemless snifter, passing it under his nostrils as he went back to the desk.

He set down the glass, picked up the little box and inserted the key. He wound it gently, to its full, and there came, as he replaced it on the table, a glissando of notes – the song coming to its end.

He raised the glass to his lips, watching the blur of the tiny vanes through the glass and hearing their whisper, before:

The brass drum crawled, but the bright notes scampered on:

He let it play. The Calvados brought him, as it always would, the stone walls and lichens of Normandy, the harsh channel air, the cry of lapwings; and the music – compressed miraculously in the drum and comb – became, for all its gaiety, the voice of that landscape.

The tune completed itself, and played again, five more times, slowly faltering out to one last note . . . then another.

Whose company had he been sharing? *He hears it not now, but used to notice such things.* He drank again, before rewinding the spring, nudging the lever to the right and waiting as before . . . .

Moderato

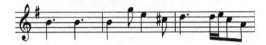

These were harp notes, surely, measured and lingering:

Had he been listening with an ear mechanically tuned, Mr Dyce would have noted the almost subliminal descant, the phantom harpist's left hand barely rippling the strings, sustaining the time. He might have marvelled, too, that the same procession and escapement, the same array of brass studs plucking the same steel comb, nudged barely an eighth of an inch to the right, could utter such different musics. And certainly he would have bowed to the shade of the unknown craftsman. But he was groping for the song, as one might for the air of a place. His mother was somewhere in it. Her figure or her face, or her voice itself – all three perhaps. The song played itself on, and down:

But the words, and the world they should conjure, eluded him.

Out of discipline perhaps, or from simple defiance of old age, Mr Dyce had no tolerance for forgetfulness of any kind in himself. "The mind," he told J.J. often enough, "is the laziest of mainsprings –" And the boy just last week had chimed in with him, laughing, hands flourishing like a conductor's, *"We must keep it wound.* And oiled too, Your Honour," he'd added, "for *rust never sleeps."* Mr Dyce had been truly impressed with that, but J.J. had laughed again: "It's the name of an album, Chief – just rock'n'roll, but I like it, like it, yes I do!"

And twice tonight Mr Dyce's memory had failed him. There had been distractions, certainly – both good and bad – but they did not excuse him. And for a dizzying moment he could not recall what the first lapse had been, in the Queen Street route where the tattooed boy had wept. Then the painting came back, and the steps of association – *a witch – the Bible – King Saul and – Endor. Of course, it was Ensor – the Belgian, James.*

At moments like this the recovered names spelled themselves out in Mr Dyce's mind and now *ENSOR*, the word itself, floated before him as he turned to the window. His hand checked before it touched the hasp. He wanted the air, but not the invasions. The smell of wet streets and the communal night, but not the inevitable sirens, far or near, with their nightmares of fear and damage, and not the sudden girl screams from the park which left you unsure whether it was giddiness you were listening to, or rape . . . .

Yet everything out there had a desolate peacefulness to it. The red and amber lights at the intersection pulsed to the empty streets. He looked down to the gates of the yard, and saw himself, hours earlier, gazing up at the lamplight and the evening's promise. As though he were saluting both that self below and his reflection in the window, he brought the glass of Calvados up to his lips, and at that moment the song came back to him, and with it the intense and gauzy smell of roses and face powder – his mother's – floating above the orchard fumes, the weather-ghosts of the brandy.

He did not drink, but stood immobile, listening. Never mind that the words would not come: his mother's voice had been for that moment as close, as present, as that other whose laughter the little box had released. As the rose-scent faded, the two women merged into one, as if they were walking together away down that sandstone terrace.

Mr Dyce turned back to the table.

Lo hear the gentle lark – was that it? He thought that perhaps it was. The words did fit the first line, if you allowed for grace notes, though the rest would not come.

He rewound the spring and took the box through to his bedroom. On the bedside dresser, less resonant than the table in his study, its sound was smaller, sweeter, yet it filled the room as he prepared for the morning.

Who knows if the music played in his dreams, or if the Ariel vanes whispered on? He did not remember. But he woke with a light heart, at his usual hour, the bedclothes as firm and undisturbed as when he had settled to sleep.

Mr Dyce had his Saturday rituals. He replaced his razor blade; selected a necktie; opened wide all the upstairs windows. By the time the metal grating slammed back downstairs, signalling Carla's arrival, his morocco valise was packed – his weekday suit and his shirts folded in together – and he went down at once.

Carla was brewing coffee at the back of the shop, and he had wound up the music box and set it to play on the counter before she noticed him. When she turned, though, it was with a sullen impatience, as though she resented the intrusion. "Just listen, Carla," he said. "The owner cannot guess what a treasure she has here."

She shrugged, not meeting his eyes. "Why don't you buy it, then?"

The little music was dimmed by her indifference. "I am not a museum," he told her. "I enjoy the thought of a home, of people, finding delight in this." She looked at him now, galled by that note of reproof. He felt the closed resentment that her parents must sometimes endure: her features puffy and distracted, her lips edged with contempt.

He could only guess. Some trouble, anyway, with that young man of hers. He felt at a loss. "See here," he said, as the music limped into silence, "I can be home by one o'clock. If you would like to have this afternoon to yourself, that will be all right."

"You mean that?" He saw hope catch at her throat. "But you'll miss your time at the zoo."

"I can go tomorrow," he said. "Who knows, the weather might have cleared up by then."

She had transformed into the Carla he knew. And there was nothing so lovely, he thought, reflecting her smile in spite of himself, as a young woman accepting a gift. It was a rueful thought, though: there was no real generosity there, just the selfish grace of the young. No, that was unfair; she was so radiantly grateful. For a moment he feared she would hug him.

But, "Oh," she said, "I forgot – J.J. left this for you. He said to be sure that you read it."

It was a flyer from one of the giant malls up north of the city where the subway ended. Circled in thick black marker was an advertisement for a Compact Disk player, with "remote, multiple functions," and scrawled across the whole page: *Come out of the dark ages Mr Edison this is a fantastic deal – would you trust me for once on this one!*

Carla was at his shoulder. "He's right, you know. And now they're reissuing all those old records, with way better sound."

The photograph was one of a dozen that filled the page. He took in the architecture of the thing – the rank of black modules, the ports and beacons, like a fortress in nightmare's valley. *Childe Rowland to the dark tower came . . . :* the Pandora's Box of microwaves, quartz actions, lazers, and everywhere simmering screens.

He reached over to close the music box and realized as he did so that the glass shelf would hold exactly a divided pack of those small Victorian playing cards.

Ladies' hands at euchre: that bay window again and the sand-stone terrace, a perfume just out of reach . . . .

"So, are you going to buy the stereo?"

"I think not, Carla." He set the music box on the shelf with the carriage clocks. "And since I am taking your place this afternoon," he said, "I have my excuse!"

"Don't be surprised if he goes out and buys it for you."

Mr Dyce was touched, and dismayed. "That would be black-mail, Carla," he said, "not generosity."

She laughed. "It might be for your own good."

Mr Dyce took up his valise. "I'll be back by 1:00," he told her.

She followed him to the door and "Ciao, Capo caro!" she called, as she closed it behind him.

Mr Dyce felt at once that he should have brought his raincoat. The damp air was still and full of night's lingering odours. He walked down to the corner, and hesitated. There was a feeble, dif-fused brightness towards the lakeshore, as though the sun had inten-tions of burning the clouds away, but behind him, to the northwest, the sky was blank, leaden November. He went back to the shop.

Carla was speaking on the telephone, twisting its cord in her left hand, tense and distracted. She lowered her voice and did no more than nod to him as he went to the below-stairs closet. "Of course," she whispered, "of course I will – you know that." Mr Dyce hurried by, waiting to put on his coat till he was outside again.

In the window, the bronze bead pursued its course, back and forth. The platen tipped; the bead returned on its way. Slowly he buttoned his raincoat. How often he had watched men and women standing in fascination where he stood now. Like solitary children on a bridge, lost in the flow of water beneath them. And some, like Justin, impelled to come inside and talk.

Dimly, behind the fish tank, Carla was clutching the telephone, her young face lifting in helpless anger. He went on down the street.

Committed now to an afternoon in the shop, he'd the truant thought of closing an hour or so early. There were two antique stores he could think of, up on Bayside, that might have old playing cards, for he was certain now of the music box's function. He would be a restorer indeed, if he could find such a pack and present the owner – whoever or whatever Justin's "old girl" might be – with her treasure complete.

My object all sublime, I will achieve in time, his footsteps kept pace with the tune, all the way up to College Street. He dropped off the laundry valise and discovered himself whistling his minuet – the Boccherini that since his childhood had signalled glad thoughts. He bought his *Globe & Mail* and found his favourite table in *Dante's* just vacated. Here, with his croissant and coffee, he could read at leisure and look out, when he chose, into glimpses of people's lives. An hour and a half would usually pass this way, but today, after just a few minutes, he put down his paper and went back out to the street.

The district had on its Saturday air already. The sidewalks were filling up, families were drifting in from the residential streets. But the clouds hung over the rooftops like a pall.

Somewhere in the city a little girl was missing. Would the poor child sense, if improbably she was still alive (and the terror, alas, not yet behind her), could she *guess* at the tide of feeling that yearned towards her, the communal love on imagination's wings, horrified, tender, that was always the nature of prayer?

If there were no guardian angels to call upon, he thought, then that commonality would be all the comfort we had.

Yet it troubled him that having thought this he had walked only twenty paces and then put it from his mind.

"I am becoming dulled," he thought, "a stranger to my life."

And it troubled him still more that such a thought could come to him, from nowhere. For he scarcely knew the meaning of it.

He was standing at the corner of Palmerston, waiting unconsciously for the lights to change, and his eyes, unconsciously too at first, turned with the eyes of the people waiting beside him to the youth on the opposite sidewalk.

The boy was staggering. He clutched a long handkerchief up to his face. "The lad's been hurt," Mr Dyce said. "His nose has been broken." The woman beside him laughed, "Oh give me a break." And as the lights changed and they all stepped out, he saw the boy lurch sideways, as if he would fall from the curb.

It was not a handkerchief – he was vomiting into a plastic bag. People stepped away from him, disgust on their faces. So young to be drunk, Mr Dyce thought, and at ten in the morning, too. He went up to the boy and took him by the shoulder: "Come on now," he said. "Let's get you somewhere you can sit down."

The boy swayed forwards, the bag still pressed up to his face. And he *was* just a boy, with fine, delicate hands and skin that was almost golden. There was the uncanny sense, looking into that young face, of a mask more real than the eyes which glared out from it.

Two women stopped, and stared, and one of them crossed herself as they hurried to catch the light. Mr Dyce took his hand away, and the boy reared back. The bag dropped to the sidewalk. Mr Dyce averted his face from the stench of ether.

The boy's mouth hung open, his teeth were an old man's.

"How can I help you?" The question itself seemed helpless; and stranded there on the corner, with the boy down now by his feet, scrabbling for that poison, Mr Dyce looked around for assistance. People glared at him, or avoided his eyes. Could they not see?

He stooped to touch the boy's shoulder: "I'm going to get help for you," and heard himself, ridiculously saying, "Just wait for me here."

Closest to him was a donut store, then a pizza franchise, but a little further on were the buckets of cut flowers, the fruit and vegetable display, outside a Chinese convenience store. He would use their telephone. For what could he do but dial 911, though he asked himself if this would do anything more than relieve his conscience. The thought of that desperate boy staring round at a hospital ward made him falter as he entered the store.

The young man at the counter was already using the phone. He looked up at Mr Dyce, his eyes vaguely attentive.

"I need to call an ambulance," Mr Dyce said.

The young man pointed out through the window. "Ask him," he said. "He's got the hot line," and went back to his conversation.

Across the street a policeman was dismounting from a white motorcycle. He was pulling off one of his gauntlets as Mr Dyce threaded the traffic towards him.

He did not look up. "Just hold your horses," he said.

"I think this is more important, " Mr Dyce said firmly.

The face that swung round at him was a mask of helmet and dark glasses, expressionless save for the surly thrust of the chin. Mr Dyce found a pen levelled at his chest: "Just get yourself onto the sidewalk," the mask said, and turned away.

Mr Dyce was nonplussed. He watched the man's weighty tread – as much a plod as a strut – as he moved to the front of the offending vehicle. He caught up with him. "I must ask for your help," he said.

The policeman gestured – as one might tell a youngster to calm down, or to pipe down for that matter. There was no mistaking the amused contempt in the gesture, the public and theatrical condescension. As the officer proceeded to write out another parking ticket, Mr Dyce took in the bull neck, the swaggering bulk of the man, and imagined the rest. He would sooner leave the boy to the mercies of the street.

In a craven moment he looked back across the traffic, saw a knot of young people there, where the lost boy stood, and quickly left the scene, *unloading hell behind him,* the words came, *step by step.*

There was no offloading his anger and guilt, all the same.

Emotions quite alien to Mr Dyce hounded him as he walked on, past the concrete planters with their bare trees, past panhandlers and street musicians, a dejected girl, an old woman whose shopping cart, crammed with frayed castoffs, rattled and veered through the crowd; past storefronts and public buildings.

He stopped, and turned back.

The girl was sitting, slouched over, on the edge of a planter. Her face was half masked by disorderly hair and as she stared in front of her, watching the passersby without seeming to, she looked – with her stained jeans and tattered sneakers – the picture of defeat.

He stopped beside her. She looked up, and then quickly away.

"Excuse me for intruding, Miss—" She looked up again, the flicker of alarm in her eyes replaced at once with a stare of insolent boredom. "I would be happy to buy you some lunch," he said, "if you are hungry."

Her eyes took in his clothes, his polished shoes. He felt huge discomfort in this place where his impulse had led him. "You *looked* hungry," he explained, "as I walked past."

There was dirt on her cheek, and a greasy wilt to her hair, but behind the uneasy scowl were the eyes of a child, still clear and alert. "I'm not going anywhere in a car," she said.

Mr Dyce flushed. "I should hope not," he said. "There must be somewhere close by where we could get you a hamburger."

"I hate hamburgers."

He smiled, "Well – that was just a suggestion. Whatever would fit the bill."

She smirked. And then stood up abruptly. "Alright – there's a place along there." Her faded blue sweater, much-washed and short in the sleeve, compressed her young breasts. She nodded past him, and set off, her slouch becoming a stiff, defiant stride. It was clear that he must follow, and not too closely.

He watched her young body, moving through the people, its pathetic pride as if she were the only one on the earth. How many, he wondered though, like her in the heartless reaches of the city?

Yet something about her – her attitude, her youth? – attracted attention, whether she knew it or not. Three teenage boys watched from a doorway as she approached, and one of them called to her.

She marched straight past them: "Go fuck yourself, creep," she flung out.

It was not the language that distressed Mr Dyce, or even the hair-trigger rage – what else should one expect from a child of the streets? – so much as the boy's confusion. He had meant no harm.

His overture had been innocent. He was affronted, though, at the sympathy in Mr Dyce's face. He nudged his friends and sniggered. Mr Dyce heard, distinctly, the word "pervert" in his wake.

The girl turned in at a doorway, then stepped back again. She waited for him, uncertain, distrustful. "This okay?"

"Of course," he said, and opened the door for her. "Go ahead, please."

All bleared and smeared with toil – the long formica counter, the open kitchen, the cracked leatherette of the booths, the shabby customers. Of all the places for a girl her age to choose – a "greasy spoon" that seemed to date back 50 years.

She scooted herself into a booth and leaned her head against the window. He folded his coat and sat down across from her.

"What's wrong with your leg?" she said. "Is it, like, artificial?"

"No, it's my own."

"What happened to it?"

"A wartime accident," Mr Dyce said, as he always did, in careful memory of poor Raine and Hodgson who did not survive the ambush.

Her forefinger toyed with the plastic sugar castor. "You talk funny," she said, glancing into his face and away again. "You Australian or something?"

Mr Dyce smiled. "What's so funny?" she demanded.

"Just that nothing could be further from the truth. Actually, I've been a Canadian for far longer than you have – I would guess three times as long."

The line of vexation between her brows marred what was really a quite pretty face.

"How old *are* you?" he asked.

She jammed the sugar back with the other condiments. "Fifteen," she said to the window. It could have been true; or not.

If only, he thought, she would stop biting her lip, and grimacing so. What could he find to say to her? He wished he had Justin with him.

She sighed loudly. Her fingers beat a tattoo on the edge of the table. Her hands were disfigured by the chipped blue varnish on her nails.

A waitress set glasses of water in front of them, and stood. "I'll have a chocolate shake," the girl said, without looking up, "and a plate of fries."

"Gravy on your fries?" the woman murmured. There was a weary meekness about her full, pale face. Almost an innocence.

The girl scowled. "I hate gravy on fries – it's gross."

Mr Dyce winced at the rudeness, though the waitress must be more than used to such manners. "That's not very nourishing, is it?" he said.

"Ice cream's good for you isn't it? And milk?" For the first time her eyes looked straight into his. He was taken aback by their alertness, the challenge there. He shrugged.

She snatched a menu from the holder. "So, can I have a denver too?" she asked, without taking time to read.

"You may have anything you want, my dear."

Was that a quirk of mockery on her lips? "Don't toast it, okay?" she told the waitress. Who stood with her patient eyes on Mr Dyce.

"Oh," he said, "just a cup of tea for me, thank you."

"You just going to sit there and watch me eat?" The girl's voice was disconcertingly loud. She was glaring at him.

"I see your point," he said. And to the waitress: "Perhaps you could make me some brown toast?"

The woman nodded, and walked back to the counter.

"I thought maybe you were going to pay for it and take off," the girl said.

"Would you prefer that?" He almost hoped she would say yes.

"No, I don't mind." She spun the menu on the table. There was a pale line on one grubby finger, where she'd once worn a ring. Had she pawned it, perhaps? It was hard to imagine her owning anything of value.

"You might want to wash your hands," he said, as mildly as possible, "before your meal comes."

She flushed. "I hate people telling me what to do." But she got up, and stalked off to the back of the room. It was that same tense, defiant stride, and it attracted the same attention. Eyes followed her as she passed the booths, assessing her as though she were at auction. This must be what fathers dealt with all the time, as their daughters grew, though what kind of father this child might have Mr Dyce chose not to imagine.

He felt, all at once, bone weary. Something nagged at his heart, like the aftershocks of the day. He wished to be anywhere else. Behind the counter the lean, near-cadaverous figure of the cook stooped under the fan hood. How many years had he stood there, in his grease-smudged apron, his spine slowly shaped to the task, flipping eggs, turning hamburgers, scraping? He and the waitresses never looked at each other; he took their written orders without a word.

Were they Ukrainian, Polish? There was something Slavic, to Mr Dyce's eyes, in their cheekbones, their stoicism.

The cook's arm over the griddle took on a life of its own. Its pallor, the almost skeletal knob of the elbow, yet its strength and precision too. It brought something to mind that Mr Dyce could not pin down. It was a painting, he was sure – an arm in the light from a window was part of it – but it would not reveal itself to him . . . .

And where was the girl? The waitress set down the milkshake, in its fluted aluminum beaker, and beside it a glass with two straws and a long-handled spoon. How long had she been? He could see no back door, down by the washrooms. She was not a drug user, surely – there was none of that spectral unhealth about her, for all her shabbiness. But what was keeping her?

The waitress came back with his tea and toast. She gave a brief smile that might have been timid, or sad, or simply mechanical. As he thanked her, he realized that she and the other waitress were sisters, and this one, he guessed, was the wife of the cook.

He saw them at home, before bedtime – their faces in the light of a half-open door – never quite free of the café's smell, in their hair, on their skins, never quite free of the details of ordering, cleaning, repeating things. This poor café would be the theatre of their dreams.

And as if he stepped past them, into their living room, he saw the photographs, on the mantel, the television, the old upright piano, with their children and grandchildren – at weddings, on holiday, in orderly suburban backyards – and knew how much he had belittled them.

"You got a smoke?" She was standing beside him, jerking the hair back from her face, biting her lip.

"No, I have not."

"Okay, okay, you can skip the lecture."

She slipped back into her seat, and concentrated on the milk-shake, moving the straws from the glass to the beaker. Her cheeks drew in, her eyes stared back at him over the metal rim. Her hands and wrist were clean now, and all the better for it, but the streak of dirt on her cheekbone had not been touched.

The sandwich and fries arrived and it was left to Mr Dyce to thank the waitress.

"You can have my pickles if you want," the girl said. "I hate pickles."

"Thank you, no," Mr Dyce said. And, "You seem to hate a lot of things."

"So don't you hate anything?" She squirted a crescent of ketchup around her plate, and dabbed into it with a french fry. "Well, don't you?"

Mr Dyce hesitated. "I would hardly call it hatred," he smiled, "but I do feel something like loathing for that clock behind the counter."

The girl anointed two more french fries, and fed them slowly into her mouth. "What's wrong with it?"

"Well, look at it, " he said. "It's ugly, to start with, I hope you'd agree with that. But worse than that, it doesn't express time; it merely records it. There is nothing to see – no face, no hands, no march of the seconds, just one slot for the hour, and another where the minute sits until suddenly another drops down – there, you see? – and replaces it. Time isn't meant to be like that. 'Telling the time' isn't meant to be, either."

She stared at him, a french fry hovering between plate and mouth, the ketchup slowly gathering into a teardrop. He watched for it to fall.

"Doesn't your brain hurt?" she said.

"I beg your pardon?"

"You think a lot, don't you?" and she tilted the french fry just in time to recover the sauce, and ate it.

"Perhaps too much," he said, embarrassed. "Forgive me." And he asked her her name.

She mumbled something, and flushed pink when he asked her to repeat it. "Tracy," she said, and "What's yours?"

"Mr Dyce," he told her.

"That all?"

"I am always called Mr Dyce."

"Yeah, but I mean, like what does your wife call you?"

Her directness amused him. "I have never married," he said.

"So are you, like, gay?"

Was she speaking so loudly on purpose? "No, I am not," he said, with what he hoped was an air of finality.

She had not touched her sandwich yet. She took up the ketchup again and made a large pool beside the french fries. Mr Dyce often wondered if people would eat half so much without this all-purpose lubricant on their food.

"Are you a teacher, or something?"

"Not really," he said.

"Shit, you're not a social worker, are you?"

"I'm a watchmaker, Tracy. A watchmaker and a repairer."

"No kidding. That's why you made the big deal about that stupid clock, right?"

Mr Dyce felt slighted somehow. He took his pocket watch from his vest, flicked it open and held it before her.

"This watch is a hundred years old," he said, "and it keeps perfect time. It has a heartbeat, as you and I have, and I wear it next to my heart. The second hand sweeps around, as the world sweeps round. And it has been in my family for three generations."

At that moment he knew that he must bequeath it to Justin, rather than to the nephew he knew only from photographs.

The girl dipped her fingers in her water glass and dried them on a napkin. "Can I look at it?" And when he flinched from her touch, "I'm not going to steal it, you know."

He felt that he had repulsed her, at just the wrong moment. "I meant no discourtesy," he said. "It's just that nobody else has touched this watch for forty years."

"That's wild," she said. "It's okay." She dropped her lips to the straws and drew at the milkshake.

There was an instinctive courtesy there, at odds with her uncouthness.

"No, please," he said, and unhooked the watch from his fob. "By all means, hold it."

He closed it and handed it to her. The chain fell in a loop against her wrist. Her face was all innocence now, and it seemed to him that a shampoo would make all the difference to that worried hair; that some decent clothing could go a long way to redeem her.

She turned the watch over, tilting it to catch the light from the window. "*Age creepeth?*" she read, and looked up at him.

"*Age creepeth, wisdom sleepeth, folly leapeth,*" he told her. "It was a saying my grandfather was fond of. He had it engraved."

"That's wild," she said again.

"If you open it," he said, "there, with that catch on the side," though she'd found it already, "there's another inscription."

She studied the watch face, almost as though she remembered his little speech earlier, following the sweep of the second hand. He had his loupe ready for her when she turned her attention to the engraving.

He almost *felt* like a teacher, watching her fit this new toy to her eye; then her young voice, faltering through the words:

> "*I am a little world made cunningly*
> *Of elements, and an angelic sprite*"

"I have a fondness for the poets," he explained, and was suddenly shy.

She handed back the loupe, then the watch. "Thanks," she said. But was biting her lip again, scowling at a customer who waited for change at the counter. It was as though she'd forgotten herself for a moment, and resented the lapse.

She took half of the clumsy sandwich and, as she ate, her other hand scrawled idle designs with a french fry in the pool of ketchup. She chewed sullenly, her eyes fixed on her plate.

"Have you friends in the city?" he asked gently.

She grunted, without looking up.

"I mean, are you living – safely? Forgive my asking."

"Yeah, yeah," she muttered. "We look out for each other, you should know that."

But how safe could she be? How steadfast would her guardian angel prove? He felt a real dread for her; all the damage that lay in wait.

"Your parents," he said. "Do they know where you are?"

"As if they'd fucking care," she said, and began eating furiously, a dark flush creeping up over her face.

"I just—"

"Look," she said, almost snarling, her face crimson now, "you don't want to know about it. Just drop it, will you." Her vehemence appalled him.

Mr Dyce toyed with his toast. It was saturated with melted butter, limp as damp cardboard. He sipped at the tea instead. If he were this child's uncle, or grandfather, as the servers and customers probably assumed, what different worlds from this weary, sad-smelling place he might lead her to. And the thought of the world she would return to, when they stepped outside – when he, as it were, would abandon her – made him feel something close to nausea. He thought of Justin, alone on the streets too, just four years ago, but with such different prospects.

He leaned forward. "If you came to my shop," he said quietly, "we could show you something that I think might intrigue you."

He told her about the shop, and where she could find it, about the watch hanging in the aquarium, about Justin and Carla, about the little music box he had explored the night before, catching her eyes every once in a while, but carefully, as if he were talking a wild creature into trust.

When he got to the perpetual motion clock, he cleared his plate to one side, took out his pen, and began to sketch the design on his paper placemat.

"Fountain pens are cool," she said. "So is there a poem engraved on it?"

"On my pen?" he laughed: "I hadn't thought of that." What came to his mind was the ludicrous *I am no poet here, my pen's the spout Where the rainwater of my tears flows out*, but he didn't offer her that – the joke might take too much explaining, and break the spell.

He drew the platen, and the zigzag grooves; the spindle, the pivot and the trips that reversed it; the little bead on its progress.

"But it must stop when it gets to the end," she said, "even for a second, before it starts back again." She had left one crust of sandwich among the fries on her plate, and had finished the milkshake. She was sipping her water now, absorbed in his drawing.

"No," he said, "though you're quite right to wonder. You see," and he made a side-sketch of the mechanism, "there is a cove at each pole which the bead runs around, and it nudges the trip there, you see, as it passes."

She was looking at his face. "*Cove,*" she said, "*poles* – you're funny." If it was mockery, there was a sudden fondness in it that wrung his heart.

"Can I have it?" she said.

"This drawing? Why, of course, if you wish."

She took his placemat and rolled it up. "Can I borrow the pen, now?"

He stifled his hesitation, and held out the pen. "Don't look," she said, and pushed her own plate aside, curving her arm on the table in front of her placemat, like a student who conceals her exam paper from a neighbour.

She made two or three strokes, as though testing out the nib, and then began scribbling, her face so close to the paper that all he could see was her hair. The fair skin of her scalp showed through at the crown. She could have been eight years old.

Mr Dyce looked away. He fixed again on the sinewy arm of the cook, still scraping, turning. That picture – he almost had it. Was it a birthday card from his sister a few years back? Something Pre-Raphaelite. A carpenter's workshop. What *was* it?

"Okay. Thanks." The girl handed back his pen. He could see her writing, tiny but full of loops, at the centre of her placemat.

She was on her feet. She tapped him on the shoulder with her scroll of his drawing and was gone. By the time he turned to look at the door, there were other customers standing between him and the street.

The pen was still warm. He breathed a small prayer for Tracy's safekeeping as he returned it to his pocket. He felt dizzy with the world.

He pulled her placemat towards him. There was a streak of ketchup across the corner, above her writing. He turned the mat around.

I'm sorry to have lied to you. I actually come from a GOOD HOME with kindly & supportive parents a cute little brother & two cats. (And a harpsichord.)

I just like to make-believe sometimes. Having an adventure or as some would call it SLUMMING. Spoiled & shameful? Yes I'm quite embarrassed.

You are a very interesting man & I thank you & wish you very well. When (if?) I get up the nerve I will come & see your TIME MACHINE.

Yours sincerely

Adrienne Henders

PS I should feel guilty about letting you buy me the meal but I expect (hope?) you won't mind very much.

Mr Dyce folded the placemat carefully three times, then folded it once more and slipped it into his inside breast pocket. He reached across the table for one of the french fries left on her plate, and dipped it into the ketchup. It was cold and greasy, and bore no resemblance to potato, but he ate another. And then another.

His last day, not even a whole day yet, had been like a novel you have read too quickly, absorbed and forgetful; delaying your bed-time, courting exhaustion. If only the world would recede and leave him sitting, alone here, for a long, long time . . . .

He could not resist the lightheartedness, though, that came surfacing for its own reasons, and it was this that got him to his feet, to pay the bill and smile at the meek-eyed waitress and go back on the street where the air felt so clean and unfettered, though the glass was still falling.

Carla was waiting in that other world; Justin would just be waking, no doubt, in some room in Lindsay. Mr Dyce breathed to the "Gentle Lark" tune as he left College and walked south, under the bare trees, towards his home. Occasional flits of rain touched his brow, or perhaps just droplets from the branches overhead. He would be fortunate to get home before the real downpour came.

He carried the girl, Tracy, with him, and "Tracy" she would remain until – if she ever should – she came to see the "Time Machine." How Justin would relish that name – it was a wonder, really, that the boy hadn't thought of it himself.

More than anything Mr Dyce wished to be a presence, a guardian, a fond household spirit, as ancestors once used to be. But that presupposed remembrance. Though he'd always believed that the watchful dead were our true protectors, what influence could they have in a world that denied them?

Even so, there were the claims of love – one could choose one's own patron saints, from the dead or the living, and something must come of it, if only comfort. Just as prayers to a heedless god might do good in the world.

For years Mr Dyce had listened each afternoon to a pro-gramme of classical music. The voice of its host, long retired now, still haunted the old workshop radio. Thirty-five years ago, the hours between one and three were reserved for the "Time Machine," as they were in later years for the jobs that were close to his heart.

The host was a dear, good man, you could tell: a fount of knowledge, of taste and judgement, of prejudice and humour, with all his quirks and quiddities (the microphone ticks of his dentures, the priceless lectures to record companies – *I'm sorry, Phillips, but it's really not good enough* – the rearguard deployment of words like con*jure*, even his love for organ music, which Mr Dyce did not share).

That man, Bob Kerr, was the one person in the world he could rather be than himself – in part because loved so much, without asking to be. Across this muddled land, Mr Dyce was quite sure, an implicit freemasonry lingered – of people who had adopted Bob Kerr as their uncle. Mr Kerr might never guess how unlonely he was.

In this medley of introspections Mr Dyce approached the high gates of the park. He had been unaccountably touched by young Tracy's teasing, her *"coves"* and *"poles,"* and he knew that Justin must mimic him sometimes – with Carla, surely; perhaps with musician friends. As he himself, or another afficionado, might relay the unvarying, anticipated adieu: *This is Bob Kerr in Vancouver, wishing you a very fond good afternoon . . . .*

The park was almost empty – no children or family groups, just isolated figures slouched upon benches, two black dogs racing in circles ahead of their master, a woman beside a tree, performing her *Tai Chi* exercises in defiance of the elements. For the downtown highrises were swimming already in mist, the CN Tower completely hidden.

Mr Dyce checked his watch. It was barely ten minutes to twelve; he would be home a good hour earlier than he'd promised. He buttoned his coat to the neck, thrust his hands in his pockets and set off again briskly, making a small wager with himself that he would outpace the rain.

On the pathway ahead, a young gull was dragging at a paper sack, comically trying to get at its contents. As Mr Dyce drew near, the bird made a frantic lunge with its beak and took flight, with what looked like a half-eaten hamburger, twice as big as its head. Two adult gulls came swooping in at that moment, scream-ing together as they chased the upstart scavenger low across the grass. As he turned his head, Mr Dyce felt a wrenching in his neck and up through his scalp, as though his skin were tearing open.

A nauseous heat filled his face and mouth, his eyes clenched against the light. There was the smell of eggs burning on a stove-top. His good leg tremored and then went leaden. When he opened his eyes, the grass was a flat board, tilting away from him. He heard the loud *shush-shush* of his own blood as though it were outside him, filling the park.

He was still standing. *"Steady, the Buffs,"* he told himself, and headed across the grass, with what dignity he could muster, to the nearest bench.

The uproar gave way to thick silence.

An arm settled, with great gentleness, round his shoulders. Close to his ear a voice soothed: "Easy now, friend – relief is at hand." A hand closed his fingers around cool, blessèd glass.

"Oh thank you, thank you," he blurted. He would soon be himself again.

But the sour fume of wine made him lurch back, choking. He saw things for a moment as they really were. The drunkard's smile on the lined face beside him, the cheap jacket, the filthy cuff at the hand which held out the bottle.

"I am not drunk," Mr Dyce declared, though his tongue made no sense of the words. "I have just had a dizzy spell."

"Whatever you say, friend." The man took a drink from his bottle, and smiled companionably. "Here she is," he announced, "here's the rain that falls on the great and the small." He eyed Mr Dyce's clothes with sly approval. "The rain takes her time," he confided, "she takes her time, and she has all the time in the world. Like I told a feller in Maryland one time, we were fighting a brush fire the whole of a jeezly week, *She's a right whore,* I told him, *and she'll let down her drawers the minute we got no more need of her."*

Mr Dyce felt the lovely, light rain on his face. He dispelled the man's voice, as it jangled on, and tried to focus on something, anything, that might restore him to himself.

He closed his eyes, and found the lynx waiting for him, glaring out from its narrow shelter. Each week, of late, he'd been drawn towards that cage, the naked tree limb its only furniture, to feel those implacable eyes upon him from the darkness. It was, he believed, the one wild-born creature in the zoo, with a memory more than instinctive of what it should be.

The fancy had entered his mind one evening, on the bus ride back to the city, that there might, in some wild otherworld, in a brambled clearing, be an idol of stone with the lynx's face, waiting out time. He had named it Remorse, and now he was somehow struggling to utter that name.

He heard himself moaning.

The man at his side nudged his arm. He was proffering that bottle again: "Last call till Blighty – she's about done."

Mr Dyce looked up and saw in him the complicit devil to whom all things are the same, without value – that ghastly tolerance which nothing could shock, or betray, or bring joy to.

In his mind he cried out *I know you, I know you – you threw away home and family and trade, for this: your children, a thousand miles away, never think of you or speak your name to their children.*

He pushed feebly at the bottle. "I am not well, can't you see?" he pleaded, "I tell you, I'm ill." And felt the last warmth drain suddenly out of his face.

The man looked hard at him. "Well, I believe you are," he said. "Don't you go and die on me here." He got to his feet and pitched the bottle away. "Keep ahold of yourself, now," he said. "We'll see you to rights."

"Just leave me alone," Mr Dyce whispered. "Just go away, and forget about this, I beg you."

The man pulled up the collar of his jacket. "I'm going to get help for you, friend. Just stay where you are."

More than anything Mr Dyce wished to be at home; to draw the walls round him and drift like a child in his darkened bedroom, while the rain spat and whispered its news at the window-panes.

There was something he had to remember.

KEEPSAKES

The little town covers a Tuscan hillside, below a pass through the mountains, and looks out down a terraced valley where a road built by the Romans, or perhaps the Etruscans before them, criss-crosses the shallow river on twin- or single-arched bridges with low stone parapets.

When the rains come, the road turns chocolate brown; in high summer it is a tan-coloured thread stitching the river into place below the orchards and vineyards; but if the hard wind blows up from the south, along the face of the mountains, the dust from the road dulls everything under a grey coat – the young olive leaves, the roofs of cars, the washing strung between walls and balconies – and fills people's nostrils with a scorched, excremental memory.

Up this road a German division retreated, to make its stand at the top of the town around the higher of the two plazas, and higher still behind the old Benedictine walls where the small plateau of the monastery gardens allowed their guns to cover the road to Milan.

It was not the first time in their history that the steep and twisting streets had been the stage for skirmishes, duels and ambuscades while roofs collapsed into flame and the dogs ran howling; but the valley was shaken as never before by the new machinery of war which churned the river banks into soupy morasses and shattered the terrace walls, all the time hurling lead and copper and iron, ton after ton, into the hillsides and staring, abandoned houses.

The war marched north. The foreign armies departed. The voice of the waterfall below the first bridge could be heard again. The town recovered itself. The monastery was repaired and the townspeople's hands, with ancestral stoicism, built back the terraces and irrigation rills, doctored the trees and grafted new shoots in the savaged orchards.

But the earth was confused. A spadeful turned up in a garden or orchard might discover a Roman denarius lying closer to the surface than a Medici scudo or a British half-crown. Sometimes such relics worked or weathered their own way up into the light. It was a process the gentleman who sat each afternoon in the lower plaza, outside the *Café Etrusco*, understood very well.

Half a century after the battle, little drifts of shrapnel still moved through his flesh. A majolica bowl in his study back in Ravenna was half filled with the metal fragments his wife had picked out of his skin with tweezers, month after month through their thirty years together.

Now that he was grown so thin, the shoals of shell-dust were like cloudy tattoos on his thighs and buttocks and across his shoulder blades. Morning and evening, after the scalding baths which he took to bring warmth to his bones, the grey-blue particles lay like grit in the tub and had to be flushed away.

He'd returned to the valley five years ago and had spent each summer there since, renting the ground floor of a house in the lower town, spending most of his waking hours on the *Etrusco's* raised patio.

He was recognized now by the year-round patrons of the café. They greeted *il professore* with a cheerful respect, tinged with pity, and it was understood that the small table in the shade of the mulberry tree was reserved for his use. There was space there for his wheelchair to be tucked in and he could lean his right elbow on the table where his books were laid out beside the habitual glass of chianti.

He was so still, so seemingly absorbed in his books and in the notes he would make from time to time in a slender calfskin journal, that no one – except perhaps the *padrone* – realized how closely and intently he watched. If anyone caught his eyes upon them he offered a courteous smile, as if he were the one who had just looked up and found himself under scrutiny.

He was watching now as a young foreigner, eating alone on a bench by the café's door, went through a strange, internal convulsion. The boy's face reddened, he sat arrested, his mouth half-open upon a mess of panini and cheese as a conflict of fear and shame broke out in his eyes.

He was an interesting case. He had turned up at about this time, the last two afternoons, to eat sandwiches with untidy haste, drinking beer straight out of the bottle, avoiding people's eyes. He was a cross and awkward youth, with no instinct for courtesy to the patio's waiter or the other customers, yet his unwavering sneer was clearly the mask of a child besieged by self-consciousness. And he hid between the earphones of his portable music player, its clashing, monotonous rhythms sounding clear across the patio.

Now he lurched to his feet, fumbling money from his pocket to lay on the bench, and headed across the patio to the steps into the street. His beer sat unfinished, though he'd grabbed up the rest of his panini as he left.

He came into sight again, across the street, hurrying down towards the first bridge, beside the old mill race, his leather field-glass case banging against his hip, earphones askew upon his neck.

How old was the boy? fourteen? fifteen? The padrone reported that they were a family from Canada, staying for a week at a *pensione* up by the monastery. Just the parents and the boy, and the parents went off every day in a rented car. As for the boy – the *padrone* shrugged: "*Maleducato.*"

The older man was not so sure. The day before, the boy had removed his dark sunglasses for a moment, while he changed the tape in his little machine, and the eyes behind the surly mask were quite beautiful. The *padrone*'s own son, Tomasso, had just moved to America, and one might wonder how *he* had fared in his first few days if he'd stepped out alone from his uncle's house? Imagine this child as an immigrant, rather than a tourist, and — *dovrei avere compassione* . . . .

But the boy was engaged already in a commando assault on the old mill, teetering along a rusted girder above the dry sluice-way, lobbing grenades into the sniper's nest that had pinned them down for three days. The panic which had launched him from the café was forgotten — the binoculars would, of course, still be there, he told himself, lying where he had left them in the graveyard. No one else was around, and he'd been gone less than an hour.

He dodged through the shell of the mill, between the fallen beams, and the pigeons clattered up from their nests in the walls as they had this morning. Then he was out on the terrace which skirted the whole lower town, alone in the sunlight where the crickets chanted and everything seemed to drowse.

There were so many scents here — dry scents, for the heat seemed to spring from the earth as much as the sun — the soil was as red and baked as the roofs of the town, yet so much was growing and every green smelled different. It was sexy. Well, everything was sexy.

He could not have explained to anyone — least of all to himself — what he really thought about the world outside him. He held certain beliefs and notions, but they were for the most part borrowed, and could change.

He lived through sensations, situations, the glamour of *things*, in a vague but leapfrogging train of emotional states, and would, if he were honest, have doubted the truth of almost anything that he said. Yet he saw and felt things more intensely than he ever had, or would again, in his life.

Here, as the graveyard cypresses came into sight, was where he'd stopped this morning to train his binoculars on the third bridge. Imagining himself a German commander looking down at the battle. And then that weird bird had called, flying straight past his face, crying *pou pou*, with its tiger-barred wings and crested wild face, and it had led him, as he tried to follow it with the binoculars, to the girl below who was also watching the bird, but whose blouse was open to her lover, sprawled in the orchard grass.

He could see where they had been lying. He could not resist it. He clambered down to the next terrace and went to the spot.

It was like an animal's lair – the twin body-forms quite clear where the grass was flattened, the pale stems at the centre like the parting in someone's hair, the dry earth showing through. He stared down. Just an hour ago. He was bewitched.

There were fruits on the trees around him; apricots, still green, though some had begun to ripen. The place smelled of them. He plucked one down, and held it to his face. It held living heat, the soft hairs on its skin teased his lips. One half of it was flushed, like Snow White's apple, the half that he tasted.

He knelt down where the man had lain, and put his palm, with as much wonder as lust, on the place where they had joined. Their heat in the heat of the earth.

Something grey, not a stone, lay just by his little finger. The zigzag lines on it made it stand out. A shard of pottery, not much bigger than his thumbnail, from the rim of a cup or bowl. Its rough skin drank in a smudge of apricot juice from his fingers. This would be his souvenir. He got to his feet and dropped the little fetish into the binocular case.

The wall of the graveyard stood above him: between those two cypress trees he had lain and spied. And here, ten feet below the buried dead and the dark trees which fed upon the graves, he had watched "the act of generation."

He laughed, and set off to retrieve the spyglasses.

They were gone. There was his form in the grass, and the dry yellow flowers that smelled of curry; and there was the white slab he had lain beside, and read when the lovers had gone – the grave of a young girl, with a poem 19 lines long carved upon it, each line ending with *Clara*. But the binoculars were not there. Anywhere.

Tears sprang into his eyes. He sat on the grave, quite honestly unsure why it mattered so much. The fact that someone had watched him, and could be snickering at him in the town? The explanation he'd have to make up for his father? Just having something stolen? No. He broke off a few of the curry flowers, and put them in the binocular case. He didn't know why. And the tears wouldn't stop till he got up and left the graveyard – he'd shamed and betrayed his grandparents, and this was his punishment.

He walked slowly back into town, and up towards the *pensione*. If his father asked he could say the binoculars had been stolen – well, they *had*. He could half tell the truth and say that he'd left them somewhere, bird watching, and couldn't find them. He didn't want to deal with his father, didn't want to see those eyes disappointed by a lie they could not understand. Most of all, he didn't want to feel this guilt.

He had just passed the café steps when he felt a hand on his arm. It was the waiter from the patio, gesturing, "*Venga, vieni.*" He followed him up the steps: perhaps they would give him a beer, for the one he had left unfinished. Up on the patio the café's owner stood waiting: "Come," he said ungraciously, "*Il professore* he like to speak with you." He led him towards the table in the tree's shade.

The old cripple with the white face was smiling up at him, extending a hand. "Filippo Redi, *dottore*," he said, his voice incongruously deep, and soft: "You will excuse me if I remain seated." The hand was like a thin glove over bones; you would not dare squeeze it.

"What do you want?" the boy asked and then – because he really did not wish to seem rude, especially since the *padrone* showed such deference to this old man and was glaring now at the boy's demeanor – "*Scusi*," he said, and mumbled his name, "but how can I help you?"

The old man folded his hands on the light rug covering his legs. "Please, please be seated," he said. "I would like to buy you something to drink, a small 'bite to eat' perhaps, and to take a few minutes of your time in conversation."

His speech was gently accented and deliberate. Was that his illness, or his carefulness with the language? The boy sat down. "Your English is very good," he said.

"How kind of you. You are much *too* kind. I regret that English is not my most fluid tongue." His face had been full once, perhaps – there was loose skin below his eyes and at his jawline. The dappling shade of the leaves played on the bare scalp.

"So how many languages do you speak?"

"Ah. I can only, with honesty, lay claim to five."

"That's amazing," the boy said. "Why don't you get them mixed up?"

The man leaned forward intently. He had green eyes, and it was hard to imagine what he'd been like when he was young. "It is said," and he paused for a moment, checking the boy's face, "it is said that the truly original mind, the *inventive* mind never ceases to explore the world through the mother tongue. For those like myself who are – let us say – clever, I think is your word, *clever* but not truly original (some would use the old Italian word *dilettante*, which in fact means to delight in something, which is not so bad, heh?), for us, the exploration of other languages – their genii, their different ways of, of appre*hending* the world – is our best path to understanding."

The *padrone* hovered without impatience – he listened in awe to the sentences unfolding in another language. The boy was more eyes than ears: the repulsion he'd felt at the old man's closeness was shifting to fascination.

"Well, well – now you understand why they call me *professore*, though I have not stood in a lecture room for twenty years. Perhaps I have written things which might be instructive, I hope so. And now we must provide you sustenance."

The *padrone* moved closer. But, "No, excuse me," the old man intervened, "forgive me, but you should not drink beer, as I have observed you to do, not in the afternoon – it will 'muddle your wits.' There is a saying in Tuscany," and he rattled off something which set the *padrone* laughing. "In essence it says that a man who drinks beer in the afternoon is good only for siestas or – for something else."

"Do not be offended, please, by our laughter. Signor Portali will bring you food and drink that you never would find in Canada. 'When in Rome,' *si?*"

The old man seemed quite at ease in the silence that followed. He reached for his notebook and on a page that was crowded already with tiny writing he began a new entry. But he did look up once, and smiled into the boy's eyes as if they shared in a happy secret; and strangely enough, when the boy looked around the patio, he got nods and smiles from a couple of tables.

The patio waiter approached with a tray, and the notebook was put away, by the pile of books on the table. "It would please the *padrone*," the old man said, "if you followed our custom of removing our hats when we eat."

The boy grinned, and took off his cap. "You sound just like my mother."

"Ah," said the other, "an old woman, *si?*" And then ducking his head, holding one hand up in protest: "No, no – no offence. Believe me, I understand. I do take a delight in the small vernaculars and I know that in English 'old woman' means *fussbudget* (am I correct?) but it also means 'wife' or 'mother', yes? 'Old lady', too. Such a language!"

Now his eyes flicked to the earphones, and when they too had come off, he sat smiling while the waiter set down tall glasses of *orzata* for them both, a demitasse of *espresso* by the old man's elbow, and, in front of the boy, a tray full of tiny appetizers.

"Wow, thanks," the boy said, "this looks great." And then, "What are you smiling at now?"

"I am actually watching the bones in your face, the bones in your wrists." And the smile grew wider. "I am thinking of that peculiar word 'rawboned.' *Rawboned* – are you familiar with the expression? I have noticed that in English fictions the Canadian male is most often described as 'rawboned.' I am pursuing its meaning!"

Ironically, though, that smile exposed the man's teeth, up to his gums, as though the skull were leering through, eager to take over.

"And now, if I could persuade you to remove, to *doff*, your *mafioso* sunglasses, we could perhaps have a conversation."

"Okay," the boy said, and began on a saucer-sized plate of crushed olives and some kind of fish. "What shall we talk about?" The salt and the spices brought saliva springing from every part of his mouth. He reached for the glass of soda: it tasted of mandarins, though it was clear. He drank half of it down.

"Taste, *taste* – give your palate a chance, I beg you, to savour our food."

Yes, an old woman, but generous too, and—

"Tell me, did you recover what you had lost?"

It was strange, like watching a Japanese film and forgetting, after a while, that the faces were foreign. The wasted body, the skeletal hands, the total pallor of the features had yielded already to the personality of this man, this talker, those searching green eyes. And now – did he have the binoculars?

"Why do you ask me that?"

The man shrugged: "I saw, when you were here before – I saw the distress in your face, and I thought, 'That young man has left something behind, and now he will have to rush off and retrieve it.' And you did rush off, and you interrupted a meal, which is always a bad thing to do, and my hope is that you will find this small repast some recompense.

"Now, if I may suggest: try that morsel of *bufala mozza* – there, mounted on the slice of tomato. It is exquisite, believe me – quite the best."

But the question was not forgotten, nor was the boy's impulse to confide.

"I left some binoculars in the graveyard. They're gone."

"Ohh. That *is* a misfortune."

"No, they were my grandfather's, you see. It's not like I can replace them."

"And your grandfather will be distressed – angry with you perhaps?"

"No, he's dead; he was killed in the war. It's – I don't know really . . . ." He wished he had kept his mouth shut.

There was a clamour of voices from across the patio: shouts, whistles, cheers. The waiter came scampering by like a child, doubled over with laughter, and a volley of bread rolls chased him through the café doorway. A huge man was dancing, beer glass in hand, round and round upon one leg, while his friends beat time on their table, until he finally fell, but held his glass triumphantly aloft. He toasted them from where he lay: "*Salut, professore!*" The old man raised his glass. "*Salut, Americano!*" The boy raised his: "*Canadiano,*" he called. "Ah, *Canadese,*" the man boomed, "Pea soup, C.P.R., Gordie Howe!" He lumbered up and approached them, but some small gesture from the old man changed his mind. He gave a flamboyant salute, winked at the boy and went back to his friends.

The old man touched the little coffee cup to his lips. "These are soldiers," he murmured. "They are just home from Yugoslavia, they have perhaps met some of your compatriots there."

"Good only for siestas or – something else?"

"Bravo," the old man nodded and nodded. "You are 'acute', I believe is *le mot just,* or is it 'astute'? No, 'acute' it must be. I shall have to teach you the original proverb before we part. And by the by, the American word 'cute,' did you know? it derives from 'acute,' and my good friend Professor Powers of Trinity College Dublin assures me that in his country 'cute' is still employed to mean 'sharp' – in reference to a man's mind, or to a knife."

He moistened his lips and placed one hand flat on the table. "Attend," he whispered. "About your grandfather's field glasses." The boy leaned forward.

"My young friend, these things that we treasure, these objects charged with memory and significance, you must learn that they

– how shall I say? – they *walk away* in their own time. It is true. I suspect that they move into Limbo, but if not – if they fall into the wrong hands – do not fear for their purity. They can not be defiled. Their *vertu* departs from them and they are merely *objects* again."

He winced, as if a cramp had taken hold of him, and leaned back from the table. "And sometimes," he continued, "we find that the time has come to give such things, such treasures, away. They are no longer ours; they have work to do elsewhere. If you do not understand what I am telling you, at least try not to forget. One day you *shall* understand."

"This is different," the boy said, "none of us knew him. He died before my father was born. My brother's got his medals – my dad gave them to him when he left home. I got the binoculars from my grandmother: she only gave them to me last week, before we left. That's all there was, except photos."

"Ah, photographs." The old man reached for his notebook and drew it towards him. "Tell me about your grandfather's pho-tographs."

"Well, there's the one on my grandmother's piano . . . ."

"*Sì?*"

"Well, just a young guy in uniform, looking off into the dis-tance. He had a moustache."

"In uniform? I find that strange, my friend, strange but – typ-ical. That public disguise, that *sacrifice*. Surely your grandmother knew the man behind the uniform. Surely she had memories more human than that . . . ."

The boy had the sudden vision of his grandmother young and naked, in the arms of her husband – of her fiancé. It seemed quite natural, a different thing altogether to imagining his parents. He knew they were making love often on this trip – maybe out in the fields like the couple this morning, but it made him cringe. His grandmother, though . . . he thought of the picture of *her* on the piano, 19 years old. Patricia."

"There is a Frenchman," said the old man, "a *thinker*, I would call him; he is too playful to be called a philosopher. He has interesting things to say about photography. He claims that because of the photograph our species has lost the ability to conceive of the *sequence of time*."

"I don't understand."

"That is all right. Just try, if you please, not to forget. Certainly you will understand one other thing he has written. He says – I will do my best to render this in English – he says, *A photograph of the deceased touches me like the deferred rays of a star*. That is very fine, do you not agree? Now I will show you a photograph."

What a character, the boy thought. What a weird mind. As the old man carefully opened his notebook and drew a small envelope from a flap in the cover, the boy was trying to imagine meeting someone remotely like this at home, trying to imagine how he might meet him if he did exist, trying to imagine sitting like this, in a Burger King, and listening.

"Now that is my mother, Francesca Redi, *nee* Porelli. The year is nineteen hundred and twenty, the year of her wedding. The place is Ravenna."

The little photograph, trembling slightly in the hand which supported itself on the table, showed a young woman in a short dress on a balcony, turning to smile at the camera, her hair styled to curve in and frame her cheeks."

"She's pretty."

"*Is*, yes, that is the word precisely. For us she is dead many years, in our Italy of television and jet aeroplanes, fifty years after a war she could not have imagined. Yet there she *is*, as you say, and pretty, as you say, and the Kingdom of Italy – which is lost beyond dreams – stretches before her beyond that balcony in the eternal sunlight."

"That's very poetic."

"Ah, no. I translate poetry. I understand it too well to imagine that I could write it."

The old man replaced the photograph in its envelope. He leaned back in silence while the waiter, who had appeared with fresh glasses of soda, removed the tray and wiped the table, skirting the twin pile of books. "*Grazie,*" the boy tried, "*bene.*" The waiter smiled, and murmured "*Ciao*" as he departed. "I thought *ciao* meant *goodbye,*" the boy said. "Ah yes – *goodbye, hello* – it literally means *your servant!*"

A narrow shudder went through the old man's body. The little envelope began shaking in his fingers.

"Let me help you," the boy said. He stood up and leaned over to take the envelope and the notebook. A faint, fungusy odour came from the man's skin. "*Grazie.*" "*Ciao.*"

The boy took a drink of his soda. Was the old guy having some kind of attack? And who looked after him, anyway? But the moment seemed to have passed: the bony hands lay folded again on the rug.

"Have you always carried that photo of your mom?"

"Ah, no. I 'dug it out' as you say, before I came up from Ravenna last month. A man who is close to death always thinks of his mother."

"Are you – 'close to death?'"

The old man smiled. "I do not wish to depress you. Young people can be so sensitive. The point I was making is this: I shall be buried beside my wife in Ravenna, as we both desired; but I shall sleep in my mother's arms."

"Do you believe that?"

"Hah!" The old man leaned his head on the back of his wheelchair and spoke to the branches above him. "I have yet to arrive at any firm belief. Nor do I wish to. It seems to me that we must believe many contradictory things, or we cease to be human."

He looked down again. "Please, enough about me. Tell me something of yourself – or, if you prefer, tell me about your parents. I see them every morning, but then they are gone – without you. They have brought you with them, but they do not know what to do with you?"

"I guess so – but it's not their fault."

"I implied no fault, my young friend. To find fault is to value the frame above the painting."

"Yeah, well, they were due for a holiday, and my dad always meant to come and see his father's grave."

"His grave?"

"Yes, this is where he was killed. So we saw the grave in the war cemetery, and the place where he died, and now they're exploring the district. Two more days."

Somehow, without his noticing, most of the customers had left the patio. Outside this half-circle of shade the afternoon sun blazed full on the tables. He had reminded himself of their first day in the town, the walk by the river through the cemetery, with its trim lawns and uniform white stones and his own name, when they found it – *he* found it – somehow unreal. The flowers they had laid were the only ones there, except for the beds of geraniums round the cenotaph. But then came the drive to the third bridge, where the trout swayed among the weeds in the parapet's shadow and where his grandfather's blood must have flowed. And his father then, lurching towards him like a frightened child, all arms and eyes, offering him weakness, which he could not respond to but his mother could, drawing her husband's face, with its tears, down against hers, while he turned back to the fish, and the swallows skimming beneath the arches, and wished to be anywhere but in their company.

He looked up. The green eyes were watching.

"I should perhaps tell you that I too was a part of that – engagement. Among the defenders of the town."

"But you're not a German."

"No, no – how to explain the confusion. You see, we had two governments then in Italy. The new one in Rome was at war all at once with Germany. The old one, up in Milan now, stood as before, on the German side, to fight off the invaders.

"You cannot expect too much of young soldiers – 'soldier boys' as I heard an Englishwoman once call them – except for loyalty to their comrades."

But the boy was barely listening. "Were you in the fighting by the third bridge?"

"Yes, there, and then at the mill, and then in this plaza, retreating all the time evidently, and at last, with nowhere to go, at the monastery. Very few of us were there to fight at the monastery when the tanks came to 'finish us off.'"

"But you were at the bridge."

"As I said." Then he drew a breath, and let out a long, low sigh. "How foolish of me. It was there your grandfather died, *si?* I am sorry. But as for what you are thinking, it is not so likely. And really, if it were the sad case that I – well, very soon we shall be able to laugh about that together, he and I."

"Do you think he'd be laughing? How – I mean, how must it feel to see your child growing up without you, to see your wife—"

"No, *please!*" There was a fierceness in the old man's voice that cut him short. "No, no, no – even for an Italian Catholic that is too absurd."

He swallowed twice, with real difficulty it seemed, and beckoned for the boy to lean closer. He spoke very quietly: "How could they *bear* to be watching? Can you *imagine* the state of impotence? You have just described *Purgatory*, young man, a Purgatory beyond Dante's imagining."

"Yeah," the boy grinned, a little scared by the intensity in those sick features. "I guess that is kind of stupid."

"You think that your grandfather watches you in the bathroom?"

"Hah! I sure hope not!"

The green eyes were laughing briefly, tracing his thoughts.

"Attend. The love, the concern, the protection is the part that we leave behind when we die – as a benediction, a blessing, *si?* It is alive, I believe, in this world." He cleared his throat, the Adam's apple trembling through the loose skin. When he spoke again, his voice was harsher, thick-tongued. "Of course they – the dead, we – leave other parts of ourselves, too. Parts that have loved this world, perhaps, all too much."

The old man was obviously feeling discomfort. He reached for his glass and worked his tongue through the bare mouthful he took. "I should not have had that *espresso.*" He ducked his head and shrugged, in mock guilt: "The pleasure principle, it will just not lie down and die." And then, looking off towards the valley, "Has it ever occurred to you that the soul is a stranger to the self?"

His voice was different, his eyes had strayed off, there was no point in trying to respond. But his hands were plucking at the rug in agitation, and one of his legs, you could see, was shivering.

"I shall have to ask a great favour of you," he said, bringing his eyes back with an effort to the boy's face. "I am most sorry. I must ask you to help me – to help me to reach the lavatory. Forgive the discourtesy." His brow was drenched in sweat, his whole face was damp.

Oh god, the boy thought, he couldn't imagine anything more scary or disgusting. But he was trapped, wasn't he? *Do I have to undress him, will I have to wipe his ass?*

He got up and edged himself round the table, past the tree's trunk. The old man was breathing fast, but contrived a smile. "It was the Englishman Coleridge," he gasped, "who imagined with horror a human mind trapped in the body of a fly." Yeah, I saw the movie, the boy thought, and then, as he shifted the wheel-chair around, "Ah," cried the old man, "saved by the bell!" The white face lolled back to stare up at him: "B – e – l – l – e!"

And there stood the girl from the orchard.

The blood rushed so fast through the boy's face that his scalp grew wet. He had seen her breasts, he had seen the inside of her thigh, seen her thrusting back at her lover, her fingers clutching those buttocks. But now she was only concerned, running forward to kiss the old man on his brow, those same fingers stroking the palsied wrist, soothing.

She looked once into the boy's eyes, and dismissed what she saw. She pulled the wheelchair out towards her, and swung it quickly around. "Do not worry," she said, as she steered the chair towards the café door, "he will be fine, fine."

An old hand lifted, like a feeble papal salute, as she manoeuvred the chair inside. She was all brown skin, the short cotton skirt celebrating her legs, the sleeveless blouse her arms, and he was free to stare until the door swung shut.

The patio was empty. He retrieved his earphones and cap, and when he stepped out from the shade a dizzying "head rush" came over him. He reached to steady himself on a chair back – it was too hot to be touched. He walked slowly across to the steps, and down into the street. The light off the house walls was blinding.

What time was it? He had no idea how long he had spent back there.

"Hey there! Hello, you! Come back!"

The girl was standing at the top of the café steps, beckoning to him. She came down two steps as he returned. She smiled down; he could see almost to the top of her legs.

"My uncle had said that you would leave," she said. "He demanded that I intercept you."

Where the old man's vowels had seemed English, her's were American in resonance.

"You speak English, too?"

She put her hand on the railing. "In my family there could be no choice. Besides, only the English world could be so lazy as to trust one language."

"Shouldn't you be with him?"

She tossed her head. Her hair flew back like a shampoo commercial. "He needed his medicine. He's okay. I will take him straight home."

The boy stepped closer. Partly he wanted to take his eyes off her legs. Now they had to avoid her breasts. And her eyes laughed at him; whatever she consciously thought, they were saying *You're a kid, I'm a woman, understand that and we'll be friends.* Yet she couldn't be more than eighteen, maybe.

"He's your uncle, then."

"Great-uncle. Same difference. But listen, he invites you to a dinner, a genuine meal, before you leave."

"Tonight?"

"Ah, no." Her eyes became darker, confiding. "The medicine he must take, he says it makes clouds in his head, you understand?"

"So when?"

"Eleven, eleven-thirty, is okay?"

"It's our last day tomorrow," he said. Her eyes were really amazing. "I promised my parents to go out with them."

"Too bad," she shrugged. "My uncle thought we would have a good time."

"I'll ask them then – they won't mind."

She came down, to the step that he stood on, and folded her arms, leaning back against the wall.

"Understand this," she said. "Me, I am two-a-penny'; my uncle is a great man."

"I've never met anyone like him."

Her laugh had a disconcerting rasp of vulgarity. "He thinks you were sent."

If his parents were put out or hurt they didn't show it. "At least," his mother said, "we'll have the three days together in Florence. And you'll really love it there." And his father asked, "Is this friend of yours – forgive the expression – *respectable*?"

"He's a cripple, Dad," the boy said, "and he's some kind of university prof. He speaks a zillion languages; he talks like a book. I like him." He felt uninclined to mention the third bridge; or the girl.

They ate that night at the *pensione* and then went out with the other guests onto the narrow balcony to watch the moon come up through the pass. The town's shadow filled the whole valley with darkness till, little by little, as the moon crept over the monastery walls, the shadow was drawn in towards them and the tiled roofs below swam in moonlight

"It's so goddamn peaceful," his father said. His mother's hand covered her husband's on the stone balustrade.

When they had gone to bed he spent half an hour in the darkness of his room, leaning on the windowsill. Here and there down the valley a metallic gleam picked out a bend in the river; otherwise the moonlight was like mist on the terraces. There were few lights anywhere and virtually no sounds, except for the waterfall's hush. A bonfire was burning, though, off to his right – a glowing smudge in what must be one of the orchards . . . .

He thought of the nest in the grass under the apricot trees.

There was a double tap at the door and his mother was there, tentative in the doorway, hands in the pockets of her dressing gown, feet bare.

"It's not much of a holiday for you, is it?" she said.

"I'm fine," he said, and, "you're the one who needs a holiday."

He turned from the window. The light from the corridor slanted across her face. He was quite conscious of things changing. He felt the old tug of her concern, drawing him towards her breast, but he could see himself, as if through her eyes, solitary and unreachable by the window.

"I should be worried about you," she said.

He laughed – a kind of laugh. "Forget it, Mom." The gold chain with its locket glinted at her breastbone; he realized that she was naked under her robe. "Go back to bed," he told her, speaking as he might to a child.

She lifted her chin: "We're on your side, you know."

He turned back to the window. "Of course you are," he said.

The door closed softly. He shut his eyes for a moment before he looked out again at the night. A bat swooped up past the window and tumbled away towards the rooftops. He saw another, then another, and, from somewhere below, the plaintive madness of a cat's cry, like a soldier lost in the mud calling *Help*, sounded and kept on sounding.

He watched, as he undressed, a cloud swallowing the moon the way a snake swallows a frog. "Taste, *taste*," he declaimed. "Give your palate a chance, I beg you, to savour our food." He made it onto his bed with one leap, flinging himself back upon the pillow. "It is exquisite, believe me," he told the ceiling, "quite the best."

He started to think of the girl's thighs, but her face got in the way.

They were walking down for breakfast at the car park's café when he saw the wheelchair approaching. The girl's face was close to her uncle's as she leaned forward, easing the wheels over the cobblestones. She was talking, and laughing.

"That's my friend, Dad," he said. He could not avoid introductions. The old man seemed tiny out on the street, slumped down in the wheelchair with a light rug, in the same pattern as the one that covered his legs, draped on his shoulders.

The boy saw with surprise that his father instantly took to the old guy. In fact, he saw more to like in his father than he had for a year or more. There was a lack of phoniness, an easiness with who he was, a grace in his body. If it had been someone else's father he could have felt envy. But his mother was repulsed, even scared, by the meeting. He felt her distress when she took the old hand. Yet it was she who made conversation and lingered, full of polite concern and gratitude.

"It is I who am indebted, Signora. Imagine the generosity of a young man to indulge an old scarecrow."

The girl stood, smiling and distant, in a blue sun dress and wedge-heeled sandals, waiting for them to move on.

The sun was already too hot; there was no movement in the air; the sky seemed more white than blue. They ate beneath the café's awning, and the boy introduced them to *orzata* sodas, discovering that there were fifteen different flavours.

"Your friend is very refined," said his mother, "but oh, Stevie, he's at death's door."

"I think the Professor's companion's the main attraction," his father said. And relished his son's blushes.

"Don't tease him, Jerry."

"Well, she really is stunning. I don't blame him. Hard to imagine that in twenty years she'll be built like a tank."

"They don't all, darling," she said. "Think of Sophia Loren."

"There was a time," his dad said, "when I did little else."

He watched the green Fiat drive off down the valley, coming back into view as it crossed each bridge, stirring brief dust behind it. He ordered another soda *orzata* with two and a half hours to kill before his lunch date.

At death's door. Knock-knock-who's-there? The old man would probably just have fun with that if he told him. *Such a language!*

Was his mother afraid he would catch some contamination?

He wandered off at last, along the terrace. He revisited Clara's grave, and the nest in the grass, but he just wanted time to pass. And tomorrow this would be nowhere.

Some boys had started a soccer game beside the river. He stood and watched. They were about twelve years old, rowdy and sprinting about, ignoring the heat. *"Ciao,"* he called out, when he saw they had noticed him. *"Canadese!"*

They waved him in, shouting and laughing without interrupting the play, pointing out the side he must play on. He went easy at first because of his size, but some of them were quite miraculously skillful. His first competitive burst was foiled by a kid who didn't come up to his chest, dancing around like a terrier to steal the ball and then score. They cheered and jeered and whistled till it was easier to feel like an adult among them – clumsy and indulgent. He was exhausted in no time. But at least he had learned the Italian for "penalty kick" and "pass the ball" and "fuck off."

He got up to the *Etrusco* half an hour early, but they were there at their table, heads close together over a book.

She looked up, and immediately uncoiled from her chair and strode across the patio. She was fierce with urgency.

"Listen to me. You must forget about this eating together. He is too tired, though he will not say it. He did not sleep in the night."

"Alright, I'll leave."

"I will give you money to buy for yourself a meal somewhere else."

"It's okay, I said. Tell him I had to go with my parents."

She took hold of his forearm. A shiver went down to the pit of his stomach. "No," she said, "you must come for a little while. He has something to give you."

The teeth in her uncle's smile looked too big for his face. "Good," he said, "good. *Benvenuto!* Sit, sit, we have a chair for you." There was some mischief in his eyes as they moved from the boy to his niece and back again.

"And you have met Francesca," he said. "My angel. My guardian."

"Wasn't that your mother's name?"

The girl broke in: "My *piccola nonna*. She was one funky dame. I love her completely." Her right hand touched her uncle's brow, then his arm. She seemed unable to stop touching him. And he took her hand in his and raised it to his lips. Then held it against his cheek.

"I have been at work," he smiled. "I have this for you." He held out a small sheet of paper in his other hand. "It is a poem that I made, discovered I should say, in translating a German philosopher. A man many people despise, and a man who feared death terribly. But he is still a great man, I believe. So, there – for you! An English translation of my Italian translation."

The writing sloped boldly forward in purple ink, the *g*'s, *y*'s and *f*s with jaunty underscrolls:

> *Man puts the longest distances behind him*
> *In the shortest time. He sets the greatest distances*
> *Behind himself, and thus sets everything*
> *Before himself at the shortest range,*
> *and yet*

The frantic abolition of all distances
Achieves no closeness

"Thank you," the boy said.

"As I said to you once before, I believe: No need for you to understand now, just please do not forget. And I think you will especially keep this as a memento of my Francesca, who wrote it out for you, because, alas, my handwriting is becoming a mystery, even to myself."

The girl drew back her hand and swept it up through her hair. Her smile seemed completely open now, and as she rose from the table she saw the boy gazing into her dress and seemed, if amused, not offended. She actually brushed her fingers along his shoulders as she passed.

He folded the paper carefully, and unbuckled the binocular case. Its old leather breath was tinged with curry.

"So today you leave behind those earphones, but you have brought the empty case. It has found a new use?"

The boy laughed. "Quite honestly, I didn't want my dad asking questions. I figured he'd be more likely to wonder if I *didn't* bring it."

"But you will have to explain this sooner or later."

"Later, I guess."

The girl slipped back into her seat. At once her hand went out to her uncle's and then began stroking his sleeve.

"Ah, Francesca. For the miserly sum, for the pittance I give to her, she is everything to me here."

Her hand slid up to his shoulder. "He pays my studies at university," she said. "Don't listen to him."

The waiter was there, with drinks for them all. The old man asked him a question, then started to speak rapidly, but the girl waved her hand between them: "No, no, *no!*" The waiter hesitated; the girl shooed him away

"There is no arguing with her." The old man's exasperation was more real than he pretended. "She will march me back to my bed, and spoil all our entertainment." More gently, he said: "It is discourteous, Francesca, you know this, to invite a guest—"

"It's okay," the boy said.

She murmured something in Italian. Her eyes were stern, she looked suddenly much older, more heavy of feature. The woman she would become, perhaps.

"*Va bene.* But first I have something to show you both."

He reached beneath the rug on his knees, and with some effort – pushing his body sideways in the chair with his other hand – worked something free from a pocket.

"Now," he said, "I will show you." He held up a watch, the kind people have to pull out to consult.

"This belonged to *my* grandfather," he said. "It was never of the best quality, yet it seems determined to limp out its time with me.

"But now I will tell you a story – concerning that battle," he looked up at the boy, "we were discussing yesterday. Yes, I have told Francesca about your grandfather.

"So, as I told you, it ended up at the monastery. And on the last day, I was with three others, we had a machine gun, we were sheltering behind a – no, I cannot recall the English word, the wall that holds up a wall, no matter, it was on the side of a chapel.

"Yes, of course it is terrible to think of the house of God as a battleground, terrible to think of the beautiful things, the history, the prayers, the memories, etcetera, etcetera. But what were we to do? We remembered Thermopylae, we remembered Horatius at the bridge, we were young men who would die to the last man. That is glory, yes?

"Suddenly, there was a tank – it was late in the day – there was a tank not 50 paces from us, and when it fired – darkness."

His niece was motioning him to be calm.

"*Sto bene. Non sono eccitato.*"

"*Ecco.* They were not sure if I would live, and when I woke up they were not sure if I would walk."

The boy's eyes imagined the legs under that rug.

"No, no," the man shook his head. "I recovered fully, in the flesh that is to say. This is another disease, of old age – a weary heart, weary blood.

"But you wonder where this story is wending. All right. I had two, three operations and then, is maybe a year later and the war is all finished, and they 'check me over' at the big hospital in Ravenna. They x-ray my legs, they x-ray my back, then they x-ray my head – and this is what they find."

He turned the watch in his hands, trying to get enough purchase to open it. "*Patetico*," he sighed. "You help me, Francesca."

The watch sprang open in her fingers. The dial was yellowed, the glass almost opaque. But, "No," he whispered, "*il dietro. Apri la parte posteriore.*" She found a groove for her fingernail, and the back of the watch was a separate door. A fold of blue cloth fell onto the table. He gestured for her to give it to him.

"Now this," he said, "they extracted from the edge of my brain." He laid his hand out in front of them. There was a dark piece of glass on the cloth. "Look," he said, "hold it to the light." The girl took it, and held it to her eye. She gasped. "*E l'occhio della Vergine*," she muttered, and crossed herself, her fingers touching on each of her breasts. She slipped the thing back, and crossed herself again.

The old man nodded: "Now you." It was no bigger than the pottery shard from Francesca's lair. The boy turned in his chair to see the light through it. "Francesca thinks it comes from the Mother of God, but I think more likely a little saint, or who knows – a shepherd." The glass was an eye, almost complete; even the eyebrow hairs were delicately brushed in. The iris was pale blue. The sun must be throwing the picture onto his face.

"I have to suppose that the tank shattered some windows, as well as my two comrades."

"And it was in your brain?"

"So they told me."

The boy put back the eye, with some reluctance. At that moment he felt stronger, older even than Francesca.

The frail hand pushed itself further across the table towards him.

He's going to give it to me, he thought. He's going to give it to me, and I'll keep it in my bedroom with the owl's skull and the gold nugget and the shark's tooth.

He glanced with a sort of triumph at the girl, but whatever she was thinking, her eyes were fixed on her uncle.

"I would like you to tell me about your grandmother." The eye on the outstretched hand was suddenly a bribe. "Tell me, was she, as they say, 'faithful to the memory' of her husband?"

What did he want? "She got married again, after a while. She had two more kids, and then they divorced when the kids had left home."

"But your grandfather's photograph, you said, was on her piano."

"Well sure. It was always there."

"Ah, *bene* . . . I like to think of a house with a piano. And does your grandmother play?"

"Yeah, she's good. So's my dad."

"And the piano, does it stand near a window?"

The girl was caressing her uncle's arm again. But the sight of those teeth in the painful smile, and the green eyes' intense interest . . . . No the old guy couldn't help how he looked.

"It's right *in* a window. What they call a bay window."

"Ahh," said the old man, "Francesca – imagine. And can you tell me what your grandmother sees when she plays her piano and looks out from her bay window?"

This was too weird. "The main thing she sees is a lilac tree. She planted it the day my sister was born. It's twenty-three years old."

"That is courage, my young friend. It is courage and – *elegance*, and faith."

"I guess so."

"Now," he laboured to sit up and lean forward. His niece tried to restrain him, but he waved her off. "I shall ask you, and trust you, to be my Hermes, my messenger between worlds. Will you do that for me?"

"I'm not sure what you mean."

"I would like you to take this – relic, and give it to your grandmother. I would ask you to tell her the whole truth about those binoculars, and to give her my gift, and to tell her the truth about that also. I believe she will understand." He had spoken with great deliberation. Now the hand began to slip back across the table. "Take it, please."

The boy did take it. He folded the cloth around it again, and opened his binocular case. And then, on an impulse:

"Look, I found this yesterday. It's not very impressive, but I guess its really old. Here, it's for you." The old man had shrunk right back in his chair. The boy had to get up, and open one of the hands, folded on the rug. The shard of pottery lay grey upon the parchment skin; the zigzag lines had a sudden violence to them.

"*Then 'twas the Roman, now 'tis I.* Have they taught you that poem yet? Ah, you are very kind," and he inverted his hand, pressing the fragment back into the boy's palm. "You are very kind, but I must not accept. All I have left to do is to give. But I thank you, I thank you – it will not be forgotten."

The boy turned to Francesca: "Maybe you'd like it."

"Me? I would only lose it! But I thank you, too."

The old man was breathing through his nose. It was a scarey sound, convulsive and animal. The girl moved round behind the wheelchair, and started massaging her uncle's shoulder and chest, resting her chin very lightly on his brow. "Time for you to go," she said.

"I have not cared very much for my body." It sounded like an announcement, the voice more high-pitched than before, but speaking seemed to make the breath come more gently, and the old man ignored his niece's shushing whispers. "Since my Lydia died, I have devoted myself entirely to the life of the mind. And Lydia would laugh to hear me say that – she would say that nothing has changed!" He leaned back, smiling up at Francesca: "I am not without memories, though." She kissed his brow, a slow kiss with those wonderful, full lips. Her hands did not stop for a moment their slow massage.

"My body shall leave me soon." He looked back at the boy, there was mischief again in his eyes. "I frighten you, I know. I am sorry for that."

"You don't frighten me. You frightened my mother."

"Imagine that. You must greet her from me, with respect." He closed his eyes. "Yes, my body shall leave me – not so soon as you think: Francesca understands. Not so soon, but soon. At the moment I have no intention of going with it."

Softly, the girl spoke the boy's thoughts, though her tone was more playful than anything, and spoken in English: "But where will that leave you?"

"It is perhaps as futile to speculate on that point, as to sur-render." His eyes were still shut. The girl motioned with her head for the boy to leave.

He buckled the binocular case. And stood up. "Well, *arriva-derci,*" he said. One hand lifted fractionally from the rug. The girl flashed him a quick smile: "*Si* – bye."

He turned at the top of the stairs and watched. Her hands pushed steadily on the old chest and shoulders, she seemed to be crooning, or singing under her breath, with a smile that seemed quite unconcerned with sickness. Her face, and her movements, reminded him of his mother at the sink and then, even more, of his grandmother kneading bread on her long table.

She looked up and saw him there and looked down again. But a few seconds later, she moved her hands to her uncle's fore-arms, and looked steadily into the boy's face, still kneading, still crooning, but looking . . . .

Twelve years would pass, and he would be walking home through the lanes of a western city in the first miraculous daze of fatherhood, before he remembered that moment in Tuscany. He did not at once recall the girl's name, but her face was suddenly vivid in the prairie dawn, leaning towards him over her uncle's bowed head, and he understood, or felt that he did, what her eyes had been trying to tell him.

TWO

DELIVERED BY HAND

Madame Doctor Deputy,

My initials are on the envelope, so you will guess at once whose words these are, though you may have forgotten the handwriting. I cannot tell, of course, if you will read any further, but allow me to say that you should – there is information within that concerns you.

No doubt you were shocked for a moment by the letterhead – it is not many months since a letter from that office would have struck fear in your heart, yes? The irony, however, is not mine. Just two days ago I found a street vendor selling old government stationery for a song: he parted with a hundred sheets from my old ministry, with envelopes thrown in, for a half-finished tube of German toothpaste. It is the cheapest paper to be found in the city.

Well, I can still read and write, you see, and I have not forgotten how to distinguish the truth, even in age and disgrace.

It is the truth I want to speak to you about, since you will not listen to me in person. Yesterday I went back to your brother's office and waited six hours. The day before, he had passed me in the corridor with cold, virtuous eyes. This time he finally crooked his finger at me from his door, at half past six. There was nobody left, by then, to embarrass him. And what did he have to say? Perhaps he has told you.

Your brother, you must have noticed, is putting on weight. His hands are white, and soft, and that sensuous mouth is being overtaken by flab. But this was offset, of course, by the nice dash of Democracy in his Marlborough cigarette and the wide tie whose colours were like something puked up in an alleyway by a cider drinker.

He gave it to me straight, as they say now – no doubt he prided himself on his firmness – "Old man," he said, "get it into your head that the world has changed." Yes, as if I were a slow-witted peasant. "Things are out of your hands, now," he pronounced – I can just hear him quoting his fine lines to you, or his wife, after work. "Things are out of your hands, so take my advice and be happy to live out your days in peace and quiet."

As if I were fortunate not to be locked up, or shot. My hand shakes with rage at the thought of it – that prig, that popinjay, that opportunist. Your brother, my brother's son!

But let me describe to you my "days in peace and quiet." I share the back hallway of an apartment building with three other fellows: oh, we get on very well together, there is a true Democracy there, two city folk down on their luck, two village refugees looking for old connections, we are the best of friends. Oh, we would not leave anything of value unattended for a second, but that lack of trust is its own kind of honour and besides, who among us has anything of value anymore? Sometimes there is a roll of tobacco, an occasional shot of liquor; winter is far away, and enough cabbage leaves, stale loaves, vegetable peelings come our way to keep body and soul together. We do not smell like roses, that's true (oh, I saw you pinch your nostrils and avert your face when I turned up at your door last Thursday!) but we understand each other, and we have stories to tell. Very interesting stories, without fear or favour!

It is easier, more than likely, to come down in the world than to climb. I have done both, of course. You and your brother have done neither, though it must seem in the last 14 months as if you have risen.

We shall see.

As for you, Madame Deputy – what has your new position, your "heavy responsibility" made of you? When I stood in your doorway, you looked as though Lazarus had risen. I could hear your visitors in the room behind you, the laughter of your daughters, some black music. "What do you want?" you said – you needed to ask me that? And when I suggested that I might come in for an hour and talk, have some coffee perhaps, a piece of your famous seed cake, a little glass of pear brandy for old times' sake, you said, "Are you mad?"

Am I mad? Well, Madame Doctor, disgrace may be a disease, old age may be contemptible, but do they add up to madness? It was your word – you, the respected, influential psychiatrist. Or has Madame Doctor sacrificed life and career for the higher calling of Deputy?

It is easier, believe me – though you will not believe me – for the old to understand the young than the other way round. Not just because we have *been* young (for you will say, and quite rightly, that our youth belonged in another world) but because we can see where you came in. We are your context.

Besides, you are not young. You are middle-aged pampered folk made giddy by the feelings of change and self-righteousness.

In your own eyes you represent freedom, hope, high spirits – the power to make reforms. You are not the first to have felt that way. I could speak about that. So could your Father and Mother if they were living.

Our country is less than a century old; it is falling apart in your hands. You are willing to let this happen – very soon you will be fighting to make it happen. Forty years of compromise, you say, and then fifty more of "slavery" to the Idea – just an eye blink of time in the true history of nations.

You are time travellers, you people – going back into the Dark Ages in your gleaming machines. And the air in that place is swarming with viruses, plagues and succubi against which you have no defences.

You cannot climb back into your machine, and return – the air of that place is not friendly to aliens, your fuel will have been exhausted, the controls seized up. You will be stranded in that stinking future which is the past returned, triumphant and free to be worse than it even dreamed possible.

You have yoked freedom to Glory. Glory is what spews out of a drunkard's mouth, when he loses his mind at the back door and the mad ghosts of his ancestors seize hold of his tongue.

Will you listen? Will you let me tell you a little about our country, the land I was born into, divided as it was, and which you are preparing to blast off the map?

I am a Blackbird – first and last but not, I insist, most importantly. And we shared the land, which you would describe as a cage, with many others. With the Sparrows, the Robins, the Larks and the Canaries – and in the later years of the Idea, with the migrant Whitethroats who came and stayed because our land was more gentle than theirs.

Our songs were different – some more, some less – but we could all understand each other.

And for 50 years, under the Idea, we were all just Songbirds. You will laugh at that, I know – and in many ways it is right that you should laugh: it was far from perfect. I remember your Father saying that a land that flew so many flags – on every lamp post, on every bridge and factory and hotel – was not yet a real country. "When there are no more flags," he said, "then we shall have relaxed into being ourselves." He was right – I did not deny it then, and I do not now. Your Father – that gentle, unworldly man who had no head for politics – was very often right, for all our disagreements.

But 50 years of peace is something! Never in history had it happened before. (And I ask you, do you see it happening again?) Your Father and I could disagree about most things and still be brothers, still welcome in each other's homes, imagine that! You could not say that of other countries which embraced and betrayed the Idea.

For we made the Idea our own. I was about to say that that is the way of our people – but no, the truth is that our people learned that practical, absorbing way with things in the 50 years which saw you grow up, in safety, and which you have now consigned to Hell.

Oh, our buildings were ugly, it's true – we were mediocre in many ways, unfit for the challenge, unworthy no doubt of the Idea we proclaimed. But could it not be that our best hope lay in that mediocrity, a generation learning to govern? Was it not part of that compromise I have just referred to. Might it not, given time and the coming of your generation, have forged a reality from the Idea?

But this all smacks of rationalization, self-justification, "revisionism" as you revisionists would call it. And I must not allow you to throw down this letter with a smug dismissal. I do not want to let you, as they say, "off the hook." And there *is* a hook – though you will not have guessed it, even if you have read this far – a hook at the end of my line, set out for two sweet troutlings, your brother and you.

So let me acknowledge what you both will discover and bow to, if you have not already begun – there will never be power without influence, toadies, bribes and advancement. Never. We are no exception – currency hard and currency soft, as they say, was what got things done. But the question must always be, not who benefits, but who suffers. I do not accept that the people suffered under us. We are a poor country (and we look to become poorer), but poverty is not suffering, least of all in a country which has always been poor. Destitution is suffering, persecution is suffering, war, famine, disease (you will see) are suffering. But no one suffered as they suffer now, with the money a worthless joke and the threat of war on every horizon.

And no longer do the rich tourists come to indulge in our brilliant history and the innocent idyll of our poverty.

I must speak a little more about that "corruption" of ours, about the "perks," about who benefited, because it concerns you, as you full well know. Oh, you will have excuses ready at hand – it was none of your doing, you will say – but then I have found that only the privileged find it easy to denounce privilege!

Was there ever a time in your childhood when you wondered about food, or clothing? You were my little "Lubi" then, with your braids always coming adrift and your make-believe world among the goldenrods. How you'd tug and swing at my hand in the park, while your sharp little mongrel raced after the squirrels and your ruffian of a brother scared up the ducks by the pond. Remember? Standing there waving his arms as the birds lifted above the trees. Yes, those times. Have you truly forgotten?

Did I not come every Sunday to drink and play chess with your Father, bringing you candy, wind-up toys, and picture books – some of them not strictly legal? Did your Mother not have good shoes, pretty underwear, and an English wristwatch? Was your Father ever without liquor or Cuban cigars for the old cabinet painted with Blackbird designs, the cabinet made by his Father and mine? Did you not have use every August of a government villa in the hills? Did you not both get permission and scholarships to take graduate degrees in Germany? Did your Mother not go to a Swiss sanatorium in her last illness? All this for the family of a poor unambitious professor!

What have you done for me, these days? Is this the new purity? Is this the blood loyalty that you fling out on the airwaves to Blackbirds everywhere?

Do not mistake me – I ask nothing of you. And all that you have refused me is my *existence*. But when I lie at night in my sweet nest under the back stairs, sharing my snores with another old Blackbird, a Sparrow and a Canary, I wonder about those things.

There were materials, you remember, that no one might read, or watch. There were prison cells, I admit, for our hostile critics. But there were no tanks on our streets, no salt mines, no show trials, no torturers. And did we not treasure the Arts and Sciences? Do not laugh – we acknowledged their power, and so we sometimes suppressed them, as the Roman Curia, perhaps, silenced Galileo – knowing that History will take care of Truth, but the truth for one time, Madame Deputy, may not be the truth for another. All parents know this, with their white lies and prohibitions.

You may know very well that children will find ways to eat candy, or read comic books, or listen to trashy music, or look up each other's skirts or mistreat animals – but that is no reason, no reason at all, not to forbid those things in the home.

And look at the trash – you know it – that your children read and watch and wear and listen to now. You call this freedom?

Again, I find myself shaking with rage. That you, who are so wrong, so disastrously wrong, are so sure of your correctness.

My niece is an eloquent woman – more impressive, perhaps more ambitious, than her paunchy twin brother in the Ministry of Supply. I have followed your career: reports in discarded newspapers outside bars, your photograph once on a magazine cover at a newsstand. What a schedule you have – I wonder you find time at all for the children, or for your practice (and there must be a call for psychiatrists now, for those who can afford them – these are nervous times). Just last week I saw you on television – I watched through an open door on the third landing – wearing your twin mantle, Madame Doctor, Madame Deputy, describing the "Gerontocracy" you had overthrown.

It was that programme which led me to turn up at your doorstep, and crave an audience.

A fine word "gerontocracy," and one that it is hard to quarrel with. But you forget that the old and the young are much closer to each other than to those who come between them. Ask any grandparent, ask any grandchild. And it is you who will send our grandchildren off into war. For an alphabet! For a midday prayer!

Consider this: in the time of the Idea, was there anyone who did not pray in his or her private hours, if only for comfort of nostalgia? The praying man or woman is a child. Good. In a world where God is denied, nobody's God, nobody's childhood, can be taken away from them. And now? – the Cross is raised as a sword, the Crescent is swung as a falchion, our "brilliant histories" reenact themselves.

I am a Blackbird, as I told you, through and through, and I thrill to the old glories, still, victories and defeats, like any child. But they live in the same place as prayer. The Idea taught us the lie of such Romances. You people have fallen in love again with literature, and you are going to turn it loose upon all children.

It is war, finally, that I must talk about. None of you understands war – you with your 50 years of peace and security, your children with their American films and heroics. You will understand soon enough – you are more in love with machines and engines than we were (and our faith in them was perhaps our greatest sin), but a war cannot be won with them, with the long-distance tilting of airplanes and rockets, by remote control. Sooner or later someone will be invaded, and then you may learn what an enemy is when you are staring into his eyes – it is closer to the schoolyard or to alleyway rumbles, than to any Romance.

Above all, you will learn what war feels like: filth. And what its smell is – death, putrefaction, a sewer-pond of torn-open bodies that lurks on your palate for months afterwards.

The air smells now as it did at the end of the German war, when the occupation was over, and our scores were about to be settled. It was the last blood-letting between us. We believed it would be the last. The smell is like electric stillness before thunder. There is madness inside that held breath.

Your Father was 24 then; I was 27. We were disbanding, heading home through the hills, nine of us left after two weeks of ragged fighting with Robins and Canaries. In truth we were on the run. A week before, we had been called over to the far side of the valley to bury our Father. His section had been ambushed and pinned down with mortar fire. We pulled down strips and tatters of his flesh off the apple trees, and put them together with what was left of his body. His wedding ring was in my brother's pocket; his old silver cross, bent up like a fish hook, was around my neck. I wear it still.

In wartime your Mother no longer watches over your shoulder. When she sends you away, she draws a veil down over her face and behind that veil there is one question only: will he come home or not? Nothing else concerns her. This you will have to learn, because you are a mother, with a son, and soon you will reach for that veil.

You denounce the Robins as fascists, collaborators, extortioners – we thought so too. You call the Canaries barbarians, heathens, criminals of the 13th century – our very words.

I will not tell you the name of the village that we came to that afternoon – though it is not very far from the villa where you picnicked with your children beside the crystal waterfalls. And I will not say if it was a Robin or Canary village – perhaps both had been living there, side by side, for years.

It was any village in the path of a war, and it is easy to describe.

There was a stain which had once been a man, on the short humpbacked bridge. There were homes without roofs. There were animals in the street, a wild barnyard turned loose – chickens and ducks and hogs by the doorways, and the dogs slunk away from us, behind the houses, fat and ashamed. There were lines of crows on every rooftop, and the storks sat up there by their nests, staring at us and cleaning the dark muck off their beaks and soiled white feathers.

There was a smell of smoke, but there were no fires, no sign of anyone. But in a small house, set back from the street, we found an old woman, and her daughter, and her daughter's son.

War has its logic and you, Madame Doctor, who must so often have counselled the victims of rape and assault, will have to learn that in wartime rape is another thing. The soldiers who survive and rape understand this logic, it is somewhere in our blood, and whatever you may believe now, you will learn that the women understand it too.

My brother laid his rifle down on the floor and took hold of the younger woman. And he set to work on her at once, not in the fast, angry way you would imagine, but slowly, tearfully, moaning like an unhappy idiot boy. And then her son – he was ten, perhaps, maybe younger – threw himself on my brother, scratching and screaming, while the old lady scolded him.

War has its logic. I pulled him away by his arm. "Come outside," I told him, "this is no place for you." We went round to the back of the house. "Look at the plum tree," I said, and I shot him.

When I came back inside, the woman was crouched by the stove, staring at me. As my brother bent to pick up his rifle, she flew at him with a knife. It gashed his ear, and cut through his shirt, into his armpit, not much of a wound. When he knocked her away, he saw beads of milk across her breasts. "Where is the child?" he said, and she set up a wail, and the old woman too, threw herself into the corner where the cradle sat, as if to shield it.

War has its logic. My brother's words hung in the air before he spoke them – either one of us could have used them. "I'll take care of your baby," he said, and then shot her twice. She understood him. And a mad understanding crept into my brain, in that deafening room: *You have blasted your own seed at the mouth of her womb.*

The old woman died too – what had she left to live for?

You might think it easier to kill a baby than a youngster, but it is not so. A youngster's eyes ask you questions, they stare back at you from a happier world. They are witnesses.

We went up into the hills before nightfall. I carried my brother's rifle for him, and he held the baby inside his shirt. We tried to sleep at the edge of the forest, but the child grew fretful, the water we gave it was not enough. Only when your Father dipped his fingers in the water and let the child suck at his finger tips – the middle finger, the trigger finger – did it settle a little bit.

In the morning, our group split up and headed for our different homes. There were Robin and Canary patrols out everywhere, but we evaded them. And we found a goat and milked her dry for the child, before we cut her throat and roasted her for ourselves.

I will not tell you if the child was a boy or a girl. But it was happier then, it slept on your Father's breast.

In two days we were home. The veil came away from our Mother's eyes as she turned our Father's wedding ring in her fingers. She slipped it on, over her thumb. Your Mother was sitting beside her, nursing her firstborn. When your Father gave her the baby, she drew it at once to her free breast. "Is it a Canary?" she asked. Both of us said, "What difference does it make?"

You will never find out from me which child was which.

I am writing this in the antiquities hall of the National Museum – it is one place that is open each day and where nothing changes. Oh, the windows could do with a wash, there are less attendants and one in three light bulbs is out of commission – but it is much the same, still, as when we built it 35 years ago. In Winter, you'll see, there will be crowds of fellows like me in here – if the heating still works, if the bombs have not started to fall – but at the moment it is almost empty. No footfalls, no tourists, no parties of school children.

I am a private citizen. How very strange it is, at the end of my life, to become that thing. I have been staring at my stained old hand, on this windowsill – hands that till only two years ago were firm and manicured. And my suit, the only one I have not sold, is ragged and loose on my ribs. I had become quite broken-down, I admit, and I have found myself thinking about my Mother, late at night – a sure sign, they say, that a man's death is at hand.

But standing here, writing, I can feel the blood perk up in my veins. I am reminded of my days at the University.

And it seems to me that if I could find something to trade for a good, unfashionable pair of shoes, and one of those plastic raincoats from the West, perhaps – why, I could set off in the afternoon, through the city's outskirts, and walk on, at my own pace, into the country. No one would pay any attention to a ragged old man, walking against the tide.

I would rather die under a hedge, come death how it may, than under a tenement stair.

I will tell you my plan – for you will not be able to hinder it – and perhaps you will learn how we private citizens get along. It is "Currency hard, currency soft," the same old song in any language.

On the third floor of my apartment lives a mechanic and his family. He will let me have a ten-litre can for, say, a safe half-share in my enterprise. On the fifth floor there is a man who keeps tropical fish. He will lend me a couple of yards of plastic tubing, for a package of Marlboroughs or Winstons. On the ground floor, just over the stairs, a woman has just had her second child. She will part for a day with the baby carriage she keeps in her kitchen for the promise of rubber teats and some formula. (They like to get them off the breast quickly, these days!)

So out I will go, after midnight, with my old coat thrown over the can in my baby carriage, and I shall deliver this letter at your side door. But first I shall siphon ten litres of gasoline out of your nice grey car. And before dawn, long before you awake, I shall be talking to the street vendors in a certain parking lot. The cigarettes – easy. The shoes and the raincoat – of course. I may have to dig and wheedle a bit to find the baby supplies. And a couple of Deutschmarks, perhaps, for the mechanic.

Before you discover this letter, I shall have done all my business and be on my way, with a spring, as they say, in my step.

There are certain trees I remember, that may still be standing. A stretch of riverbank where the yellow flags grow thick at this time of the year. If it is to become a battlefield again, let me get there first.

Ah, what a success story, our family's. A Doctor, a Manufacturer, both of them Deputies.

I was your uncle, your sponsor, your benefactor.

This curse upon both of you . . . .

CROSS FOX

There were two young boys who thought they were young men, and one of them was me.

It was in a coulee down by the Border that it happened, and this was a time so long ago that you might not find it in your books, even.

The other boy was Patrice Sinclair. He was my cousin, my mother's sister's oldest. We called him Cross Fox.

So I think you know what I am telling you about. No? Well, perhaps not. I thought your Auntie must have spoken about it. And if she did not, what on earth could have made you come hunting me down?

In any case, it is the only story I have to tell you.

Patrice would have been your uncle, you see.

It is strange to be thinking about that Valley suddenly, here, so far across the sea. It comes back, because of you, the light and the smells and the distances. And I have not thought of it once in this way, these fifty years. But, you know, not one day passes without my remembering what happened in that one coulee.

You know what a coulee is, yes? I have used the right word?

The thing is, in the years in between I have learned to speak and to think in a language that was not mine then. It is a language that has taught me to understand many new things – perhaps too many – but it does not have the words for that time and place, or for what those young boys experienced.

All the same, it is your language too. It is what we must use.

It was a coulee from which the trees had not been taken, very wide and deep; and above, where the plain grass hills began, was the place where our people once had their winter houses.

Now at this time I'm telling you of, a few men came back every autumn, very late in the year, to hunt for meat. The herds were long gone of course, even then, they were only a memory, but the coulees were rich with game – with deer and wapiti, and the furbearing animals, too.

That Autumn – you call it the Fall now, don't you, like the Americans, that *is* a good word for it; we used to say *Itakwakik* or *Automne*, which is the same of course in French and in English – that Autumn, Patrice and I made our plans to go down to the Valley two weeks before the men, to do some hunting of our own. The men would go in *sections*, sections of ten, with one leader, as they had in the buffalo years, but we planned to hunt on our own, with just one rifle and a handful of traps, and to wait for the men there, to prove that we were men too.

It is so long ago. It must all sound as foreign to you as this sleepy backwater where you tracked me down. The truth is, I feel myself as if I am talking about someone else. I ask myself, which is real: those young boys trekking towards the Valley, five thousand miles and forty years in the distance, or this old fellow sitting among these gravestones and telling his story to a pretty young girl? – oh you are very pretty – in her WAAF uniform, under these ancient trees. And both things are real, I suppose, aren't they? – they are part of one life, and for all that has happened, always one thing must lead to another.

There was a time, you see, after there was nothing, when there was plenty. First there were things as they had always been, and then there was nothing, suddenly, in less than a child's lifetime, and then for a little while there was plenty. A different plenty – a plenty of different things – but plenty. For a little while. Less than a boy's life.

And some things came back from the nothingness, out of the time before, that we thought had gone forever.

I hope you can understand what I am telling you, because it is happening now, all around us. I lie in my bed at night, in this village with all of its lights blacked out, and I listen to the aeroplanes high overhead, the German bombers moaning their way towards Coventry or Birmingham, where factories will burn and children will die in their beds, or hiding in the cellars, and it seems to me that Time can lie down on its side and sleep, and maybe dream, and be so still and quiet, and then suddenly it is up on its feet and racing upon us like a runaway horse.

Yet this place feels immortal, to me. That church has stood here for nearly eight hundred years; those yew trees are almost as old; the peaceful ghosts of this place make the air like the air of a nursery; and the same birds sing among the graves that have always sung here, and build their nests and share the crumbs of my lunch . . . that one is a chaffinch, I will show you his nest in a little while, see how unafraid he is, there, right by your feet, and his wife will leave her eggs before I go home, and come for her share . . . .

Yes, I have ended up in this place of peace, tending the grass and the flowers among the graves, but the bombers fly over each night and the children burn. And when we go up to the church in a little while – for it will be raining soon, you can watch the weather coming in England, it is not like Canada with those wide skies – you will see when we go in that this peacefulness is built out of war and death, out of nothing and plenty ebbing and flowing like the tides. That is my other job – to show our visitors round the church, and point out the things of interest . . . oh you may smile if you want, but I do not talk to them as I'm talking now – I am quite unobtrusive!

I was taken aback when you spoke to me, by name – I thought you were just another visitor, come to see our church. "Taken aback," – what a language we have, full of secrets. But I must take *you* back.

I remember the dust upon the roads, and its singeing taste in my nostrils. We had a long way to go, and we went slowly, because

Patrice had gone to Regina that Spring, hoping for better prices for his furs, and he had fallen under a *charette* there, a wagon, and his leg had not mended properly. But still he carried the rifle, which had been his father's and had seen action against the Police. It was a Winchester *Trente-Soixante-Quinze*, with a six-sided barrel – when you looked at its mouth it was like a three-penny bit with a big hole in it. It was a famous make of rifle, just then, because of an Indian boy up north who had had some trouble with the Police and the Military, and that was the gun he had carried.

We walked for four days, going south, and slept under the stars, and then we fell in with three families, taking their goods in to start homesteading at the east end of the hills. They had come from Saint Victor, I remember, with beds and stoves and ploughs all piled up among the children and sacks of food, and we went with them for two days, sitting on the buckboard of one of their drays, till we came to Dollaire, at the mouth of the Valley.

If you have not been down to that part of the world, you must understand that the prairie, the plains, finish there. To the west it climbs up to the hills covered with forest, *Les cypres*, but to the south it falls away into the Valley, and that is where the Hudson's Bay Men built their post. But that post had burned down twenty years before those boys went into the coulee.

There are coulees along the whole Valley side, and some with big trees and deep shadows. There was a lake there, too, every Spring, and they said that the water ran out in two places, and one led north, all the way up to Hudson's Bay, and the other flowed down to the Gulf of Mexico. And that may have been true. But the Valley was a dry, yellow place for most of the year, except down by the river banks and back in the coulees where the trees had not been cut.

And that coulee must still be there. That is strange.

I remember the smell, and the light echoing off the dry grass above the coulees. It is a world away, and a lifetime, but I can smell it now – I want *you* to smell it, even as those clouds draw in on us. It is a wide, dry smell that you would never find in this country, but I will be truthful with you and admit that those smells and that light are confused in my memory with the light of Africa.

Yes, I was there too, for a year and a half, and that is where I really became a young man, perhaps. But that is another story, a story for someone else; it has nothing to do with what you came looking for.

Those two young boys, then, Patrice and I, we trekked across the Valley in the dusk towards the high butte with the four shoulders. And we made a fire on one of the old hearths where the houses had been, and ate the small quantity of food that the homesteaders had given us, and slept until just before dawn.

I think you will understand when I tell you that that was the place I loved best in the world back then. Coming there, and above all sleeping there brought me the only feeling of peace that my young heart knew. I felt safe there, I slept as if I had come home. There is a comfort in old things, you see, even if they lie in ruin like the scattered logs around those stone hearths in the Valley, when you feel you belong to them. That was where our people had come, year after year – oh, for nothing like the old generations who watch you everywhere *here*, but a long history as we understood things – and the trees and the stones knew our people and the stream that ran out of the coulee seemed late at night to speak with our voices. I think you will understand, because that is what you have come looking for, isn't it? Ancestors.

Ah, see how dark it is getting. Well, we have not far to go for shelter when the thunder comes. Yes, your search has brought you to an English churchyard – is that not ironic? But what I was telling you about that old winter camp in the Valley is connected to this. I have come to see that it is not just your own ghosts – if that is what they are – which make you feel you belong. I have lived here, mostly, for much more than half of my life and – except in my dreams – I am very at home with these English ghosts.

If you go to that Valley some day, when this war is over and done with, you will find all along the rim of it old stone circles. They were the bivouacs of the Indians, the Cree and Saulteaux and Siksika, the stones which held down the hems of their tents, and they may have been there for centuries, who knows? because nothing much changes on the face of the prairie. Some of their blood, of course, ran in our veins as it does in yours, and though we were enemies, and rivals for the herds, and much blood had been spilt between us, I have learned that without blood and loss there *is* no history – they get changed into peace and belonging. And I think that those Indian spirits were part of the peace which I felt in that place. And perhaps the coyotes that cried all night were calling with *their* voices . . . .

Patrice had brought traps for those coyotes, and for marten and badger, but above all for foxes. And so I should explain to you how he came to have that name, Cross Fox, an English name, for some of us almost the only English words we knew. You see, he had a gift for trapping – he was only eighteen, but for three years he had brought in the most *pelages*, furs, skins, you understand? And the best quality too, in all our district. The cross fox was a new thing to us, it was part of that plenty of things which I spoke of that followed the nothingness. We knew the *reynard*, of course, the red fox, and sometimes a silver fox would be caught, or even a white fox once in a while, but no one had ever seen the cross fox. Now, some people said it was given that name because it was an *hybride*, a cross between red fox and silver fox, and others said it was due to the black cross which runs down its back and its shoulders. In any case, the traders were hungry for it and *they* gave that name to Patrice because he was the first to catch one, and he went on catching them; he had an understanding for animals.

When we were very small he explained to me that if you wished to find a bird's nest, you must put yourself into the mind of that bird and seek out the place where you would build your nest. And I think that is how he went about setting his traps.

So that was our chore for the first afternoon, but first we would go up the coulee with the rifle to look for some meat. If we found a deer we would be able to *cache* it down by the stream where it was so cool at night that the meat would not spoil, and then we would have food for ourselves, and for the men when they turned up, and we could leave the animals undisturbed for a week, for the main hunt.

But I think we should go in, before I tell you this story. The rain will not hold off much longer. No? Well, you may have to run – the rain can come very suddenly here, though it's nothing, I know, like the thunderstorms back in Saskatchewan. Still, there is no light like this strange green light that steals upon England before it rains. Smell that – how the trees and the flowers breathe out now around us. We are drowning in history, I like to say. You like that, do you? Yes.

But look at that headstone behind you, no – the one across the path. Can you make out the lettering? It is a mother and her seven children, Mary Downham, all of them dead within three days of each other. 1807, you see? Cholera. The visitors love to take pictures of that stone. And on the other side of the church there is a plain grey stone, an obelisk, with no inscription – it was set up in 1740, when 300 people, men, women and children, died of the plague. They were not buried in here, of course – the plague pits were outside the old town walls, where the football fields are. And up by the lych-gate where you parked your car, there's the headstone of Janet Kirby, *foully murdered by Thomas Buckle*, 1864. Those are the favourite monuments, outside the church.

And all of them part of this tranquility . . . .

There – there's the thunder now, over by Market Rushton. Perhaps it will pass us by, after all. I doubt it, though.

We are very troubled by thunder these days – these nights, I should say. Thunder of the bombs and the ack-ack guns in the distance, and the sudden flashes that light up the horizon. And it is like in a thunderstorm – you see the flash and then you count until the sound comes, and that tells you the distance. You can tell whether the bomb fell in Coventry or Wolverhampton or Birmingham. But the dead will be dead by the time the sound reaches you.

And some of the aeroplanes that we hear, I suppose, are flown by those boys from your airfield, climbing into the sky at night to hunt for the bombers. Yes, I can see it in your eyes – do you wait up to see how many brave hunters will come home?

Ah well, there is still much in common between hunting and warfare, even today. But, you know, when I had my first taste of warfare – and I was barely seventeen, not yet seventeen – it was *all* hunting. We hunted them up and down, and along the rivers, in a land that was not very different to my eyes from the Territory, and as often as not it turned out that they were hunting us, because they knew that land, the Boer *Kommandos*, and they could appear and vanish out of thin air. And that is what became of *our* hunting, that morning, to Patrice and me.

When you go into a coulee, you must have a hill at your back, so as not to stand out on the skyline, but you should have the light behind you, too – so that you may see into the trees and the shadows. That is the trick. And if there is a breeze, and it is coming towards you, so much the better. And everything was perfect for us that morning, as the sun came up and we started towards the trees.

But to think that that coulee still sits there, remembering. Even the trees perhaps – the tree which I climbed into that morning – holding it all in their memory. You could go down, when the war is over and you go home – unless, of course, you should fall for one of those fighter pilots of yours! – you could go down and stand in the exact place I am telling you about.

Ah – you are laughing at me again. No, no – I am not offended: "Here we go round the mulberry bush," is what Captain Richard would say when a tale was too long in the telling. He was my employer, Captain Richard – his family, the Comrys, have lived in this village since the church was built ("since the Conquest," they liked to say): you shall see their memorials when we go inside. And we should go in soon: believe me, that rain is coming. It will make short work of my story!

But bear with me, Marie – I do not talk to many people these days, except by way of reciting the guidebook to our visitors, but I read every evening, a new book from the lending library each week, and I think – I think in *words*, which I believe too few people do – and I do have things to tell you.

For there we were, coming out of the valley at dawn, and you know how the world over there smells at daybreak – not like here, washed clean and starting the earth anew, but clear and alive all the same and trembling with excitement. You understand?

We went in through the first scrub of trees – the buckthorns and berry thickets – and down over rough open ground to where there is a kind of *shelf*, a space of land where the big trees begin before the ground falls away to the stream bottom. That is where the game trails ran. So we were not into the shadows yet, but they were closing around us, and the sunlight slanted down between us into the trees. There was no sign of life yet, we could scarcely hear the stream rustling below – and then we saw something move, up ahead.

It was actually above us, among the scrub trees, and it stopped as soon as we saw it, and watched us, too. And we could not make it out.

Patrice raised his Winchester, but there was nothing to aim at: it was big, but it was not a deer, and it blended in too well with the thicket.

So we stood and watched and waited. That is when your heart makes more noise than the world around you.

I was watching over Patrice's shoulder, trying to focus my eyes into the bushes, and when it moved again he turned his head to me, with bright eyes, and said *"Loup!"* Wolf. It was far too big for a coyote. But then it ran on again, fast, and it passed through a patch of sunlight, and I saw that it was a bear! And then it was gone.

There had been no bears, in the valley or the hills, since long before I was born. They had vanished before the herds did. My grandfather told me that one year the Hudson's Bay Men took out a thousand bearskins, and in two years they were all gone. They were extinct. But there it was – out of the time before.

Imagine how you would feel if a bear came now, prowling between the tombstones. As soon as you could believe your eyes, you would look for an explanation, wouldn't you? You would think it had escaped from a zoo, or a circus. And, you know, just a few years ago there was a mountain lion loose in these parts, people kept seeing it, a few sheep and calves were taken – and when it was shot by the Comrys' gamekeeper it had a collar around its neck, a collar with turquoise stones on it! And I wonder how many, many centuries it is since there were mountain lions in England. But there were bears here – not so long ago, not so long in the English sense of things. There were still bears in the woods when this church was built: there is a carving in the choir of a bear playing the bagpipes, I will show it to you later.

Now that may seem too long ago to count, to you, but believe me, when I knew we were sharing that coulee with a bear it was just as if a wild English bear were to appear now. Because the nothingness which fell upon our world was sudden and swift, as I told you, but it was complete. The time of the bears and the herds was as dead as if ten centuries had fallen between.

But Patrice had not seen it as clearly as I had, and he did not believe me. He laughed. *"Nitawapinketak"* – *Let's go and look"* – he said to me. And so we went on, very softly, taking a deer trail into the trees, till we came to a little dry watercourse filled with sunlight.

It was then I got frightened. "Perhaps he is hunting us," I said – *apotikwe emitititoyak awa*. And my fear made Patrice frightened too, though he did not admit it and still did not believe. So he told me, "Skwa*tawe l'arbre là*" – *Climb up that tree* – so that I could look around. He could not climb up himself, because of his leg.

There, did you feel that. The rain, yes, just as I thought, just when I'm telling the story. Well, let's walk up to the church, before the downpour begins.

So. I got up in a tree, just beyond the watercourse, and I looked all around, up and down. And sure enough, there was something down in the trees, where the ground fell away. It moved between the trunks and then stood still. "I can see it, I think," I whispered, and Patrice handed up his rifle to me and told me if I saw it clearly to shoot. *"Pas*kisaw *li cou*," he said – *Shoot for the neck.*

He walked backwards up the streambed a way, to be out in the open. And when I looked again into the trees, the bear was gone. Or perhaps I had only imagined it.

It was then that I heard Patrice, talking loudly. He was speaking as though to a policeman or a priest – frightened but very brave. I looked around and he was not where he had been. Then I heard him cry out, and I heard the stones scatter in the watercourse, like this gravel under our feet, and all of a sudden the bear was walking towards my tree, and he was dragging Patrice along with him. He had Patrice by the neck, and I could see the blood running into his shirt, and they came right underneath me.

I had the rifle, but I did not dare shoot at the bear's neck for fear of hitting Patrice. So I aimed at the hump between his shoulders, and just before I fired the bear dropped Patrice, dead still on the ground, and looked straight up at me and let out a great sigh. Like a woman. And perhaps that spoiled my aim, for when I fired he did not fall, but galloped off into the trees.

Remember, I was sixteen. I was trembling all over, and I was alone. I had never been alone in all my life. And I was sure Patrice must be dead. All so suddenly. I dropped down from the tree, and as I did so the bear came back out of the shadows.

Yes, yes – run on to the porch, I will catch you up. Oh – you don't run like a girl. It must be your Métis blood!

There – safe and sound! We can enjoy the storm from here and still be dry. No, I haven't forgotten, I assure you: I dream this story at least one night in the week. No – be careful how you shake your cap – there is a nest up there. A swallow, you see – *hirondelle,* yes? – she is tight on her eggs. See her black eyes watching us? We must talk softly.

And your hair is so blonde – what is your father, a Swede, with a name like that? Icelandic? Hmm. And you must have grown up feeling that you were white . . . . Well, I have spent more than thirty years feeling that I was white, that I was English! I have been a white man longer than you have! Though I do tell the children who come down after school to play, that my great grandfather was a Red Indian Chief! Chiefs and princesses and braves, that is all that they can imagine!

Listen to that! And look! Soon the rain will be coming off the roof like a waterfall. We are like animals in a burrow, aren't we? Or Indians under a teepee! So sit – I'll get on with my story.

I told you that the bear came back. I was standing at the foot of the tree, and he came as far as Patrice's body. I could see that Patrice was as dead as a stone, and the bear's mouth was open, he was panting, and my cousin's blood was trickling over his teeth.

Oh, what a crack! We are right in the middle of the storm.

They said those old bears stood twelve feet tall on their hind legs. It was said they could run down a buffalo, or a man on horseback. And their skin – can you hear me alright? I said there would be a waterfall – their skin was so tough that the Hudson's Bay bullets would skate right off their hides if the shot did not come from straight on.

This will not last long – do you see, behind the village, blue sky already. Well, this bear, I must say, did not seem so big. He was big *enough,* but he did not seem like a monster. Even when he came closer, and lifted up, and reached out his arms towards me.

He was very thin, and his hair was greyish, and moulting in patches. And the smell he gave out – it was not what you'd think: it was like cobwebs in a cellar.

150

I did what I could, but it was not enough. I fired the Winchester into his chest – he was only five feet away, at the most – and then, to my shame, I dropped the gun and I ran. I ran for my life.

He did not chase me. I looked back once, as I went through the scrub trees, and he was lying under that tree, beside Patrice, but still I went running – I was a boy after all – and it was only after I had been out in the wide sunlight for half an hour that I thought better of it. The bear might be dead, and Patrice might still be alive.

So I went back into the coulee. And this is the truth I am telling you. The bear was not there, Patrice was not there, there was no sign of anything – just the Winchester lying on the ground beside that dry watercourse, and the two brass cartridges below the tree.

I *did* search, for a little while. I went on down the trail for two minutes, and I looked down the bankside toward the stream, among the big trees, but I saw nothing, and heard nothing. And the whole place was watching me, of course, empty as it was.

And so I ran again. I snatched up the rifle and I ran, and one way or another I kept running for a week. And if you want to know why, it was because standing there, with both Patrice and that bear vanished, I *knew*, or the boy that I was thought he knew, that one of them would get me if I stayed. I was a child running from a bogeyman. There is no more frightening bogeyman, believe me, than a friend who has turned against you.

There: not much of a storm, here and gone like tomorrow! So, that is almost the whole story, as far as my part in it goes. I followed the river down through the valley until it crossed the Line, and I sold the rifle – I had no more shells for it anyway – to a trader for some food and shirts, and a pair of Scotch boots, and I found work in a little Montana town for a month, until they caught up with me.

Oh, it will rain on for an hour perhaps, but the sun will be out again before you have to leave. This is what we English call "a gentle rain," "a soft rain" – it suits this spot, don't you think: the old stones and the trees?

Yes, they hunted me down. They believed I had murdered Patrice. I thought that perhaps some people still believed that, but your Auntie said nothing about it? Well, I am glad it has passed out of memory, but the thing is, no one believed me then, not for a moment, about the bear. And the look in their eyes, Marie, when my family came down to the jail and I told them my story, made me feel like a dead man. It was the bear in my story – that, and my running away in the first place – which got me shipped off to South Africa, and on my way to becoming an Englishman.

But that is another story, as I said before. Allow me to tell you one thing, though, which I believe is a certain truth: you cannot leave a place, or be sent away from a place, or least of all run from a place without leaving something that trails behind you, as though you caught your sleeve on a thorn bush, or on the barbed wire, and a thread is unravelling constantly, go where you may. And it is by that thread that you will be reeled in some day, or that someone will come to find you. It is as simple and strange as the birds and the fish coming back each year. And here you are, and here am I, to prove what I'm saying.

You are searching for your features in mine. I have been doing the same – it is almost uncanny when I think of how many things separate us.

But *there* is a face for you – did you notice it, there on the door. It is known as the Sanctuary Knocker. You see, in olden days, if a man was in trouble, no matter what he had done against the laws of the land, he could come to the church and claim sanctuary. No one could touch him while he stayed in the church. And here they say, once he got his hand upon that knocker, he was safe.

So, hold it. And think of the other hands which may have clung to it across the years. He does not look too friendly though, does he? More like some kind of bogeyman, or the devil! But you'll see – there are many things carved and painted in the church which will surprise you. They knew what they were doing, in my opinion, back in the thirteenth century, because this church was as much the house of the people as it was the house of God. They were not nearly so narrow and superstitious and cruel as we like to think – they included everything in their worship.

Yes, that gash in his forehead! Well, the story is that a fugitive, long, long ago, was running from a mob of people, and they were shooting at him with longbows or crossbows, and just as he grasped the Sanctuary Knocker an arrow whizzed over his head and pierced the face. It's a good story, and who knows? – I think enough people have believed it that it must be called true!

Cross Fox? The name has taken your fancy, has it? Or are you telling me to come back round the mulberry bush? Well, it seems that the men found his body, when they rode in three days later, and they said that he had been shot. They were looking for me, thinking I had been murdered too, and then the word got out I had been seen somewhere downriver, carrying a rifle, and the next thing there was a price on my head. It was a good sum, too, for a Métis boy – 50 dollars, the price of a silver fox *pelage.*

And one morning, I woke up in my little shack at the back of the general store, and there were two men standing in the doorway. One of them was a homesteader, I think, down on his luck, and the other was what I would call a half-breed. We were Métis, though they made us answer to "half-breed," and whatever you may have heard, we had some pride in ourselves.

They were not gentle to me. They tied a rope around my waist, and they rode, and I walked, back up to the Border until they could get their reward.

But now, let us go in. Come, it has brightened enough that I need not turn on the lights: you will see the church as it should be seen, in the light of the stained-glass windows.

There is no stillness in the world like in old churches . . . .

If you'd like to sit for a spell and absorb the history around you – here, this guidebook will tell you everything you need. There are always chores for me to do, when the weather is bad.

Very well, you shall have your own guided tour!

I do love this place. I cannot imagine my days without it.

The East Window there, it was set up in thirteen hundred and forty-six, by craftsmen from Flanders, as a thanksgiving for the passing of the Black Death – one third of the English people had died in two short years. Yes, it's a lovely thing, but when the morning sun comes in above the altar, the colours dapple the whole of the nave floor, and the pews and the feet of the columns. And the dust motes drift and dance in the light. It is like a stream bed in high summer, under the willows, or the floor of a forest at the edge of a clearing.

It is what I wish I could see when I close my eyes.

Try to imagine the congregation of survivors, when that window was finished, kneeling here with that light falling over their faces. And we call that the Dark Ages!

Now these are the oldest monuments in the church; they are the tombs of the Mauleverer family, after whom the village is named. This is the oldest: you see – Sir Piers Mauleverer and Lady Euphemia, twelve hundred and twenty-six is what the Latin says. They are carved out of alabaster stone, from a quarry just two miles away. You will notice how his right foot is crossed upon the left – a sign that he went on a crusade to the Holy Land. Poor Lady Euphemia could not have seen very much of him! But there, beneath her feet, they have carved one of the spaniels which must have kept her company.

But I am slipping into the same speech I give to all the visitors . . . .

Their faces are gone, you see, and his sword is broken. All of the tombs and statues are damaged – and I will tell you why.

During the Civil War, in sixteen hundred and forty-five, Oliver Cromwell's men – the Ironsides they were called – they used this church as a barracks and a stable. To them, all the old statues were idolatry, and they looted and vandalized everything. God knows why they spared the windows.

Well, it's part of the atmosphere, part of the peace! I have read that every nation must have a civil war to cement itself, and

England has had two or three. But not for nine hundred years has it been invaded. Our rector prays aloud every Sunday that that may not change.

I should not say this, perhaps, under this roof, but I am not so sure that God has very much to do with these old churches. I believe the English come here to remember who they are. To kneel with the spirits of their forebears. It is disrespectful, perhaps, to think this way, but God knows how I love this place in my heart. And to think what my Mother, or Père Calixte from my childhood, would have thought of me working and worshipping here, in a Protestant Church. Yet it was built by Catholics – a good part of the ghosts here, listening to us now, must still have their Catholic beliefs.

And those are the Comry memorials, all down the North wall. They were merchants, I believe, in the fifteenth century, and they married into the Mauleverer family. And then when the old name died out, they inherited everything. And now *their* name will die out. That is Captain Richard's tablet, there – and above it his brother's, Major Geoffrey, killed on the last day of the Great War.

I owe everything that I am to Captain Richard. There was a daybreak at a ford beneath the Drakensberg, with five dead horses and three dead men. And when we heard the boys come hallooing, looking for us, and we knew the *Kommandos* would melt away, Captain Richard sat up and turned to me – he was not a captain then, of course, he was what they called an ensign, scarcely a year older than I was – and he said, *"We are living on borrowed time, Jackie"* – oh, it did not take long for my name to get changed! – *"We are living on borrowed time,"* he said. *"We must make the most of it."*

And he brought me to England after the war, at his own expense, and gave me charge of the stables, and set me to learning English – *real* English.

You would have laughed – to see me, a big, awkward lout, squeezed into a chair in their little schoolroom, with Miss Celia, his youngest sister – she was twelve years old and, as they say, self-possessed and she could twist me round her little finger! The two of us, and the tutor they employed for her, reciting *The Lays Of Ancient Rome* and perfecting our elocution and, in my case, learning to handle a knife and fork!

But I did learn English from the inside out, and around here they would say that I speak like a gentleman. So different it was from the language I grew up with – a true hybrid language with the names of things in French, plus a few Scotch and English words, and the rest in *Nehiyawinin*. It's a lingo I only understand now in my dreams. I will say, though, after all these years, and through all the books I have read, I have come to see that English is only a *Michif* that has weathered a thousand years . . . .

Now this, you see, was originally the Lady Chapel – but the Mother of God is the one missing presence from the Church of England, so they have moved the old font here, for christenings.

Oh, I see! Well, permit an old man to ramble a little – no, you are quite right: I left out a piece of the story . . . .

I could have been hanged you know. My life could have ended just then. Though no one would have wanted that, whatever they thought of me, except for the English magistrates who were trying to set an example in those years.

My Auntie, Patrice's mother, your grandmother, came to the jail and begged me to change my story. She told me, whatever the truth might be, that I must say it had been an accident, and that I had run off because I was afraid of being blamed. It must have been so hard for her, disbelieving me as she did, and yet loving me, too. I could not meet her eyes, I remember. She had her new baby with her, still at the breast, little Marie Thérèse. Yes, your mother . . . .

She was a great woman, I think, your grandmother. Yes, your *Nokhom!* With a heart that understood even when she did not. Because the rest of my family had turned their backs on me, though I believe they would never have allowed me to hang.

And so my story was changed, and I said that the gun had gone off accidentally. And the magistrate told me, *"The suspicion still hangs over you."*

When I think of that magistrate now, I see that he was a trumped-up little pipsqueak, a nothing, and probably no more than twenty-five years old at that. But to me, a scared "half-breed" boy in a police cell, his voice – which I could not understand, of course: they used an interpreter – was the voice of the Crown. Of life and death too.

And then he asked me if I was a good man with a canoe. I told him I was, though I was no better or worse than any other boy on the Saskatchewan River, because I had no idea what he was driving at.

The Queen, he said, had need of young men on the Orange and Vaal Rivers, to fight the Afrikaner insurgents. He would drop the charges if I would enlist. It was as simple as that, and the easiest thing for all concerned. I suppose they thought they had got a *voyageur*, but it turned out the river work was abandoned, and I had a way with horses.

So I perjured myself, and three months later, in the last year of the century, I was *Marching to Pretoria* as a groom in a cavalry regiment. Imagine!

That regiment was the 15/23rd Lancers, the *Do or Die* boys. It is an old Buckland regiment, and this is its church. Yes, a good half of our visitors come to see the South Chapel, where the standards hang. Old soldiers, widowed mothers, the children of the fallen. You might hardly believe how many ladies in their middle years have stayed true to the engagement rings on their fingers. It was the Great War, you see, the *"War to end all wars,"* and it took a toll on England like a second Black Death. They come and they stare into the chapel, and feel some comfort, I believe, as if something remains here of their loved ones, and their hopes.

I will show you: that is true history, there, with its relics and witnesses. Come – this is the best place to sit.

Oh yes, I am married. For almost ten years. My wife teaches in the school here, and you must come back and visit, on your free weekend. She is spending Whitsuntide with her daughter, in Brighton. No – she is a grandmother now. Her first husband fell at Paschendaele; he was brought home and died of his wounds. We get along very well – though it is understood, of course, that she will be buried with him.

But look. Those flags take us back to the 1600's. They have seen battle: the tears and the shot-holes. The blue one is from Waterloo, and the one up above, with its corner torn away, flew in the Crimea – where the 15th and the 23rd were each so decimated that they were combined as one regiment. And there is the Colour that we carried in France, where Major Geoffrey fell. The carving beneath it was set up by old Sir Marcus, as his son's memorial. *"Stormed at by shot and shell,"* Captain Richard used to call it!

Yes, of course. After fourteen years of peace that was like a dream, a way of life which seemed to have gone on forever and that welcomed me into it, it was time to go back to war. *"The War to end all wars,"* yes. And it was a new kind of nothingness, believe me, more sudden and deathly than anyone could have imagined.

I was thirty by then, but I re-enlisted as a groom – and away we sailed for Flanders, and Compiègne. As a groom, yes. Everyone knows now about the tanks and the gas and the trenches, but we were not to know. There were cavalry charges, which no one seems to remember. But I will never forget them coming back from our last charge. It was a mere stone's throw from the scene of a famous victory, six hundred years before, and this was a victory, too, though only one third rode back from it. Captain Richard came with me, into the pickets, while I washed down Sir Nigel, his old hunting mount, and he said, *"Our days are numbered, Jackie; this is the end of us."* He told me the Bosche had broken and fled, all but one machine gunner who had stayed at his post and kept firing. And that one German had taken down thirty or forty riders. *"The longbow did it at Agincourt,"* he said, *"and the machine gun will do it now."*

Captain Richard left something behind him in France. Oh, he went through the motions of being himself, but he broke off his engagement, and if a bee or a wasp flew close by him he would tremble and sweat, and cry out for someone to *"Swat it!"*

I had my rooms over the stables, and he took to coming each evening to sit with me, to talk or just sit, with his bottle of Courvoisier brandy and Tessie, his Springer spaniel, at his feet. It was in that room that he chose to die.

And things do come together, Marie – though I did not set out to tell you these English stories. It was 1921, and Captain Richard came down to the stables with a letter from the Regiment. Someone had written from Canada, enquiring after me. My Mother, they said, was dying in Winnipeg. Now, I had scarcely thought of her in years, except in my dreams, but Captain Richard thought I should go back – he almost forced me into it, and he paid my passage, yet the last words he said to me, standing outside the railway station, were, *"Shall you come back to us, Jackie? I hope you shall."*

I should not have gone. That was a year of death, all round, 1921. I arrived too late to see my Mother; Josette, your grandmother, was gone; and my Uncle Isidore, who was the only one I could talk to, was far gone with cancer. So I spent my time by a deathbed, anyway. I blundered about in the old language, and when they spoke the English they had learned I was ashamed of them. As for me, I spoke like an Englishman – the wrong kind of Englishman for them – and I dressed like an Englishman, and I felt like one, too. Though we tried, on both sides, there was little trust or liking between us, except for old Isidore.

I wrote home, of course, what I thought of as home, and a letter came at last from Miss Celia, telling me of Captain Richard's death. But he had provided for me in his will, and she told me I had a place, whenever I wanted one.

And there I was in Saint Boniface – and I did not get out on the prairie once in those five months – for they had all moved back to the Red River, given up on the farms in Saskatchewan, and it seemed to me that they had chosen a prison and were falling away to nothing.

It was only a day or two after Isidore's death, I remember, a week before I returned to England, that your Auntie Gabrielle got word from out west that Marie Thérèse had passed away. I suppose, my dear, that that is when you were born.

Well, well – life must go on, and there is much to be grateful for. There is the sun at last, back through the South Windows – you can feel the old stones coming to life, don't you agree? Shall we go out, to the fresh air?

Sometimes I think of those coulees, you know, when I'm alone in here. There are the columns, like trees, and the same cool silence. Patrice told me that even as late as midsummer there was thick ice on the stream at the bottom of that coulee, with the temperature out in the valley at a hundred degrees. He said the biggest, oldest trees of all had ice around their trunks for nine months of the year.

And sometimes, when I've had one of my dreams, I stand and imagine that I can hear the ice melting and the water trickling away far below me. Though it is only the dead who lie beneath this floor. The old Mauleverers, and twelve generations of Comrys, dreaming, and listening perhaps, from their shelves in the old vaults.

Yes, the dreams. When your great-uncle Isidore was dying, he was terribly troubled by his dreams. His head was turned, I suppose, from the morphine they were giving him, and he wanted to know what was real, his dreams were so vivid. He got a shame-faced look, sick as he was, when he spoke about it, but he had to tell someone. I remember your Auntie Gabrielle telling him, *"It's all right, Nociwees,"* (which is to say *Great-uncle* – you could call *me* that if you liked!). *"It's not for us to say that what you've seen isn't real,"* she told him. She was right, too – a lot of people used to say that what you dream is as true as anything else.

I imagine a man could die of fright in his dreams.

And all of us suffered from dreams after the Great War. Captain Richard, I think, more than anyone.

The dream which troubled Isidore most of all was the strangest of things. He had it, he told me, every night. He found himself hunting, coming out of the woods with a group of riders, all of them dressed in red or black jackets and round caps, as they are in England, and the pack of hounds out ahead on the prairie, close on the fox's heels. I don't know where he'd have got such a picture – perhaps from the painted plates that the Hudson's Bay store used to sell; perhaps, who knows, it was a memory from his grandfather who was half English. But it was very strange for me to hear it, because every week, in the season, I would help Captain Richard get dressed just that way, riding to hounds in all weathers.

The gunroom in the Hall is bedecked with the masks of foxes and otters that the Hunt has taken over the years.

But the thing in Isidore's dream which he kept coming back to was this: as the horses came out into the sunlight, and set off in pursuit, he'd look down at his hands upon the reins and they were growing red fur upon them, changing into paws! And that is where his dream always ended.

Funny things, dreams . . . .

Ah, look at that! There is nothing so bright in the world as the earth washed clean. And the swallow has gone from her eggs, see – she could not resist it! A little exercise and food in the sunlight before she comes back to her duties.

So, touch the knocker for luck, and I will walk with you up to your car.

And you will come and visit us, won't you? I've been a great talker today, but I can listen too! I would like my wife to meet you – she might be relieved to see I have relatives like you!

Here's the stone I told you about: *Janet Kirby, foully murdered* . . . . One short, young life.

I would like to tell you a dream of mine, before you go. I have it more often than I can say, and it never varies.

I dream I am sixteen again, just that – I have no knowledge of my life since then, I am looking back across nothingness.

I am in the coulee, below that tree, with the Winchester in my hands, and the bear is looking at me. I shoot him in the chest, and he cries out and falls. He makes the kind of moan that a man makes when he is being beaten and robbed at the same time. And he lies there.

Patrice is not in my dream.

Then I am kneeling over the bear, with my skinning knife in my hand. I want his *pelage*, and I cut in under his ribs and open his belly. And then I am looking at us both from the outside; it is like a coloured picture in a boy's adventure book.

And the bear has sat up, and is looking down into my face as I cut him open. His mouth is agape, and his tongue is red, and his eyes are laughing at me, and his claws are lifting.

BEGGING QUESTIONS

When my Father was 43 he began to see things in his eyes. Threads, he said, and circles and smudges that sailed wherever he looked. He noticed them first one night on the porch after supper. Every clear evening in Summer he used to stand there and watch, staring up over the rooftops until the third star came out, and then he'd squat down, with his back to the house wall, and tell me it was time to go in and leave him.

He told me when he was a boy they used to row out round the point from their village and sit in the bay until the third star came out. Then it was time to start fishing. They didn't use rods, or nets, just let the lines down into the sea through their fingers. "The water was like ink from a pen," he said, "and sometimes the sky was that colour, too." But they could see down to the bottom of the bay. "White sand, like snow, many feet down."

My Father was Greek, but he didn't speak Greek at home, or try to make me learn it. "That was another place," he always said. "You belong here." But his *aitches* sounded like *kays* and when he was mad he would jerk up his chin to say No. He would mutter a cross little *po-po-po* noise to himself – and when I slip or stumble, or hoist Widow Gardiner's grandson down from the swing, I always go "Oh-pah," which I learned from him. He never went back to his island, to his home on the Lesbian shore, but I know that his Grandfather came there from Turkey, and he said that the Turks are the cruellest people on Earth. He never went back and he only got one letter that I know of, when his Mother died. I've got it still. "I'll go back to Greece when I die," he said.

That's what I told them at school, "My Dad has gone back to Greece."

There was a girl in our school who came from Yemen. I don't know if she was born there or not. When she was in Grade 9 she went back for Christmas and they married her off to someone in their village. She had two children and then some church guy rescued her. But she had to leave her children behind.

She came back to school and started Grade 10 again. That was pretty brave, in my humble opinion, but she told me she wanted to do things our way now, even though she hated school before.

She was going to get her children back some day. It wouldn't surprise me, either. She could have brought the girl back with her maybe, but they wouldn't have let her take the boy. "They're my kids," she said. "He just raped me, they're not his." Lily, Lily Rabati. Her older sister went back at the same time and the same thing happened to her, but she wasn't rescued. Lily said one day she'd get her sister and her kids back, too. She was working towards that. Her Dad sold them to his cousins.

Of all the Unmarried Mothers in Grade 10, she would have made the best Mom. And she didn't have her kids.

She lived with her Mom somewhere up by the Park. Her Mom walked out on her Dad, which broke every rule in their book, so *she* learned something at least.

My Mother was English, though she said she had Gypsy blood, maybe that's why she fell for a Greek. My Father laughed and said all Greeks hate the Gypsies, it couldn't be that.

I don't look like either of them, though my nose comes down straight off my brow, like the cutouts outside the Mykonos Café, like Pallas Athene on the blue stamp that came with my Grandmother's death letter. It is strange to say Grandmother of someone who maybe didn't know I existed. I don't know what her name was, either – Widow Gardiner translated the letter for me and it just calls her "Our Mother."

So I never had Grandparents, my Mother's parents died when she was single.

Bereft, bereft, there's no one left, I shall become a Troll.

Handsel's dictionary called Pallas Athene "A virgin goddess of wisdom and prudent warfare."

All his days my Father would chirp with his tongue behind his teeth when my Mother crossed the room. He hugged me against him on the sofa and told me to look at those shoulders. "She has the back of a dancer," he told us. Sometimes she laughed and tossed her hair. Sometimes she frowned and made her own tooth-noise, *tchi*, as if she was irritated Beyond Measure. Mostly she just ignored it.

Every so often I see a woman crossing a parking lot or going along past the shops with that lift in her walk, and her brown hair bouncing on her shoulders, and my heart reacts. I realize how beautiful my Mother was, and how my Father saw her.

I look in vain for her in the mirror.

I asked my Father why we didn't have other children and he told me some women can't have any more after a hard birth. But my Mother said later, after he was gone, that it wasn't the same between them when I'd been born. She didn't enjoy him.

But who was lying to whom, she wondered.

And that is a Begging Question. Making them up was Handsel's and my favourite game. A Begging Question turns into a Skeleton Key which opens a haunted house with a hundred rooms. Go search, go tremble. It was almost our Chief Diversion and we collected 27 of them. My favourite will always be *How many men have kissed the Mona Lisa?* A whole history, creaking with secret lives, in eight words. Handsel said that in a sane world you could publish all those words as a novel.

And I blew across the mouthpiece of my flute, and fingered three keys and played three-and-a-half bars, seven notes of *The Trout*, and said that could be published as a Quintet. "Recorded," he said, and whistled across a grass blade.

But I have no trust in recordings. Where was Moses when the lights went out? I can hear what I read, and find different things each time. In a sane world everyone could.

My best friend all my days will be Handsel, although he is lost forever. He could finish things I'd started, and give me things to finish for him. We knew what we were thinking.

He should have been my brother, like we pretended. I chose him for my brother, which counts for more.

The person I'm most grateful to in the world is Widow Gardiner. Her and Herant Gavilian. The Sad Maestro. He seduced me when I was 14, after I met him in the Railway Café.

I used to go there after school to watch the people getting off the train from Montreal. And the people waiting to catch it when it turned into the 1655, number 272 for Windsor. I collected faces. If you search you will find there are only 27 faces in all the world. Every one of them a Begging Question.

He had soft black hairs, like eyelashes, crowded on his wrists, and eyes even darker than Handsel's. I had never seen such a melancholy face, like a prince's. And he had elegance, too, though he hadn't shaved that morning and there was a coffee stain, like the map of Italy, on his shirt.

I have a birthstain on my left shoulder blade. My Mother was frightened by a spider in the bathroom when she was carrying me. That's what she told me when I was little, and for years I got the story wrong, imagining it wrong, till I realized that by "carrying" she meant she was pregnant with me.

She tried to knock the spider off the basin and it ran up her arm. She said she nearly lost me, and that was where the mark came from. What did I think she meant by "lost"? – I can't quite remember, but I was full of her fear.

It's not raised up like some people's birthmarks. It's just a mulberry stain the shape of a spider. My Spider.

I asked him if he was an artist. He was rolling his own cigarette and his hand quivered when I spoke to him and he looked up at my face. The whites of his eyes were shaded blue around the irises.

He stared for a moment, with the cigarette near his mouth. Then he licked it and his eyes almost closed. He looked like a man playing a soft harmonica.

"A sort of artist," he said. "Why do you ask?"

His voice was shy and mumbled for a grown, princely man.

"I just guessed," I said. Though what else could he have been?

"Well, I don't paint pictures," he said, picking up courage, "I can't ask you round to model for me." I laughed. I think he would have been blushing if his skin wasn't that colour. Caramel. His accent was driving me wild.

"If you came to see me, I would play for you," he said.

He had this long room in the roof of a friend's house, for when he was in town. He wouldn't let me be there when his friends were at home, not for the first few weeks. Not till our Carnal Relations were a thing of the past.

I lay on the couch under his window while he undid my blouse. He sat on the edge of the couch. "You can't stop now," I said.

But after Spring Break, though I still went over three afternoons a week, he did stop.

"I suppose you don't enjoy me any more." I was trying to keep the childish whimper and whine out of my voice, I was trying to stare him down but it was me who looked away. I watched him spurn me as I had watched him seduce me. "It is my fault," he said, "I am responsible. I should never have let it happen – you are such a child." Those boring words – it seemed the most unfair thing in the world. He knew some parts of me better than I knew myself. Till he introduced me to them.

But he still played for me, though it was not the same as when I was lying naked and drowsiful in that window-bay, wrapped in his blue and green afghan with the picture of Mount Ararat above my head. Except that now I was playing, too.

The first thing he ever played for me was *Humoresque*, and he found sadness in it like I never could. I thought he had written it himself, in fact I thought he was making it up for me, there and then, imagine. Not that he told me so, he never deceived me about anything.

What could there have been to deceive me about? (B.Q.)

I'd lie there and he'd get up and lean his butt against the desk and play his flute. And my skin would settle down and dream until my brain woke up. He always put his shirt back on. It was always brown cotton. Half open at the front, like curtains.

Until the day he fell asleep instead. And I leaned up on my elbow and played with my fingers across his shoulders. His beautiful back – I guess it hadn't changed since he was the handsome, boring young man in his photographs. My fingertips followed his backbone down, no knots or bumps or ridges – it was like a braid of hair, like a soft rope under his skin. He smelled of Passion, and Me, and like Cinnamon Dough. "Oh Doctor Gavilian," I whispered, "you are the Very Devil." The words came to me without a thought. But why is the Devil so weak and sad? (B.Q.)

He was asleep with his cheek against my leg. I reached across him and took the flute from the bed table and tried to blow the way he did. The flute was so cold – I thought it would be warm, like his skin. And when I got a note from it his eyes opened and watched me, as if they were someone else's, behind a mask.

Then his hand came up and took the flute and he said, "Watch. You must learn how to kiss the Air. She will make the Music."

That was the last time we made love, as they say. After that he regarded me differently.

No, there was one other time, of course, two years later, a year-and-a-half ago. Things were very different by then, I seduced him.

"I might have your baby," I said.

"You could not have my child. You would take upon you a thousand years of grief," he said.

I guess he felt superior because his people had suffered so much. That probably got in the way of his success.

Because he was a failure. The Devil, the Very Devil, is sad and suffers and is a failure. Behind that silken, brilliant mask is a bewildered soul calling out. "Oh, who will know how to help me, if you do not?" (B.Q.) That is the song the Sirens Sang.

But can a Mere Slip of a Girl comfort and nourish a vain man who's as old as her Father and a failure, too? That is by no means a B.Q. because there is one simple answer. Yes. Naturally. Often.

But we are not Princes, like them, or Princesses. We are little Sneak Thieves, and we make off in the end with treasure they were wasting. With only a nod to Pity.

Sometimes I was so trivial with him. I thought it was because I was so young, but it was just that he was so naturally sad.

He said he was teaching me a new language. He told me I had an Amazing Natural Aptitude.

Three days ago the cold ridge from the Arctic finally passed away and the birds came back for the second time. I wonder what they do when Spring gives up and a cold spell drives them away. They can't go back down South. Do you think they just die, and the next birds that show up aren't them but the slowpokes from Mexico?

That can't be it, they must know something.

I guess they must pull in their bellies and huddle in the cedar swamps and barns and hide their head under their wing, poor thing.

This is what Handsel wrote two years ago, when Spring arrived, the week he dropped out of school—

The Southwest Wind has been skulking behind the suburbs
His coat is ragged but the lining is full of pockets
And he's letting the crows loose on us now

Scattering black confetti, rags and seeds and feathers
Across every skylight. They are the asthma
Of a lean old man whose time has come again
Their laughter maddens my lungs, and the Gypsies
Camp in my brain and steal away from their fires.
But down in the street my sister wears her face to the bone
And thinks she is happy, whispering that Spring has come.
We are beside ourselves
We have too much time . . .

I shall have it by heart all my days, though I do not need to because it is written in this book – the only thing they did not take or break. If I turn back the pages to when he wrote it I will find all those times, in his writing and mine, even the smells, which are stronger than words, and closest of all (because it has been a year, almost exactly, since this book was written in – this is the first time I have opened it since he shrugged his shoulders in that New Mexican bus station and said, so offhand, "Well, those things are all yours now"), closest of all are the butterfly wings, and the leaf from the creosote bush – just a page back from here, I can feel them through the paper though I will not look. And the snakeskin diamond and the feather and the flower from the Desert—

And oh I could cry, sitting here under Widow Gardiner's roof, with my face looking back in the lamplight from the night window, holding my book of ghosts.

For he found his lean old man, and learned devotion.

Tchi-tchi. Po-po-po.

This room was to be Dr. Adam Gardiner's study. It has his desk and his chair and his boxes of music, but it never had him. Because he died in the pasture two days after they took their savings and left the city and bought their farm. Who writes the story of our lives? – that was our first B.Q., but we left it off the final list. And to think that she looks at *me*, once a week at least, and sighs and says, "Oh, my dear . . . ." She is the bravest of the brave. She is my Fairy Godmother and here I am in this room beneath her south gable. My Nook, my Treasure Trove.

With my view in the afternoons of the grey barn and the long, long pastures down to the creek. And the sugarbush beyond that, climbing the hill, its winter sky-lanes almost filled in by the young leaves. I believe in those things – I must learn to trust things that I see only parts of. For although it is dark now and the window is only a dusky mirror for me and my room, those things will be there when the light returns. And it *will* return. The Blackbirds say *Yoouuu'll see youu'll see!* The Killdeers circle the house and cry their names, the Meadowlark bargained away her tail for a song but the song is the heart of the pasture, from her yellow breast, kissing the air. Try to catch that in musical notation, and you'd take all its life away.

The Sparrows chant all day and do not know what boredom is, the Swallows are here, zig-zagging low in the yard, lifting into the barn door. And now, as I write, the Owl is calling her two-bar warning and ripping the heads off sleeping chickens. Widow Gardiner calls it Le Grand Duc.

And the little doves with the black eyes are Les Colombes Tristes, she says, are Les Tourterelles Pleureuses.

She told me this afternoon during practice, watching me by her window, that I had brought Youth and Grace back into her house. She turns mice into prancing steeds and pumpkins to coaches, she turns cinders into diamonds. And I said, "Shall I dance for you?" The words came to me without a thought.

And I would like to say that I played for her in the sunbeams beside her piano, for that is what I imagined, but of course I did not. I danced, though – and she tried to play for me at first, but then her hands faltered on the keys and she laid them in her lap and stared at me. A little astonished, a little afraid, determined to feel delight.

So much has happened today, and changed. I danced on tip-toe, slow, half-crouched, with one foot pointed down in front of the other. An elf who played upon a flute, the Elf-Me that Handsel drew last year, back near the start of this book, but now I play upon a reed of course, and could only hold my clarinet as if it were a flute, and mime it. There was no music, once she stopped playing, just the dust specks like notes in the sunbeams round my shoulders. A naked elf-marionette in my mind, daring to play the flute again, in charge of the room.

She was small in my eyes, Widow Gardiner, for the first time – unsure and helpless. I brought the dance to a close and stood beside her and said, "The thought came unbidden" (which are her words), and then she looked up at me with her blue girl's eyes and said, "Oh, my dear . . ." in that voice. Watching us for that moment you would have seen a dear old woman and a damaged girl embracing, her cheek held to my bosom, my eyes closed for her. And when we drew apart, who were we Each?

And who are *You*? B.Q. B.Q.

I could turn back the pages now, skipping The Desert and the roads, and the hopeful, remorseless year, and find that Elf-Me birthday sketch, but I never will. I fear it will be Slick and Unoriginal, and I must never be disappointed in Handsel. He went as far as he could, nobody dies before their time – I did not know there were walls around us, that my open road was a closet beneath the stairs for him, waiting for the Southwest Wind, that elegant, brown old Texas man, to tug the door open and rescue him.

When people die, their ashes return in cardboard boxes. There are numbers on them in blue marker and inside, a plastic bag of them.

A Mother's dead face on a pillow is all Begging Questions rolled into One.

What have I done to deserve good fortune?

My Fairy Godmother is a Lady. She has English ways with a French accent. She has taught me to speak again, but first she taught me to play upon a reed. When I play that clarinet I am touching the place that only her husband's lips ever touched. The three of us play together. She prefers the harpsichord to the piano ("I would rather pluck than strike!" dit elle) but there is no one in these parts to tune it, after all.

It came to me last night, half asleep, that I should dance for her again. I'll say, "Would you like me to take off my clothes?" and she'll rest her hands on the keys, or put down her cup in its saucer and say, "What an extraordinary suggestion," and then she will tilt her head like a sparrow and give her determined nod and say, "Well yes, you know, I would like that very much."

The room full of sunlight. The deep dark mirror of the piano.

But where (B.Q.) do such Quaint Delusions come from?

I was always a mimic. I pick up the way people talk and I never forget their words. It's true. Handsel and I used to make up scenes, on the buses below the Border, or walking the back roads – and all the characters in them were people we knew, saying the things they said. Doing all the things they'd never do, of course.

We laughed so much.

Now that the sky is clear I go out each evening, as far as the witchy old elm tree down the concession road, and wait for the stars to come out. The first one is there, suddenly, in the West, halfway up the sky, a minute after the sun is gone, while the horizon's still red. It sits there in the yellow-blue West. It is Venus I suppose.

The second one is higher, but in the same part of the sky, a few minutes later. You would not expect to find light beginning where there is light already.

It takes you into a trance, staring for stars. Thoughts *do* come unbidden, or words, or notes. Are thoughts unbidden the whispers, B.Q., of the Devil? Do memories ride upon thoughts, or the other way round? The hidden, unbidden departed?

Les Tourterelles Tristes.

Venus gets stronger and beats like a heart, and the second star is almost green – you cannot miss it once you have found it.

The first night I walked back to the house after Venus.

Last night I turned back after the second star.

Tonight I waited for the third. It took five minutes more, at least, and then there it was, almost straight overhead. Time to start fishing, I thought, and looked back at Venus. But then I lost the third star, though I knew it was there. Then there it was, clear as ever.

A big bird flew over. A heron, or perhaps a hawk, with slow, big wings ever so high. I followed it as it flew West – soon it would stand out against the pale half of the sky. But after I checked my three stars again, the bird had vanished. It was not to be seen though I knew where it was. But there were dark smudges up there, that shifted with my eyes, black confetti, rags and seeds and feathers, and when I turned my head away from the West I found a fourth star, instead.

I meant to come home before I saw it, I wanted one new star for each evening, but by the time I had reached the gate I couldn't stop myself looking up, and there were dozens more stars already,

I could see the constellation shaped like a W.

I guess the fishermen didn't look up. I guess they knew that the third star sets all the stars loose. I guess they could see the sky in the water.

It's like searching the sky for memories; searching your mind. I don't like to do that, though. I forget as much as possible. You keep what you have to. What belongs to you.

The *almost there* things that people search for. That's nostalgia, I would presume. The damp evening smell of regretted places. I've got no time for it, with all its lies.

I know what Comfort is.

Piped she.

I am a traveller in Time. I have come to a wide land, without streets, where silence has waited all my life. The farmers pass on the concession roads, slowing down so as not to strike you with flying gravel, and smile shyly from their tractors or pickups, waving and passing – I am a stranger here and safe. At the heart of this country is the Widow's House, with its soft lamplights and music, and a garden where flowers embroider the vegetables. "Appetite," she says, "but Appetite without Greed." It is her motto. We feast upon a single "exquisite" tomato, an "immaculate" avocado, the clean, fierce layers of a rose-tinted onion. Seven herbs hang in her kitchen window, her knives are bright and accurate, olive oil is a sacrament, our plates of food could be shown in a gallery. "Presentation," she says. She is a wise and tender Witch.

The furniture is old and full of memories, it breathes out light and lavender. There is an oboe in the Armoire, and three recorders. "Armoire." A quince tree espaliered around the piano window. "Espaliered."

And the books have memories, too, so many of them, tended and dusted each week while the Chinese Nightingale sings in its lacquered cage.

As I dust and polish this desk each week, and shine the window, and bring things in of my own, from my walks, making it more mine. Though it will always be *his* room, his dream at least. But as I recover myself in his room, the boxes whisper – they have treasures for me, when I am ready. This morning Monsieur Saint Saens introduced himself, inviting me to draw his Tarantella from its nest – *Tarentelle pour Flute, Clarinette et Orchestre* and I was able to think of my flute again, after all this time since I rose from the dead and learned to play upon a reed. For there were the Flute and the Reed together, at play, and in handwriting on the third page of the score were his words. "Soloists here *as one*: two skaters glide from the opposite sides of the pond and move hand in hand for six bars before parting." A humorous voice in pencil from the dead – the elegant loop of his *gee*. I place his lips upon mine each time I take up the clarinet.

All at once I am blessed with ignorance. Is that not, B.Q., what Sanctuary must mean? How can you pity yourself when there's still so much you don't know?

My flute played *Humoresque* in the shade of Catalpa trees in a town called Troy. It played *Tom Hark* on the embankment above the brown Missouri. It sang for its supper outside the arcade in Spring-field, with a guitar and a mandolin; it had found itself friends.

It should never have left them.

Is that really me, on the roads back from The Desert? She is a Friendless Waif, tiny and far away, with her backpack and flute and her See-America bus pass. With her tail between her legs, however brave, a speck moving North up the map, looking for signs, trusting her Guardian Angel.

But she came to a city by the river – how could she know there are streets there so blind that the Guardian Angels must close their wings and weep? She was broken in half.

They turned my flute against me. Blood and hair upon the keys.

There!

I was found and delivered. I will never know how. Why was the wife of a doctor in Detroit possessed of a Mother across the river? A Mother she thought must be lonely – in this wide safe land without streets.

Tonight when the stars overtook me by the gate, I stayed and looked up at where there was still some light in the West, and I saw the threads and circles and smudges sailing again. I was not frightened, I am not 43 – besides, my death is behind me. They floated and settled, as my eyes grew still; they were notes – half-notes and quarter-notes, with ties and slurs, all ashiver.

Across the pasture, where the land rises by the swamp like a fairy fort, with cedar trees and lilacs, the young spring frogs started up, the Peepers, their tiny thousands like the voice of the stars.

I stepped back, scuffling the gravel beneath my feet, and there were telephone wires overhead that I'd never noticed before, but they formed a perfect stave – five lines drawn fine across the sky, with those floating notes of mine clear all at once, and set in their place there.

I read them and did not linger; I knew if I did that the stars would drown them out.

I came back to the house, and waved from the hall without speaking, and ran up the stairs, singing them under my breath.

So I dared after all to take out this book, and write them down.

They are only a phrase of the music, a hint of the story, but in a sane world it will be enough. It is a skeleton key, I think – go search, go tremble.

There will be ghosts from the future too, I suppose.

But what is Youth for, I beg to ask, if not to give itself away?

ITHACA

The coming of age has cast me back into childhood.

The tender, flushed parchment of the fruit, the clear print of my teeth glistening in its flesh. The last taste of memory.

The day's heat shimmering off the hillside. Blind light off the portico. A boy's laughter.

Oregano, marjoram, mint, dry under bare feet.

Duósmos, thumári, phaskomiliá.

My little shadow, huge on the path through the olives.

Breathing not air, but the dear confusion of scents that is place. Time. Home.

White. Blue. Yellow, tan, olive, rose, charcoal.

The lazy white shoal of waves, tracing the headland.

Itháki.

❀　　❀　　❀

I must rehearse my name, over and over. I must detach it from the face it belonged to for thirty years. It is mine now, it is me.

And the girl who last night took on my old name is standing, I know, at her window, looking out to the hills, rehearsing like me, relinquishing.

I have been her. She will become me in turn, at some god-given time down the years, when she holds the drug to my lips. How shall our names change us? How much will I be myself, and how much the woman whom we let go last night, who has no name now, who is nothing, who lives only in me?

The girl with the name that is no longer mine looks out on the wild hills and asks herself the same questions.

And behind her, in that room, waits the child whom she brought from the orphans' quarters, to witness and share in death, to receive her name. That child relinquishing, too, dazed by her lack of sleep and the terrors of death, crouched by the bed, watching for the woman who stares out at the hills to turn and explain things to her.

I have no one to guide me now but a dead woman with no name.

❉   ❉   ❉

Before dawn, while the tongueless ones carried their burden down into the darkness where I, where this flesh I inhabit, shall be carried one day, I came out under the trees and heard the cranes flying. The town was asleep still, not a light down below (no sickbed vigils, no fishermen yet awake). The dark of the moon, as it shall be, most likely, when my own time comes, and the cry of the birds high above me, like the clamour of frogs in a faraway swamp. I saw them, the vaguest shadow staining the Milky Way.

Others hear messages in their calls, or read portents into the skeins they weave on the sky. To me they were a season passing finally, as it has passed and will pass again, until Time has devoured all its children.

❉   ❉   ❉

Now the town sleeps again, the heat-numbed sleep of the afternoon where voices blurt out of half-dreams and hang in the room, pregnant with meaning yet with no midwife to deliver them, where purchases and betrayals incubate, where children are conceived. The lizards cling immobile to the walls above the beds, the crickets drowse.

And this wall, too, patient in the heat under my hand, as I look down on those roofs and lanes, its stones quarried by giants in a time before songs or story.

❖   ❖   ❖

She had nothing to give me.

I saw no trust in her eyes, no future. It was the look of an athlete defeated and alone at the end of a long foot race.

She tried to refuse the poison. Turned her face from the bowl that the child, without understanding, held out to her. I took the young hand and guided it. I closed her nostrils, so she must drink.

We breathed with her, then without. I said, Break the bowl now, and it fell from the child's hands. And I told her with kindness, but with half a heart only, You are an orphan no longer. As I was told, in my turn, long ago in that room, not knowing then that the world had just closed behind me.

❖   ❖   ❖

And I asked her (as I should not have perhaps, but it is for me now to judge and decide such things and she was more than ever a lost girl, and I remembered that), I asked her, What was your name before they brought you here?

The Maiden-no-longer turned and stared, as though to reprove me, and the child shivered and clung to her arm. They were afraid of me, in their separate ways. Afraid of themselves, too.

Long ago, I told them, my mother would call me Koré.

The Maiden-no-longer looked away. Was she thinking of her own first name in the world? Or of mine, never spoken before, as though I had broken a promise?

The torch shook in her hand as her eyes came back to meet mine. By daybreak she would be what she has watched me being these thirty years: the creature who chokes in the smoke above the pit, raving and weeping with mad and agonized calls from the underworld. And I would be the Midwife, Mother-no-longer, to unravel and deliver those secrets to men's ears.

Our eyes, then the child's, the new Maiden's.

Chosen by her for the same inescapable path.

Maiden to Mother to Midwife.

Parthenos, Mitera, Maia.

I closed the dead eyes and came out to the cranes flying below the stars.

❉   ❉   ❉

In the courtyards, down there in the taverns, and far away, too, in the halls of the magnates and generals, the lies are repeated and taken for truth. I have heard them.

Overheard them.

They come on the wind, in the dust upon travellers' cloaks.

One above all.

His music. His triumphant, beautiful lies.

Stronger than history. Lovelier than truth.

A song from the tavern, on the shore wind at night, scaling these walls from the lives that commingle below, with their wine and laughter and kisses, their brawls and couplings and betrayals, their getting and spending, all sharing the story.

A song that has poisoned the story.

❉   ❉   ❉

He was a boy to be loved, and not trusted.

Where had he come by his charm? He told me that pirates had taken him, he'd been sold as a slave in the Troad, his new master, a merchant who had travelled the world – had been with the eyeless shepherds, had steered through the jaws of Messina, had been shipwrecked on Ogygia, had looked into Hell's mouth, wore a bracelet woven from a Siren's hair, had scaled the world's head where the cold turns the waves into stone and crushes the ribs of ships – had adopted him as a son.

My mother laughed when I told her the story. Her white throat against the myrtle leaves by the window. A laugh to preserve me from charm, yet to honour it, too.

His gift won us all. He became our mascot, we took credit for inventing him. But alone with you, there was always a secret shared, a winking conspiracy.

He'd be there, by the well, in the grove, on the rock shelf over the bay, out of nowhere. You were glad of him, even as he broke into your solitude. Eyes laughing and dancing under the black curls.

One green eye, one brown.

The cat and the dog.

But his gift . . . .

When we practised, or at meal times, he would pounce on a story midstream and leap to his feet with a bird's laugh and head for the doorway. He would call back a phrase or a cadence or name that the speaker had used, and be gone.

And we sat in the silence of the broken story, or continued half-hearted with our lesson, knowing that he was pacing under the portico or out on the cliff's edge, and we waited.

Then back he would come with his song, and the notes to go with it, built from the words or the tale he had borrowed. Uttered from the doorway in that voice that my mother called silver – effortless, yet with every rule observed.

And there was no envy. He would finish, and bow, and then, with the lop-sided shrug of a faun, he'd break out in a giggle, his voice not yet wholly a man's, as if there was no help for it, as if the song wrote itself.

And he'd slide back into his seat, and lead us in laughter at his song's audacity.

Then wag his hand in dismissal, as if it were done now and could be forgotten.

He forgot nothing. Ever.

Phemios.

Our prodigy.

In everyone's confidence.

The cat and the dog.

❊ ❊ ❊

Where do we come from? Out of the land of ghosts. *What are we?* Only our thoughts, our memories and the dreams that the ghosts send to us. *Where are we going?* Into the land of ghosts.

I watched him, open-mouthed, the sweet juice drying on my lips, the fragrance of it on my hands.

We come back again then? I said.

But he'd looked away. His fingers were shredding a leaf, piece by piece. He stared out at the water.

I asked him again.

Then he nodded, and I turned to see the ships coming round the headland.

The ghosts have come to fetch us, Koré. Though he spoke my name it was as though I was not there. There was a misery in his eyes I could never have imagined, and a crease of pain through his brow. See, he murmured, they come with black sails.

He saw the doom clearly, yet to me, as I lifted the fruit again to my mouth, the three sails below were gay in the sunlight, white as the lazy waves they came over.

❊ ❊ ❊

The falcon who nests on the headland hangs over me, riding the shore wind. Her young ones have scattered, her mate has flown south already towards the Troad. She hunts for herself now.

She disdains the swallows that are gathering on the roofs below. She watches our doves, pecking beside the pool, the white and the black. They know better than to fly up at this hour, but she is patient.

The hoopoe comes unafraid, swooping down through the sanctuary, out past me into the air and back to feed on the path beside the doves. The falcon could never catch him, she does not try.

I am halfway to the sky, watching the swallows weaving like fish over the roofs below me.

The hoopoe nests in filth, but the gods set a crown on his head. *Opou*, he cries, Where, where, oh where? *Pothen pröerkamen? Poi aperhkometha?* His breast is like rosy silk, the sun picks out the bars on his wings when he flies. His brow is golden. His eye a black mirror.

❋   ❋   ❋

The gods touch the earth with colour, it's true. My mother knew this. Colours die with the light, and in our sleep or our deaths they are only wraiths, fading perfumes, cold figures. My mother taught us to hear the music of colours, like our voices echoing from the cliffs.

We may not become immortals, but we may answer the gods and touch their lives, as long as our songs are remembered.

❋   ❋   ❋

And Phemios was our bright singer, conjuring words when the mood was on him as if from the notes of his lyre. He led the dancers on, carrying each song beyond itself to where gods walked with men, and centaurs came down from the hills to taste the dark wine, and cowards were changed into golden heroes, and mothers ran wild in the groves with the children of Pan.

He was so young, so thoughtless, in love with wine and blood, with famous lies and betrayals, with every kind of wonder. He wove all of the songs into one.

A god speaks through me. I sing to the gods, and to those who are worthy to listen. The words in the Song were his own, but I alone of the living remember how they were spoken – the terror in his mismatched eyes, his pride, or was it cunning, defying the knife at his throat. The stench of slaughter, and wine fumes mingling; the weary sounds that the dead still utter as their bodies settle.

> *here in the dust and the reeking blood-runnels the singers*
> *and dancers*
> *lie in their blood-boltered heaps, brought to naught by*
> *the homecomer's vengeance*

The vaulting words that outlive him.

❖   ❖   ❖

The god who spoke through him spoke first with the tongues of merchants and sailors, for he would vanish whenever a ship put in at the harbour. That god spoke first through the old songs, too, the bedtime stories, the wild tales of market and tavern – songs that come with the wind on the open sea, filling the sails, muttered in the holds, spilling out with the cloths and amber and slaves upon the wharfs.

The god who has spoken through me these thirty years is a cruel stranger, riding me up from the darkness, strangling, stealing my tongue. His voice is a serpent's, bursting out of my lungs, voiding my bowels. There is no music. I know nothing of what he speaks.

❖   ❖   ❖

The doves croon, the town sleeps, the fish rise and fall in the pool. A white boat, its sail slack and brown in the sunlight, is becalmed out in the bay. This is all the world I have known for fifty years.

❊   ❊   ❊

The Mother has no dreams. I was told this, and told it in turn to the Maiden-no-longer, for it is true. The god steals the dreams. But now, I wonder, will that olive tree, alone above the rocks where the seals lay in the sun, so old and black that it seemed made of stone itself, come back to me as it used to, out of the land of ghosts?

And the cavern on the way down, where the stone hives were sheltered, the bee song loud in the creepers upon the cliff. There we went in late afternoon, to bathe at the stream's mouth, and wash our clothes, and play. The girls took my hands by the water's edge, and afterwards my mother sat under the olive, in the throne of its roots, and talked to us. Behind her, across the straits, the two low islands and the misty gap between them – the path that my father had taken before I was born, to be with his dark-skinned lover.

My mother's words had wings – they carried us across time and ocean to the Spartan shore, and the sea cave where she and her sisters would dive and play. The mermaids had their great looms of stone there, she said, and purple draperies that opened and closed with the tides. The sand below was gold in the light, and silver beneath their shadows, and a ship lay down there, on the threshold, its cargo of wine jars studded with shells, blue and yellow, where the bright fishes darted.

Her heart still lived in that place, she told us. And tears filled my eyes that I could not understand, for the story was sad all at once with no reason.

❊   ❊   ❊

But that was where my father came out of the sea. His red hair almost black from the water, as he clung to the oar, drifting towards the sands. She told that story with no sorrow, even laughing, for it was time past to her, and my angry brother had left, and peace had been ours for a year. My father pretending shipwreck, though his ship was moored out of sight behind the islets, coming naked out of the water to fall at her feet.

That oar was displayed on the wall, with the panther skin and the boar's skull and the bow, in the hall where the world came to an end.

❊   ❊   ❊

My father's world ended, too, twenty years ago now, if the priests are to be trusted. Killed by the son of that dark-skinned princess. His son, they say.

Last night the old woman whose name I bear now fought against her world's ending. *Into the land of ghosts.*

My mother's world ended twice, before she left me here. I looked back at the hilltop, to the smoke rising out of the grove, as the sea floor vanished beneath us. Will we go to your father's home now? I asked her. She would not look up. There is no home, she told me. There was grey in her hair, her beauty had died in the night. Before you were born, she said, the raiders came. The lovely old house was burned. Her eyes were fixed on the boat's wake, closing behind us. They are all dead, Koré, and my sister Iphthimé carried off with the cattle and furnishings, who knows where?

I can smell the chill of that dawn, the spray on my young cheeks, the sorrow.

I will take you where no one will harm you, ever, she said.

❊   ❊   ❊

Next to those whom the gods protect, the makers have the safest lives. Those who make earth's treasures more precious yet, the clay, the cloth, the metals; things that do not age, that outlive their makers. The weapons, too. For some most of all, it is the weapons.

The makers can be owned, can be traded or stolen like the things they create – and so they survive. Not their masters, though. Sooner or later those who have peace and who care to have beauty around them, are the ones the raiders seek out.

Like wasps that watch through the slow summer days, while their cousins, the wild bees, labour from dawn till dusk plying their waxen palace with tawny nectar, till the hollow bough overflows with their winter's store; so the raiders wait till the harvest is at its richest. They come with their black sails and leave only ruin and death.

The songs make heroes of them, and they come to believe in the songs. They put themselves in the poets' hands and see themselves turned into princes and kings. Then they, too, want peace, to live out their lives with their spoils, and to see their children inherit. They hang those beautiful weapons on the wall, and their edges grow dull. But peace is no more than a season in this world, an island in our land of islands. The raiders come in from the sea.

❖   ❖   ❖

My best memory is of staggering with the basket of skeins, as big as myself – the linen threads, and the silks; the purple, the saffron, the blue. I held the treasure, and they let me carry it, laughing as I struggled up the steps, to where the great web was stretched between the columns.

The words in black letters: *Where do we come from?* A laurel tree spreading beneath them. The swallows with blood-red breasts. The outline of dolphins on the bright waves below.

All the colours of her mermaid cave.

And Antinous, the one prince among us, hoisting me up to touch them – my child's hand joining the swallows in mid-air.

I wanted him to be my father.

He held my mother's hand when the raiders came.

*   *   *

Soon the town will wake, and the people will turn to their business, leaving their dreams behind.

What dream are they living in, though, under these giant-built walls, under the gods' protection?

The town is growing – more taverns, more inns, more workshops. Our fame is spreading. Travellers have come from Egypt, from purple Sidon, from the mountains beyond the Troad, and the craftsmen follow them. There is ivory now, and amber and gold, and the carvers are taking marble from the cliffs at the headland, splitting the rocks with their fires.

The priests grow rich, new houses spread up the hillside.

And what do they think of us, truly, down in the town; we who are their livelihood and protection?

If one should look up for a moment and see, high above him, my face, like a bird's, looking out, what would he imagine?

A cloistered, old, unfondled woman?

*   *   *

Last night the girl slipped out from the tavern door, and the boy whistled softly below me from the shadows. They were part of a dance that they scarcely understood, drawn together there by something beyond them. Their cries like creatures in pain, the pale orb of her face down there, his hair dark at her neck. A desperation that turned in the end into laughter. And when she ran back in, leaving the door open wide, with the sounds of shouting and singing within, I saw him step out from the wall, and pose there alone in the doorlight, dancing.

It was a child's dance, not a man's, for all of his triumph. He was a faun, arms outstretched, face turned to the stars, and to me.

And I thought of Phemios – young, and then old.

*   *   *

189

As though he knew, as though after thirty years the time had come, now that the god had possessed me, he was there at the gate like any supplicant.

❈   ❈   ❈

The tongueless one who sweeps the cloister paths has white in his beard, and his shoulders hunch like a dove's. He makes his own music as he works, a bee song above the scraping of his broom. He must not look up, unless I speak to him, but when he does, his eyes are still those of the child sent to fetch me that day.

❈   ❈   ❈

Through the veil I saw an old man among the priests in the courtyard, silver-haired, with a staff higher than his head. And a youth beside him, a goatskin lyre-bag slung open over his shoulder.

The Midwife prompted me. Has he a question? I asked.

He lifted his face towards me, not so old after all, but everywhere furrowed except round the pale, hollow lids. His voice clear and strong, as he beat time with his staff:

> *Tell me, oh Muse,*
> *of those things that have never*
> *occurred in the past and will*
> *never take place in the future*

And he shrugged, and laughed. A young man's mockery.

Phemios, I said.

Ah Koré, he said, you remember.

The priests hissed like snakes. She is The Mother.

He laughed again, an old man's laugh this time. Then so quiet, I scarcely could hear – And I am The Hostage, he said.

Homeros. The Song, the triumphant lies were all his.

I was too weak, the moon was three nights from the half and the taste of the god was still harsh in my mouth. My hair reeked from the smoke; that morning I had shuddered above the pit for the first, anguished time – had been the creature that I, as the Maiden, had watched through the years, eyes streaming, wailing in a voice not her own.

Why did you take that name? I called down. Did my father keep you prisoner?

We are hostages to our songs, he said.

He has no question, said the Midwife. Come away.

        ❈   ❈   ❈

The priests say that his skull is lodged in a temple niche under Mount Ida. The villagers bring water from the spring there, anoint the empty brow and gather the water again. It cures the falling sickness, so they believe.

        ❈   ❈   ❈

And the cry was wrung out of me, as I was led away. The girls," I cried, "—that was not true, surely. They were not killed!

The youth stared up, as though his insolent eyes could penetrate the veil, but Phemios turned away.

In all the Song's lies, the truth that I dreaded most was that death. Twelve girls, hanged there by my brother, where the web was torn down, limp bodies under the portico.

My brother who vanished when my mother raged, and Antinous banned him from the girls' company. Who found his father, my father, and came back to destroy.

Quicksilver Phaone, and tender-hearted Melantho, all of those girls. Our family, the singers and dancers. Choking before my brother's eyes, with no one to save them.

Turning in the sea wind that stole us away before daybreak. What my mother had seen.

❈   ❈   ❈

Tomorrow night, or the next, the moon's horns will show themselves over the bay. There are travellers waiting already in the
town. Whatever her dread, the new Mother knows what awaits
her. The tongueless ones know, they will do what they always do.
But four days from now, I must carry word from the pit, shaped
into meaning, for the priests to write down and deliver.

How shall I know? I have no instruction.

Did the dead one, whose name I now bear, wonder too? Did
the past overtake her, as mine has, in the moon's darkness? Did
the one before her prepare her at all?

Poi aperhkometha?

No answer comes back, no echo, no sign from the gods.

The tongueless one's bee song stops. He smiles at me, and
shrugs, and raises his broom – as if he would sweep the whole sky.

❈   ❈   ❈

Only once did she tell me what I, as the Mother, had said.

*The spring shall run dry, and the Earthshaker tear down the
walls, and the mountain shall fall on the town.*

We stood by the pool, and she laughed. It was not her way to
laugh or be kind, even among the orphans. She stroked my hair
– I will not tell the priests this, she said.

❈   ❈   ❈

It is the slanders I do not forgive, not the lies. All stories are lies,
after all. That is their beauty – the inventions the gods permit us.

But poor Arnaeos, the crippled porter on his pallet outside
the hall. Always willing to fetch and carry within his means, his
hands still nimble, his eyes full of laughter, my storyteller.

Phemios would bring him wine, and stay to listen to the mad
tales of his sailing days. The island that became a whale, the Old

Man of the Sea and his seal flocks, the enchantress who fed men wine and turned them to beasts, the brothers who captured the wind in a leather bag.

Arnaeos beaten to death by my father – the first blood, for no reason but to show us why he had returned.

The name defaced forever. All of those names.

I see my father's hand in that, or my brother's. The knife at the throat.

❖   ❖   ❖

Three ships filled with plunder, and twenty men climbing towards us from the harbour. Their eyes seeing nothing but what they had come to find. Though I saw my brother, how could I know that the man at their head was my father?

He stared down at me with eyes suspicious and cold, then fingered my red hair and laughed out loud. He caught me up, and held me high in the air. His great hands on my ribs. It was a face that could turn from laughter to murder in an instant – I saw it, as I struggled against him and cried out for Antinous.

❖   ❖   ❖

There was blood, and then wine, and then nothing but blood.

The overturned table, and Antinous dead on the floor.

It was not the great bow from the wall, but the one that they played with to shoot at the papago – the silly bird of rags and feathers, hung from the portico roof. It was leaning against the doorway, where Amphinomous had set it down. Gentle Amphinomous who was stabbed from behind by my brother.

❖   ❖   ❖

This is the truth. That Phemios dragged me to the corner, and pulled an ox hide over us. The smell and the clammy touch of that. And it was all in darkness – the cries, the screaming, and then, behind the silence, the sounds of my mother weeping.

❖   ❖   ❖

Ti esmen?

No answer comes back, no echo.

❖   ❖   ❖

I cried out to her, and the hide was pulled away.

It was the second time, the last, that I looked in my father's eyes. They were eyes in a mask. Crazed with blood.

And Phemios, dragged out of hiding, the knife about to strike.

Think twice, before you cut my throat. A god speaks through me . . . .

Sing then. My father's voice.

I followed Phemios' eyes. The circle of killers, tall men, their passion subsiding. A swallow flew into the silence, and up to the beam above us. We heard her young in the nest, clamouring for food. Phemios seemed like a child, even to me, beside those ruthless faces, but he wanted to live. His eyes swept now where I could not follow them, across the bodies. His hand began to beat upon his thigh.

> *gaping and flailing like fish at the grey-foaming tide line*
> > *of Ithaca*
> *hauled from their element spilled from our fishermen's*
> > *meshes to sprawl there*
> *drowning in sunlight, strewn on the bright sand and*
> > *banished for ever from*
> *saltwater's haven, their silver-scaled armour befouled and*
> > *blood-crusted,*
> *outwitted and slaughtered, their fleetness and pride turned*
> > *to misery – even so*

here in the dust and the reeking blood-runnels the singers
                                        and dancers
lie in their blood-boltered heaps, brought to naught by the
                                homecomer's vengeance

The seeds of the lie already there, staving off death.

The knife moved up from his faun's throat. I could only hear myself screaming. The cat's eye and the dog's spilled out upon the floor.

And who remembers the *singers and dancers* now? They have vanished from the Song.

The raiders are changed into heroes, outnumbered and righteous, the gods at their side.

Usurpers and harlots are slaughtered without mercy.

Butterflies turned into worms.

❖   ❖   ❖

How shall I know? I asked her. How shall I understand? How will I find the words?

You were chosen, Mother, she said. You must trust in the gods.

THE BOAR HUNT

The way it turned out, there were races on that week and scarcely a car to be found in the town itself. The three that there were at the station, as the crowd straggled out, were not pitching for florins. The front driver came sauntering down the queue demanding our destinations, ignoring anyone he chose to. A big fellow with flash shoes and a burberry and a nose broken in two directions.

A young woman two back in the line from me stepped out in the rain with her hand raised. "I have to get to Crossdurgan," she called. She was English. "Can you take me there?"

The man was wise enough to the madness of tourists to hide his satisfaction. "Crossdurghan, is it?" he said, setting her straight on the name. And with something of a bow, as he reached to pick up her little suitcase, "Well get there you shall, dear heart." He pointed to his car.

"What will it cost me?" she asked. "Can we settle the price before we leave?"

He furrowed his brow, as though deep calculations were in swing. "Well, now," he said, "that'd have to be eleven or twelve pound easy. English pounds."

I stepped up then. "It's a coincidence," I told her, "but I'm heading for the very same place." She wasn't much more than a girl, determined but scared. "You ride up front," I said, "and we'll share the cost."

"I'd have to charge another five pound," the man said. "Wear and tear on the vehicle."

"We'll say fourteen pound, then," I said. "You climb in the front, miss."

The boyoh didn't like that. I set my bag in the trunk beside hers.

"Crossdurghan," I sang out. And of course, young Evans came up from the ruck, asking to come on board, and another fellow too, about sixty, with nasty teeth and the style of a failed barrister.

The driver started in again on the fare as they got seated, but I pressed his arm and steered him back round to the trunk. "Now listen, you bollocks," I said, "there'll be sixteen quid for this trip and there's the whole of it." "I can refuse to carry more than one fare," he said. "But that's the thing you won't do," I told him. "If you keep your eyes straight, there may be a tip in it for you."

Evans and the girl were seated and waiting, but the other stood hovering at the car door. "I prefer to sit by the window," he said, "if you've no objection." A college voice, and eyes that had long ago worn out their charm. A brandy gloss, too, on his nose and cheeks. A maggot.

"I'm easy," I said, and climbed into the back seat. I could see the girl's eyes in the driver's mirror. Evans was looking at me. "I saw you, didn't I?" he said, "last week at the vernissage."

I felt the Maggot stiffen beside me.

"You did," I said, "but I'm not in competition. I've other fish to fry." His innocent face looked perplexed.

The driver said not a word all the way out of town, but he couldn't keep faith with his sulk, it wasn't his nature. By the time we were past the Cathedral and away on the Corrib road, he was teasing and jesting and drawing the girl out beside him. About England, where he'd spent time himself, and the Kilburn Road and the characters. He played his own character to the hilt, there were smiles all round. I could see his eyes too in the mirror. I was well placed to watch.

When he asked us at large what our business was, though, there was frost in the air. It was Evans who opened up. He'd nothing to hide.

"I suppose you could say I'm engaged in a man hunt," he said, and gave a little laugh, his scholar's tones at odds with his hillfarmer's face. "A remarkable man, actually, a painter. A forgotten man whose time, it would seem, has come." You could picture him up in a lecture hall.

The girl's eyes widened. She caught me watching in the mirror. And the Maggot beside me, his hands were clenched in his lap, his eyes flicked away from mine.

"Fame and fortune, is it?" the driver said.

"It might be," our Welsh friend said. "There are just eighteen paintings, some drawings and studies, that came to light after his former wife's death. They are astonishing." He looked at me, but I shook my head, no. He leaned forward: "The thing is, the paintings were all done thirty years ago. Nothing's been seen since. I'm hoping there's more work, that he's kept painting, evolving. I'm an art historian you see."

The girl turned round in her seat, her pale face lit up, and the driver too was about to speak, but the Maggot could not contain himself. "It's Halloran you mean," he said. "It's Tag Halloran, ain't it, by God?" His breath was a diet of wine and blue cheese. The girl looked away. It dawned just then on Evans that he might be in trouble. Slyness didn't sit well on his honest face, but slyness it was. He stared at the Maggot. The Maggot turned and stared bitterly out of the window.

I watched the girl's eyes in the mirror, and she watched mine.

"It would be a remarkable thing," I said, "if every person in this car was in search of the same man."

All eyes were upon me then, but mine I closed.

"Do you know where to find him?" the girl said.

"I'll be working on it," I told her.

No one spoke for a while and then the driver started in on the races and the desperate soft going that was turning the odds on their heads. "I've a certainty for the 3.30 anyhow," he said, and the Maggot roused himself and growled, "Turin Dolly," and "No," says the man, "your mare will buckle in the back stretch, it's like Haney's Bog there, ankle deep," and "What then?" says the Maggot, and the driver glances back and says, "Hungerford," very smug and knowing, it's a great piece of theatre for the visitors, and Evans hugs his knees in delight. "Hungerford?" says the Maggot. "He's a frigging cart horse!" and "Those legs will bring him home," says the driver, "guaranteed." "Could I make a phone call?" asks the Maggot. "Oh, you've a bookie, then," the driver says. "We could stop in Oughterard, if you'll give me the lend of him."

They proposed a ten-minute break at the *Connaught Arms.* The rain had dwindled to Scotch mist by the time we came in through the town; there was a streak of blue sky, even, off to the west. I walked along and smoked a pipe above the falls while the others went in at the lounge door.

I was wondering should I let things unfold the way they were heading, or hold back for a day and let those three attend to their business with him, whatever it might be. Not that the Welshman's quest was any mystery. I'd wait and see, I thought – get a clue, perhaps, what the other two were about.

It was a country ten minutes, all right. The girl came out first and stood fidgeting by the car, not looking my way, and after her, Evans. The Maggot and driver appeared then, together, wiping the froth off their lips.

Then we were back on the road, with the smell of wet wool and Guinness, and the girl's soap or perfume and the Maggot's breath and cigarettes. He'd a grand silver case, with a monogram, curved to the pocket, but the smokes inside it were home rolled. The car cozied on, with the driver whistling old bar rebel songs, everyone occupied now with their private thoughts as the land opened out.

Myself, I enjoyed the ride. I didn't know Connemara, it was like scooting through half the bad films ever made in Ireland, and maybe a good one or two. Green bog and cotton grass, and cabins and turf smoke and stones through the drizzle. With the cry of a curlew or lapwing every so often, when the Maggot cracked down the window for one of his smokes. A body could lie out on that desolation for twenty years and never be found.

I thought a couple of times that the girl would say something. She would have, I think, if herself just and Evans had been in it. She didn't trust me, though, nor the Maggot neither. Who could blame her, whatever her story was?

We must have crossed over two score of bridges, bearing west and south, by the time we got in. It could turn you around, that western land – long stretches of nowhere, and was this a river or lough or an arm of the sea? And then the Atlantic smell, you couldn't mistake it, and the road on the skirt of a long bay, and Crossdurghan itself beyond, climbing the hillside. The cobbled main street opened into a square at the top. The names on the stores all Joyces, Conneelys and Kings. Tourist shops, bars, two hotels and a half, an old barracks.

The car stopped outside *The Celtic*, the one with the pillars and the A.A. two stars, and the driver went round for our luggage. I took the girl's suitcase from him. "You'll wait at the car," I told him. "I'll be out directly with the cash."

We juggled the change between us in the hall, and I went back out, where the driver was stood by his car, glowering at his shoes. I gave him his sixteen pounds. He counted the notes in disgust. "You ruined a good fare for me," he said.

"I stopped you from gouging, you mean."

"I don't like your kind," he said.

"My kind wasn't put into the world for your entertainment," I told him. "And by the bye, you weren't in Crossdurghan this day." I put a twenty-pound note in his hand, and went back inside.

It was a joke, seeing how they went at it. Young Evans, of course, was straight out and innocent, asking first off at the desk, "I'm looking for a Mr Halloran. I believe he lives hereabouts."

The woman at the desk looked us all over. "You'd need to ask Mr King," she said. "I've been here ten years only. The name means nothing to me." And she went off to the lounge bar by the stairs and talked with the man there rinsing the beer pumps.

He came out to the desk, drying off his hands on a towel. Looked us well over too. "What was the name?" he said. "Halloran? Halloran. No, I'd have to say there's been no one of that name around here, not in twenty years easy." He pushed the register over the desk to Evans. "I'd be the one to know if there was." Very smooth, I thought. A self-respecting type, with a shrewd eye.

"He'd be about seventy now," said the Maggot, over Evans' shoulder. "Tag Halloran, with a droop to his eyelid, the left eye."

"Not in this country," said the publican, handing over the room-key to Evans.

"A painter," offered the Maggot. "He might carry a cane still, with silver bands at the hilt."

"Now where would you get such ideas?" asked the publican. "What put you gentlemen onto this locality?"

"He sent letters from here," said Evans, "a number of letters, before the War."

I could see by the Maggot's eyes that he'd come the same route.

"Before the War!" your man chuckled. "Well, well." His eyes dropped to Evans' name in the book, as he swivelled it round for the Maggot. "I was barely a man myself then," he said, and smiled back in their faces. "He was passing through, perhaps," he suggested. "There were always travellers down here in the season, like yourselves today." He picked up the pen and tapped at the Maggot's sleeve to speed him along, or to bait him, maybe. "And then there's the fishing, of course," he said, "on the Lough in April."

"Is that so," said the Maggot. There was fierce sarcasm to his voice. He signed the book and picked up his key.

"Let me stand you a drink," he murmured to Evans, just leaving then for the stairs. And took his elbow, at the lounge door: "I've a head start here," I heard him say. "We should pool our resources."

"There was an O'Hanlon, now," the publican called out. "About seven years back, a traveller in gravestones. It wouldn't be him you were thinking of?" His eyes touched on mine, he was enjoying himself. The Maggot ignored him.

The girl, I could see, had drawn her own conclusions. She signed the register, said she'd be there for two nights, and went up the stairs without a glance in my direction.

"One night," I said, and signed my name *John Cudahy*. He could make what he wanted of that. He could send out the word for all I cared. I could feel his eyes on me, all the way up the stairs.

My room had a great view over the bay, with a lighthouse winking at the head. A break in the clouds, out over the islands. A postcard altogether. I dropped my bag and went down again, out across the market square and down a steep back street to the river side. I walked on past the bridge till I caught up with a twelve-year-old at the mouth of a boreen. "What's *your* name?" I said.

He drew his cuff across his snotty nose. "Danny," he said, all freckles and ears, "Danny Marken."

"That's what I thought," I said. "How many brothers and sisters are there at home now?" I was using my best Monto talk. He was wondering at that.

"There's five of us, sir."

"Right," I said. "And your Da still working, is it?"

"He is."

I'd the leaf of his jacket in my hand now, and brought him up close. "Now," I said, "it's a terrible thing when a man gets hurt, and is put out from work, wouldn't you say?"

He nodded, the poor little beggar, eyes wide and green.

"There's men in the world," I told him, "would do that kind of damage, if they were cheated out of the information they require."

He was searching my face for murder.

"It's a man called Halloran I'm looking for," I said. "But he uses the name Cudahy, and you'll tell me where he lives, if you're smart."

He looked up and down and away, and whispered a word. "Again," I said, "I don't hear you."

"Farranishg," he croaked.

"And where's that?"

He told me. I stuck a five-pound note in his breast pocket. "Keep yourself to yourself and you'll be all right," I said, and went on my way. I could hear his feet slapping the mud up the boreen.

The river fell into a loughan, and the road skirted that, rising and falling through some woodlands and round again to a humpy stone bridge where the rocks pinched in by the sea strand. The tide was boiling out through the single span of the bridge and I could see at once down the yellow sands where the islands lay, and Farranishg the nearest.

It was fifteen or sixteen acres of grass, with sheep dotted over it, lifting out into the bay. There had to be cliffs, pretty steep, where it faced the Atlantic, and the only sign of habitation was a peep of grey wall at its shoulder, just visible from the shore. I walked over the sands till I came to the nearest point. He'd a moat ready built for him there. His island stood five rods out at the most, across clear shallow water, with a sunken rough cause-way of stones that would surface in low tides.

I stood looking over, gauging the state of the tide, while the sun, which had only come out, as they say, to go down, dropped behind that island, Farranishg, and shed a blinding great halo around it. "And there you sit waiting," I thought, "as you've waited these fifty years."

When I turned to go, the island's black shape stayed afloat on my eyes.

There was a shop just down from the hotel, with a phone booth outside and a post box, and I stepped in there when I got back, and studied the tide-tables that were posted inside the doorway. It was a class of business you'd look for today in vain – cramped and dark, with that old reek of oilskins and stockfish and flour. They had dunlops slung from a beam in the back room, and I was sorting through them when the English girl came in off the street.

There was a huddle at the counter, two old shawlies and a cattleman paying down his account, and she stood there a good half-minute, chewing her lip, before they paid her any attention. Then she asked them straight out for their help.

"I'm looking for someone who lives near here," she said. "It's my husband's father and I don't think he even knows that he has a son."

The farmer was eyeing her sideways, like she'd stepped down from outer space, but the old girls were hooked right off and she knew it. She was keener by half than I'd guessed. Her eyes kept slipping back to them, though she seemed to be talking to the shopman.

"Can you please help me?" she said, standing up there in her cotton dress and her white English skin, like a sprig at the altar rail. "I've only got two days to find him, and my husband would be furious if he knew I'd come – he's too proud, you see."

You could see the yearning in the shawlies' eyes, to be in on this, and the shopster breathing down his nose, taking it all aboard.

"The name is Cudahy," she said, "but I think he might be using another name, Halloran." The flick of the shopster's eye didn't get by her. She raised her voice. "He must be an old man now," she said. "It would be awful if he were to die and not know he has a son in England, and a grandson, too."

I was wondering now if this might be more than a story. And her knowing his name. Either way, I thought, another day and she'd have it out of them.

"There's no Hallorans here," the man told her.

"Or Cudahy?"

The man shook his head.

"But he must live nearby – he's sent letters to people from here, over the years."

"And what sort of man would he be, now?"

"He's a painter," she said, "or he used to be. I heard someone say that one of his eyes was sort of droopy."

The shopman's hand tapped softly on the counter. "You'll be staying at *The Celtic*, is it?" he said, and frowned at the women. "I'll ask around for you."

"My name's Corner, Irene Corner," she said, and then, direct to the women, "Please help me if you can."

And she would have gone on, but she saw me then in the back-room, watching. We exchanged a look, as they say. "I'll come back in the morning," she told them. "Please help me to set things straight for my family." And out she walked.

I've never in my life made a purchase with less chat. They couldn't wait to have me out of there, and get on with their scandal. I went back with my parcel and up to my room in the hotel. I could see the lighthouse beam, now, sweeping the night, and a couple of lights beside, down the shore. Behind one of them, maybe, a man in his last night on earth.

I went down to the lounge, and she was at a little corner table, with a book and a meat pie. The other two were in the snug together. The Maggot saw me look in and muttered something, and when Evans looked round he'd the sheepish look to his face of a schoolboy caught out. I went off up the street for a couple of pints and a mixed grill at a side bar. A bare, pitiful place, a century behind the times like the rest of the town.

When you're on a case sometimes, you have the feeling that someone is writing a book with you in it, and the only way you'll resolve things is just to tide along with it.

And I was thinking this girl was a part of my story, and whatever the truth in *her* tale I wouldn't miss out on her meeting with him, not for the world. Which meant I must let her get to him ere I did. It meant I'd have to go with her.

And as it turned out, of course, when I went in upstairs, around ten o'clock, she was stepping out of the bathroom, along the landing. I stopped for her, and she clutched her towel and little wash bag up at her chest. She'd these tufty blue Woolworth slippers on, and a quilter dressing gown.

"You trust me or not," I told her, "but I've found your man."

Was she sly, or an innocent altogether? I couldn't tell. I don't for sure know to this day. She just searched my face and said nothing.

"I'll be off to see him in the morning," I said, "about half past nine."

"Where is he?" she said.

"Are you fit for a three-mile walk and back?" I asked her. "If you are, you may come along."

"All right," she said. She'd no choice.

"Some Wellington boots wouldn't hurt you," I said. "I'll be down in the hall."

She hung onto her questions, and ducked her head, and went off to her room.

For whatever reason, though, she must have said something to Evans next day, for he was speering out from the dining room when I came down about eight. She felt she could trust him better than me, I suppose. And he, be sure, would never shake off the Maggot. Well, I thought, we were all to be in it, then, and my mood lightened and I ordered a cooked breakfast and took a maddening long time over it, with a newspaper and a bland look, I'm sure, on my face. No hurry, anyway, going by the tide-tables. I'd had a bad night, but I was almost myself again.

I'd the taste of apprehension, though, in my mouth, when I teamed up with her at the front door. The sun was out and the place felt unnatural, somehow, with that thin light over it. I realized, as we stepped out, that I was glad of her company. I was surprised at myself.

She'd a scant raincoat on, and a headscarf tied at her throat – a juiceless stick of a girl really, with that skin which might never have been out of doors, but she could walk, I'll say that, and she kept right up to me though I was making fair time, even with those knee-high dunlops on.

The pace was harder on the Maggot, I'll guarantee, though it wouldn't have troubled young Evans. Oh, they were trailing us, a furlong or so in the rear. I saw her look back as we turned down through the trees, and there was the Maggot, trying to jook out of sight at the bend, his coat flapping loose, gasping for breath already I wouldn't doubt. I had to laugh.

She spoke, then, for the first time. "Who *are* you?" she said. "What are you doing here?" And she stopped, with her hands in the raincoat pockets, as if I should stop, too, under those dripping trees, and give her the reins. She had green eyes, I saw, and a queer direct look, and I wondered again was she foxing us all, or was she just what she seemed, with a fierce little will to sustain her?

"I'll ask you a thing first," I told her, and I set off again, so that she had to run to catch up. "Was that story you told in the shop anyway true?"

"Yes it was," she said. "Why else would I have come here?"

"There's a begging question for you," I said, "but I'll tell you this much: you don't trust me, and you're mistaken in that, but it's no matter. I've got family business, too, with him, of a sort, but it's different. I'll lead you to him, and I'll wait my turn."

The tide was low going out through the bridge-arch, but there was some body to it yet. "You'll wish you'd brought those Wellingtons," I said, for she'd only walking shoes on, "we've some wading ahead of us."

"I'll just take off my shoes," she said.

"Easy for you in a skirt," I said, "but what of your cronies behind? Can you see the Maggot with his pinstripes rolled up to his mottled hams?"

"The Maggot?" she said, and gave something like a laugh. "He's creepy, isn't he? Did you smell his breath?"

We were out on the strand now, the bit of wind skipping foam-scraps along the tide line. She looked behind her and asked me, "What do you think *he's* after?"

"I wouldn't know," I said, "but I wouldn't doubt either he's in the same line as young Evans. Something to do with the art market. Whether it's money or 'professional advancement.'"

"I'm here for money," she said, "and don't try to make me ashamed of it." I'd nothing to say to that. I was looking across to the shoulder of Farranishg, the roof of a building there. Then, "Do you know what to expect?" she asked, as though she'd a door on my thoughts, and "No, my little woman," I said, "I do not."

It was easy walking below the tide line, but the boys in the rear, still trying to keep out of sight, were making rough weather of it up in the soft sand. I saw the Maggot offload his coat on a thorn bush; he was floundering like a mired heifer, a good twenty feet behind Evans. Poor bastard could be buying a coronary for his pains.

We came down at the crossing and I held the girl's arm, limping over the first wet stones. The tide was still running a foot deep or more, with a tart whiff of seaweeds and dead crab around it. She looked across doubtfully; the ford's good half was under water and she'd no way of knowing how deep it was, or how swift. "I'll be your Saint Christopher," I said, and I swung her up and set out. She'd no more weight to her than a sack of chaff, her face turned away from me, pale and sparrow-boned with the teeth just a tint oversized, and her talcum powder smell. There was a mole on her cheek and another, smaller, just at her collar, and you knew there'd be others, too, out of sight. "I've a daughter your age," I told her, and just then a big sea-trout swirled up against my feet, breaking the surface, and she cried out, and I stumbled enough to let in a slop of the sea at my right boot, and I hugged her to me and went to dry land.

There was a cart-gate there, set in a length of drystone wall to keep stock from the crossing. You could gauge the high tides by the dulse and bladder-wrack draggling at the wall's foot. I set her down and went through, and when I turned to latch the gate shut there was Evans and the Maggot at the waterside beyond. They'd no cause to hide themselves now, but what would they do? We went on up the hill and left them to it, but a minute or so after we heard a shout, and the Maggot was down on one knee in the tide with his shoes held aloft. Evans had turned back to help him, but he at least had his trousers rolled up past his knees and was half ways dry.

"You've got such a cruel laugh," the girl said.

The track curved on up, with a stone trough halfway along set into the earth, though where the water came into it from, I couldn't guess. And there were sheep all around us, the queerest I ever saw, with skewbald flanks and four horns apiece, which goes against nature as far as I ever knew. Is he breeding freaks here, I wondered aloud, though I have to say they looked more alert and nimble than most of their kind.

It was clear now that the stonework above was no building, but a wall at a man's height curving around some trees. As we came up, though, the house roof was there, in grey slate, with three or four gulls hanging on the wind by the chimney, and then you could see there were steps going down and the house itself on a great shelf of land at the cliff top.

There was a man at the door, smoking a cigarette, watching us.

"Well, now," I said, and I was spared saying more, for a sheep-dog came out from the house side and up the slope after us, barking and slavering and hugging the steps like a serpent, and just as the girl fell back against me in fear, the Maggot himself came purple-faced over the brow, ahead of Evans if you'd credit it, and barged us aside and full tilt into that dog's path. He kicked out at it, and it grabbed his wet pant leg and swung and growled, and the man below showed no sign of calling it off.

"For god's sake, he'll have me killed," the Maggot cried out, kicking in vain at the dog and near to tumbling down the bank-side. Evans showed some of his mettle then; he darted in and planted his boot square on the dog's neck, pinning it to the ground. A swath of the Maggot's pinstripe came out in the beast's jaw, though.

The man below threw his smoke down, and stepped out from his doorway, jabbing his finger. I could see him clear now, lean and with thick white hair. "Let my dog be," he roared out, and it *was* a roar, no feebleness in it. "You call him off, man," cries Evans. "Get off my land," says the man, "and I'll call him off." "Oh

Jesus, Tag, be reasonable," moans the Maggot, plumped down on his arse now, surveying the damage.

Young Evans kept up the pressure; the dog's eye was bulging white and blue in its socket. The man came on. You could see his age, climbing the steps, his old frame loose in his clothes, the favour in his left leg.

I was glad, maybe, of the ruction. I couldn't quite fix it in my mind that this was him. And he paid no heed to the girl and myself at all. He'd eyes for the dog only till he came up to the Maggot. Then, "Jesus bloody Dunphy," he said, with amaze and disgust, and aimed a kick at him, "*You* here!" And right away he went at Evans with a two-handed shove, and backed him off from the dog. He got down on one knee beside it and held its face, for all it showed willing to go back on the attack. "Husha, husha," he crooned, the long, strong fingers on him stroking across its ears, combing the neck hairs.

He didn't look up at all. His voice had the smallest shake in it, from the rage. "You'll get off my land," he said, "and you'll stay off it." He'd been a strong man once, and his arms and shoulders had a heft to them still, crouching there. "You'll be off this minute, and not a word spoken, or I'm down to the house for my gun." He lifted the dog's muzzle to his own. "I'd have no trouble at all using it," he said.

"Mr Cudahy," said the girl, stepping forward, and he looked towards her. And then he saw me.

We were alone in it for that moment, his pale eye staring up at me. His neck brown and stringy in his loose sweater. I couldn't describe his look. He must have seen my father in my face.

He stood up slowly, looking round at Evans, and the Maggot, and the girl, and then off over my head. "Let's get it over with out here," he said. He was holding his right hand down on his thigh to stop it trembling.

I was myself again. "We'll go down to the house," I said.

He led the way. I could sense the pride at war in him, but he just said, "Come on then," quietly to his dog, and set off down the steps. With his droop-eye towards me, though, he looked like he could be praying, eyes shut.

The dog, for some reason, let Evans pass with ne'er a twitch but it fixed its eyes on the Maggot and growled in its throat. I looked down at the accident-prone poor slut and thanked my stars I didn't inhabit that skin. He was propped on one arm in the grass, with his wet lip trembling, his pasty leg bared through the slit in his trouser leg. I gave him a hand up. His shirt was pressed and clean, I saw, but frayed through all round the collar. "Did your horse come in?" I said. He stared at me, as if to defy my contempt, and a flicker of spirit showed in his brown eyes. "*My* horse came in, all right," he muttered, and cleared his throat, "but your carman's hunch was a bust." "No harm, though, in hedging the bets," I said. He edged round, to keep me the weather side of the dog. "Whoever you are," he said, "I'm not the fool you think me."

He skipped round me a couple of times, playing fence with the dog, as we followed the girl down the steps. Then he bolted before her, in at the house door.

Would Halloran be ready, I wondered, with that gun of his. But he was leaning up against a table, at the centre of the room, fiddling with a packet of Dunhills, as if debating whether to light one or not. Himself and Evans by the table, the girl just inside the door, and the Maggot slumped already in the one easy chair by the range.

There was bread, by the smell of it, baking or on the rise, but no sense of a woman in the place. Just the brigid crosses tacked up on the rafters could make you wonder, some of them faded to the point of disintegration. It was like stepping back into time, that bare whitewashed room with mats on the stone flags, and a deal dresser facing me between the two back doors.

So there they stood, like a scene, too, out of the past, like a waxwork. Each of the three of them nursing a secret and wondering what were the others up to.

And Halloran himself, just a frightened old man, to me, staring down at his hands, until Evans began to speak. It dawned on him then that this wasn't the set up he'd thought, and his real style started to show itself.

"Whatever you're about," he told the Welshman, cutting him off, "you've doomed yourself by the company you keep." He lit up his cigarette, and blew a jet of smoke towards me in the doorway.

I closed the door behind me in the dog's face.

"We have come here to *honour* you," said Evans, "myself and Mr Dunphy here. I can't speak for the others. But you are a great artist, Mr Halloran, and we wish only to advance your career."

Halloran's face was a study in changes. His eyes were, at least. There was hunger there, sudden attention like a hawk's, but a fierce distrust, too, that concealed it. I suppose any artist must want to be told that he's great, it must be what they dream of. It's a phrase, I'd imagine, they chant in their heads all their lives.

Evans had on a tweed jacket with a yellow cravat at his throat – lamb dressed as mutton, and acting the part. "What I'd like," he said, "is to see, is to track down and photograph every piece you've ever made. I assume, I can only hope, that you've kept," and he sniggered to himself, "at your 'sky blue trades.'"

The Maggot nodded and chuckled through all of this, till Halloran's glares damped him down.

"I am well placed," said Evans. "Indeed, I am authorized, to propose a full-length monograph, with impeccable reproductions, a *catalogue raisonné*, biographical and critical essays." There was a preen at the sound of his own voice that made you want to duff him, only that beneath it all was a country boy who'd come up from nothing.

If it wasn't a speech set down and rehearsed in the night, I never heard one. "It is more gratifying than I can say, Mr Halloran, to find you in fact alive and clearly in splendid health." He squinnied his arse down into a chair, and leaned his elbows on the table, hands clasped. He'd sincerity down to a fault. "I can only guess what it is to suffer neglect as an artist of vision. It is the fate of the truly original in this philistine age." The blood crept up into

Halloran's cheek. Evans leaned back: "I am respected in my field, Mr Halloran, and I say this in all humility. I would be honoured to help you, to be the instrument which sees justice done in your lifetime. With Mr Dunphy's help, and with your permission, I can promise your work the most handsome and sensitive treatment." His hands came out like quote-marks. "There is genius in your work, sir – I am on fire to see how it has developed through these solitary years."

Flattery's a hard thing to brush off, whoever you are, most of all when it strikes close to home. But I saw, I believed, in Halloran's face not just a distrust, but an honest shyness – he was embarrassed by praise.

It was a strong face, though, a healthy, disciplined face for his years – selfish no doubt of it, arrogant too, but not what you'd call self-indulgent. He'd none of those pursey flares and hammocks that appetites wreak on a countenance. At seventy his face was rendering back to the bone, and I've always respected that. I'd want it for myself. It has to be earned.

"Mr Dunphy," he said, "*Mister* Corrigan bloody Dunphy." He was cold with fury, my presence had ceased to count. "Only for a misapprehension," and his eyes flicked to mine, "he would not be under this roof." He kept his back to the Maggot, speaking only to Evans. "He's the last man, the *last* man, I would ever invite to my home."

Young Evans was at a loss now, he looked over to the Maggot. The girl's hands beside me were grooming each other.

The Maggot heaved up in his chair. "Ah, Tag," he said, with a wheedling attempt at good humour, "have a sense of proportion."

"Would you look at yourself," said Halloran, and he turned deadly slow to look over across the table. "Just the bloated, repulsive failure you deserved to become."

"Now, now," said the Maggot.

"I understood," said Evans, "that, er, Mr Dunphy was an early collector of your work."

"My work?" said Halloran, grinding his cigarette out. "Here's the very creature that denied my work. He scotched my show, he exerted his power to destroy me."

"Then I have been deceived," Evans said. He glared at the Maggot and the Maggot glared back at him.

"*A sense of colour,*" Halloran said. His voice filled the room. "*A sense of colour so crude, so limited, yet so confused that one is reminded of nothing so much as a child's 3D novelty book . . . .*" He'd the voice down perfect, a Baggot Street fairy trooping the colours.

The Maggot tugged at his tie with a kind of moan. Halloran kept at it.

"*I was tempted to ask the gallery attendant if she had neglected to pass out the cardboard red and green spectacles . . . .*"

"What in God's name is this?" said Evans. The Maggot said nothing; he was struggling at his trouser pocket, his face as near white as it'd ever be.

"*This is fiddler's indulgence,*" Halloran spat out.

"Oh God," said the Maggot, and got his cigarette case open. A drizzle of pukey water came out of it, all down his wrist. There was rage and exasperation, and a kind of buffoonery, too, about him, as he picked at the ruined fags. Each one of them fell into pieces. He flailed at the shreds of tobacco and paper in his lap.

"*Fiddler's indulgence,*" Halloran said again. He reached for his pack of Dunhills and lit one at leisure. He blew the smoke up at the ceiling and watched it spreading, and gave a laugh. "*Fiddler's indulgence –* remember that?!"

The Maggot looked back at him. "I do, of course," he said, "no less than yourself, believe me." He spread his hands. "A man may make mistakes in his younger years," he said, and he could not have known that my laugh was aimed at Halloran, not at himself. The colour came back to his face. "Minds get changed, Tag," he said. "Has yours never?" He clutched at the chair arms. "Where's the dishonour in trying to make amends?"

Halloran smoked, and gazed at him, but gave no retort. How could he, with me standing there? He'd have been answering himself.

So Evans launched in again about Halloran's pictures, and the articles he wanted to write, and the fame and justice he'd bring him, and the impertinence, by the bye, of the sorry Dunphy. Very measured and earnest and picking up steam, till the girl cut him short.

"Could I say something?" she blurted, fierce with impatience.

"Now just you hold on, Miss," said Evans.

Him she ignored. "I know you by one name," she told Halloran, "and these people seem to know you by another, but they're beating around the bush with their fancy words." Halloran put his foot on the chair beside him, and watched her over Evans' head. "You're in all the papers, whether you know it or not," she said, "and there's a film made about you and your pictures are going for a fortune, and nobody knows if you're dead or alive."

Evans turned in his chair. "I was coming to that, of course," he snapped.

"Would you shut your mouth," said Halloran. The Welshman's gob hung open, in fact, for the next half minute. And Halloran looked at me then, almost as though I might tell him what to believe. I'd my first straight view of his eye, with its lid at half mast and the pouch underneath like a blister pricked and flattened. He turned back to the girl. "Tell me about it," he said.

She hesitated, and looked at me too for a moment. She knew there was something with him and myself. Her hands were pushed deep in her raincoat pockets. "Well," she began, "after your first wife died last year in Canada – I suppose you knew that?"

"Only," he said, "my only wife. And this isn't Outer Mongolia."

She checked his face for how deep the sarcasm ran. "Well, her family inherited your pictures of course, with everything else."

"Ah those," he said, in a tone you'd be hard put to label.

"Wonderful things," murmured Evans, just for the record. He kept his face down, though.

"In the Autumn," she said, "they had an exhibition, in Montreal, and a film was made, like I said – and they showed it on the BBC and last week the pictures went on display in London. At the Courtauld Institute." She pronounced those words as if it were Buckingham Palace. There was a silence. The other two sat there like scolded dogs.

"Or perhaps you knew that, too," she said.

Their eyes sparred with each other. I could see he was warming to her. But, "Never mind that," he said, "what of it?"

"Well this," she said. "I'm married to your son. I want you to help him, now that you're famous, now that your pictures are worth so much."

"Ah get on," he said, "that's pathetic. We had no children." And he turned away in disgust.

"Not her," she said, "Molly." Her hands came out of her pockets. "Molly Corner. She told me who you were. She told me your name and where I might find you."

"Molly?" he said. "Never. She would have told me."

"Well she didn't," the girl said. "Do you want to see him?"

She fetched an envelope from inside her coat and stepped around Evans to the table. Laid down two photographs and pushed them across. "You can see it, can't you?" she said.

He looked down at the pictures, and then at her. "What would your name be?" he said.

"Irene," she said.

"Irene what?"

"Corner, of course," she said. "That's Jamie's name."

"Jamie," he said, and grunted. "Just a minute, now."

He did a queer thing then. He went off to the door to the right of the dresser, walking slow and a little stooped, as if age all at once had its hand on his shoulder. It was a scullery from what I could see, and he came back out with a cloth in one hand and a tin rackeen in the other. Then he went to the range, which took up the whole of the left wall, and bent to open the centre oven. He pulled out three bread pans, one at a time, and tipped out the loaves on the stove top. He tapped the bottom of each, with his finger tips, like a drum, and then set them down on the rack. I've seen my wife do the same, and my mother. And after that, he went to the dresser and took up a pair of spectacles, with a lace to go round his neck, and put them on and came back to the table.

He leaned on his hands, gazing down at the photos. All eyes were upon him.

"The child?" he said.

"That's Colin, our boy. He'll be two next week."

I saw the wind blow through him. And I wondered, Could any picture the man himself ever painted produce an effect like that?

He was in his solitudes there. And I wondered, too, Do the times of your life turn themselves about when you're told you're a granddad?

But that, God willing, is a thing I'll find out for myself before Winter is done.

He let down his glasses, and handed her back the photos. "What does he know of me, your Jamie?" he asked.

"He knows nothing," she said. "Molly tried to tell him about you when he was younger, but he showed no interest."

"And where does he think you are now?"

"At his mother's," she said. "She's looking after Colin."

His fingers played on the table top. "But you'll tell him?"

"Of course," she said. "I don't care, Mr Cudahy, I'll make him take any help you can give us. There's our son to think about."

I thought again, this girl was an innocent altogether or a match for Maguire.

And maybe Halloran was thinking the same. "What help did you have in mind?" he said.

"Jamie left school at sixteen," she said, "and he's been working ever since."

"That would describe me, too," he said. "Is it a pension he's after already?"

"Don't laugh at me," she said, "that's cheap of you." The trembling in her arms didn't reach to her voice. "Jamie's a good steady worker, he's clever, he's the best at his job, but it just isn't fair. If he had his papers, he'd get five times the money they pay him. He could have his own place, I could do the books, it's our dream. But he has to go back to college, and that costs money."

"His own place?" said Halloran. "What kind of place?"

"A garage," she said, "he's a motor mechanic."

Halloran ran his hand through his hair, a couple of times, and reached for a cigarette. "A motor mechanic," he told it. "A good steady worker." No stoop in his shoulders now, I thought, the sarcastic bastard. He stepped back from the table, the cigarette in his lips, tipturling his lighter up and down on his palm. "He'd be twenty-one, now," he said, with a pawnbroker's smile, "this son of mine?"

The girl met his eyes. "He'll be twenty-four in August," she said.

"Ah," he said, "twenty-four," and strolled off behind Evans, across the room again. There was no reading his face. He pushed open the other back door, lighting his smoke as he went through.

I saw a lean passage, with doorways to left and right and daylight beyond, where he went down some steps, out of sight. The Maggot was braving himself to filch a smoke off the table. Evans was eyeing the girl, with a mind to collusion. The girl's face was red with vexation, staring down the passageway. The scent of those bread loaves filled up the room.

We heard, in a bit, his footsteps mounting again. What came after was all for effect. He shuffled in and leaned up against the dresser. He'd his glasses back on his nose and the cigarette in his lips, squinting down through the smoke at a painting. All you could see was the frame and the canvas back of it. The Maggot craned up from his chair for a look, but Halloran drew it to his chest. He stepped into the scullery then, and emerged with the thing half wrapped already in paper.

He came to the table. "Would someone fetch me the twine?" he said. "There's a spool on the counter in there." Evans was out of his seat in a flash, and scampering off to oblige. The paper fell open, but the picture was lying face down, and Halloran proceeded to package it up, neat and methodical as a butcher's wife, and not a word spoken.

He held out the parcel. "This should do you for a while," he said, "if you choose to sell it." She made a half-hearted reach for it. "Take it," he said. "If my work's all at once worth the fortune you tell me it is." The two boys there were like trout with their eyes on a mayfly. "It's the same vintage," Halloran said, "as the ones Ginny had. All from my Dublin show." He took her hand, and folded it round the package. "It's ancient history to me," he told her, more gently, "but it's one of the best."

Then, "Be off now," he said, and he half looked my way. "If I'm spared, you'll be hearing from me, soon enough."

She fumbled the photographs out from her coat, and laid them on the table. She'd the painting clutched to her chest.

"Molly's well, is she?" he said.

"Yes," she said, " but she lives on nothing. She always has."

"You wouldn't blame me for that," he said.

"Molly wouldn't," she told him, "why should I?"

I measured the hunger in Evans' face, and the Maggot's frustrations, as she slowly opened the door. "Goodbye, Mr Cudahy," she said, and she tried for a smile. "Is that what they call you?"

"I'll answer to it," he said.

"And thank you," she said. "I'll write to you." And she closed the door.

It was anyone's guess who would make the next move. Not the Maggot, I'd guarantee. I stepped over to the window and watched the girl, Irene, going up the steps, with her coat tail blowing and Halloran's dog in attendance.

It was Evans broke the silence. "What I'd give to have seen that painting," he said. He'd had time to work out he should leave the soft soap. "If she does put it on the market," he said, "she could send him through college just on the interest! Mind you," he added slyly, "she'd be smarter to hang on to it."

"What'd it be worth, then?" said Halloran.

The dog was coming back down the steps, its tail feathers jaunty in the breeze.

"The three sold in Canada went for 50,000 apiece," I said.

I could picture her going downhill with her trophy. Kneeling by the water, beyond the gate, to take off her shoes, cradling the package against her. Her little English face, as she crossed the stones, confirmed in a duty done.

The Maggot cleared his throat, a couple of times. "Which one was it, Tag? What painting did you give her?"

"You would remember, I suppose," Halloran sneered. "Indelibly etched in your mind!" And he started again upon what was etched in his own. "*The images themselves, beneath the brash and glutinous impasto, are entirely derivative and banal . . . .*"

Evans was uttering scandalized clucks and sighs. "Ah quit that, for god's sake," cried the Maggot.

"*The old twilight and langour tricked out in a jester's motley . . . .*"

I heard the chair groan at the Maggot's agitation.

"*This is fiddler's indulgence. Mr Halloran could do with a dose of clear history. He might hear, then, over his shoulder, the jackboot of Fascism trampling through Europe.*"

"Listen, would you!" the Maggot shouted. "I'm haunted by that stuff as much as yourself. I didn't come here for this."

"And how did you find me here?" Halloran's voice had dropped to a deadly quiet.

"I'll answer you that," I said. I turned from the window. The Maggot was stood halfway to the table, flushed to the gills, his hands in fists by his belt. Halloran was staring him down.

"In the film about you," I told him, "mention was made of a place called Martinstown. Your wife's brother didn't know its whereabouts. These boys worked it out for themselves – that the town had been Irished, with the Republic."

"Ah," he said. "And that was your route, too, was it?"

"I've known you were here all along," I said.

His one eye and a half took that in, with ne'er a flicker. He was tough, I'll give him that, when you think what had piled on him that hour.

The Maggot was staring at me. He'd the need, I think, to offload his frustration.

"What interest," said he, "have *you* in this business?"

"In this business, nothing at all," I said.

With his eyes and snout, at that range, he put me in mind of a pig. Only, a pig knows well, if the odds were straight he'd have *you* for breakfast.

But the Welshman gave him the chance to explode.

"I must disassociate myself entirely from Mr Dunphy," said Evans. "He misled me about your connection." He drew out a notebook from his inside pocket, and opened it on the table. "I came here in good faith to do you a service; I ask you to trust me."

"Do him a service!" The Maggot lurched over and slammed both his fists on the table. "Do *him* a service! 'Tis your own advancement only that counts, your parasite career, you and your lickspittle pedantry." The walls were ringing. I thought he might burst an artery. There was a stir, I'm sure, of amusement on Halloran's face.

And Evans, he flinched at the row, and took out a hanky to mop the spray off his cheek, but he let it be seen the attack was beneath his dignity. "I'd be grateful, as a start, for any information on your subsequent work. Any collectors, or galleries. A sense of how much of your work is in your own possession."

But the Maggot was not to be gainsaid now. "Would you listen to me, Tag," he demanded. "You forget that I was a painter, too, in those days. Or I thought I was one. Did you not know that? I had ambitions, vision – but you had the talent, didn't you? The paint loved your brush." He turned from the table, and went a few steps. He'd his hands clasped behind him. "I walked through that show of yours and felt my hopes run cold . . . ." And he turned again. "Oh Jesus, I need a cigarette."

I went over and skated Halloran's smokes to him down the table. They fell over the edge and he genuflected for them and showed me his beggar's eyes – full of gratitude and hate. He took two butts, I saw. His matches, at least, were in a dry pocket.

Halloran pulled back a chair, and sat down. You couldn't have read his face in a thousand years.

The Maggot drew hard at his cigarette. "This is the thing, Tag," he said. "As it chanced, I'd my first real assignment as a critic that weekend – Mannion called me from the *Times* – 600 words before midnight. I'd be first into print. If I played it right, if I was urbane enough and emphatic, I would scare all the other reviewers out of their senses. Though to speak God's honest truth," he said, "I doubted any one of them would recognize what you were."

"You're right at least about that," said Halloran. He scowled at his hands. "Yourself and the whole damned tribe of them."

"I would make a distinction, you know," said Evans, "between critics and reviewers."

"Would you?" said Halloran, flat and sarcastic.

"The critic preserves, pays attention, casts a light."

"Ah well," said Halloran. "I've a *healthy* respect for scholar-ship."

The Maggot had tears in his eyes that they wouldn't hear him. "It was two careers poisoned, Tag. Don't disbelieve for one minute that the thing itself you hate me for has not literally de-stroyed my life."

Something about that made Halloran laugh.

The Maggot leaned over the table. He spoke slowly. "There was one picture only sold of that show," he said. "It was myself bought it. My fee for that review was what paid for it."

The old man's eyes would have cut through granite. "Have you it yet?" he asked.

"I have," said the Maggot. "*Suzanna* – the faces looking out from the willows."

"Well sell it, then, if I'm such a prize all at once."

The Maggot straightened up. "I've kept it through harder times than I'm facing now," he said. "I would sooner die. 'Tis the grace note in my life."

It was like a speech in a play, but you knew it for the truth. I've raked men enough over to guarantee that. The decent ones reach a point where you're off in the middle distance, out of earshot, you might as well not be there in the room with them, they're owning up to themselves.

I heard the fire settle in the range. I saw two men smoking and one man holding his peace.

Then Halloran reached for Evans' notebook and his fingers beckoned for a pen. He wrote with his left hand, speaking as he went. "Here's the name of a woman in Frankfurt who had some of my stuff. If she's dead or moved, the hunt will be your affair." He put out his smoke, and wrote again. "And this was my gallery there. They may have a thing or two still in their dungeons – at least I never heard they were sold."

He closed the book and pushed it from him. Evans took it – he was on his way to Deutschland already.

Halloran kept hold of the pen, rapping it on the table top. "They're all signed Cudahy, too," he said, and looked up. "That should keep yous happy for a while, I imagine."

"Is this recent work?" Evans asked him, reading the notebook page.

"Not really," he said. "Must be fifteen or twenty years."

"I'm most grateful," said Evans. "Are there any other collectors I should know about?"

"There's nothing else."

"But you've worked?" said the Maggot. "Surely you kept on working?"

You might call it a smile that came over Halloran's face but the shark, as they say, smiles for every man. "What I haven't burned is below" he said.

He angled himself towards me, though his words were for them. "If I'm spared," he said, "you may come back a year from now and look things over. You'll tell no one of my whereabouts, you'll talk to no one – your publisher breathes no word of this. There's my condition: you break it and you're finished."

"But you'll give me exclusive access," said Evans.

"The two of you," said Halloran, still with his eyes on my face. "The both of you."

Evans sat there, readjusting his dreams, but the Maggot let out a cry like a girl, and flourished his arms. "Oh Jesus, you're great," he said, and clapped down his hand on Evans' shoulder. "Would you put it in writing, Tag?"

The Welshman flinched, and hissed in dismay, as if he'd not had the very same thought in his head. The Maggot was not to be flustered, though. "There's your age, is all, Tag. A man never knows—"

"You heard it all," said Halloran.

The Maggot turned then to me. "You're a witness, anyway," he said.

I looked at Halloran. He gave a nasty laugh. Then, "I'm tired now," he said, and pulled open the door for them. I admired that. He could have used them for cover.

They were quickly gone, though I didn't pay much attention. There were handshakes at the door, I know that, and Halloran holding the dog back as they mounted the steps. I took off my coat, and threw it over the easy chair. Halloran was crouched with the dog, holding fast to its collar. "That's all right, that's all right, never mind," he was saying. Then it settled, and he stood in the doorway, looking out.

You could not ignore the strength of the man, ruined though it was. Twenty years back he'd have been a match for me. But standing there, in his loose old sweater, and the baggy corduroys with no show of an arse at all, he'd become his own ghost.

"I liked that girl, your daughter-in-law," I said.

He spoke to the open door. "I wouldn't have thought she was your type."

"She's far from being my type," I said. "I could say the same about you, but it doesn't preclude a certain degree of admiration."

He turned and looked at me then, flat on. "I know who you are," he said.

"Certainly you do," I said, "and you know why I'm here, too."

He took a couple of steps, and gripped the knob of the chair beside him. "And what's to prevent me blowing your brains out first off?"

"I wouldn't blame you for trying," I said.

"You'd beat me to the draw, I suppose," he said.

"There's no gun in it, on my side," I said.

"Ah," he said, and he passed his hand over his mouth, fingering the scrawns of his neck. "Are you telling me you don't mean to kill me?"

"I'm telling you no such thing," I said.

He shunted the chair back to the table with his hip. "Would you allow a man time for a drink, then?" he said.

"Plenty of that," I said. "I want to know you first."

He went to the dresser and opened the upper cupboard. "You took *your* time," he said.

"Well," I said, "I'd a life to live first."

He came to the table, with a bottle of Redbreast and two glasses. "*L'uomo che venchare*," he said, with a lopsided smile.

"What's that?" I said.

He poured a small measure into his glass. I've seen steadier hands. "It's a proverb from southern Italy," he said. "*The man who takes his revenge after thirty years has acted in haste.*"

I sat down where Evans had sat. "That's not bad," I said. "I'll keep it in mind."

He nudged the empty glass. "Will I pour you one?"

"I might have a drink," I said, "but I won't drink *with* you."

A flit of amusement passed through his lips. "Would that," he said, "be a yes or a no?"

"I'll pour my own drink," I said. Our hands touched when I took the bottle. I spent a minute reading the label on it.

He was holding his glass at his chin, staring into it. The Adam's apple stood out from his throat. "I'm unused to drinking by daylight," he said. "I haven't the stomach for it any more."

"You're in great shape, though," I said, "for a man your age." I poured my drink, and set back the bottle, uncorked.

He was watching me. "I could tell you," he said, "why you shouldn't kill me."

I took a flirt of the Redbreast, and held it on my tongue while the bite eased out of it.

"For one thing," he said, "there's the bread yonder, fresh made and untasted."

"Do you think I'd break bread with you?" I said.

"Well," he said, and he tried for a laugh, "but this is the best wheaten bread – you won't have tasted the like in twenty years unless you've eaten on the railway."

It was sheer foolishness. "Is that the best you can do?" I asked him.

"Indeed it's not," he said. "That was just by way of pleasantry."

"Pleasantry," I said.

"I'm an old man," he said, "and I'm trying to behave as I might have twenty years back. Put yourself in my shoes."

"I've no interest at all in that," I said.

"Well," he said quietly, "you said that you wanted to know me."

"True enough," I said.

"All right, then."

He leaned forward across the table, near to my face, as if he would dare me to strike him. I saw the fear in his eyes give way to something like plain curiosity. And then, "Look at the great spade face on him," he jeered, and sat back again and lifted his glass to his lips.

"I came by this face honestly," I said. "You're no Adonis yourself."

His good eye narrowed down to the size of his left. "All right," he said, "I'll ask you for a reprieve. Three weeks, let's say a month. I'll not run out on you. You waited this long anyhow."

"A reprieve?" I said. "Why would you ask for that?"

"I'll tell you," he said, "though I've no expectation you'll understand."

It had nothing to do with his son, or any of that. He'd this story to tell about a painter dying in Vienna. Dead of the plague that came after the trench war in Europe, just when the Troubles at home were hotting up. Your man was at work on a picture called *The Bride* when he took sick. His name was Klimt, Gustav. All this was true – I looked it up after. He'd painted this girl stark naked on her bed, and then he'd set out to paint a gown over her, so that only himself would ever know the secret of it. And that's when he died. Alone in this big house, Halloran said.

He refilled his glass. I let him top mine up, why not?

"The evening he died," he told me, "two thieves broke into the silent house. They roamed about, taking anything that was of value to them. Nothing old Gustav himself would have placed value on, naturally. Nobody knows if they found the corpse even, though you'd think they'd look in at a bedroom. Nobody knows if they looked at *The Bride*, or what they had to say of her if they did. She was watching them, sure enough, as she'd watched her own maker. But she keeps her secrets."

He could tell a story. "You look at that painting today," he said, and he sought out my eyes, with his finger and thumb beating time, "and you see all that, you wonder what she's concealing, you stare at her little half-covered limbs, but what you see truly is the heart of the painter himself, which you weren't supposed to."

He seemed to have reached an end. "If your point is you've something unfinished on your easel," I told him, "I'd say you just made a good case for keeping it that way."

"Yes," he said, "yes, you would think that," and he drained off his glass.

"Ah well, try me," I said, and I finished mine too. "Let's go and look at the heart of the painter himself."

I don't know when last he'd been jeered at that way. We were one step ahead of each other, though. "I'll just see to the fire," he said, and began to get up.

"Keep the house warm for the thieves," I said, but that he ignored. He went over to the range and I stood up. "That's a drop of good stuff," I said. "Shall we take a glass with us?"

He was bent to an old skip in the corner, gathering black turfs from it up against his chest. "I told you," he said, "I can't handle it like I used to. Help yourself, if you wish." I let it be.

He seemed steady enough, till he opened the firebox and squatted down. He lurched over then, and a couple of turfs skidded off, and he dropped on one knee. "Watch your hand, now," I said, as he reached for support. – I thought he would grab the range top and be scorched. "I'm all right," he said, and got on with the job.

He put me in mind of my grandfather, riddling the grate there. The smell of the burning turf, and the caged fire within, and the ashes swirling. At the same time, standing behind him, I saw how easy 'twould be to wring his old neck

He stood up, and brushed at the scraps of turf on his sweater. I was so close that he chose to edge by me along the range front. As he passed, I remember, his hand stroked one of the bread loaves, as you might a tame cat.

I followed him through the door, and along the passage. I had to stoop to get by. There was a small room off to the left, with its door ajar. Just a plain bed within, a crucifix over its head, and a candlestick on the dresser. It was quite the convent cell, only for the picture on the side wall. I stepped in for a closer look. "That's as near to being beautiful as a filthy thing could be," I said, but he'd gone on ahead. There was "Cudahy," scrawled on the canvas, down to the left, in the tangle of sheets.

Five paces more past that room and I'd my face in the rafters, near dazzled by all the light coming up at me. It was a barn of a place, with a staircase beside me, nine feet or ten at the least, to the floor below.

There was more glass in it than any stone house has a right to – two shop-sized windows inviting the bay into the room. You could see the cloud shadows even on the floor matting. And the smell was of dry wood and sacking and turpentine.

He was standing below, facing the view he'd made. He looked upright again from here, and no hint of scalp through that white mane of his. There's not many keep their whole thatch to that age, and the most of *them* alcoholics, which I don't believe was his case.

I went down a few steps, down the rear, I suppose, of the old house. The weathering showed on the wall, and the mortar was frayed, but there was lovely stonework after, a full man's height, until the floor. The fastening above of the new roof onto the old was a marvel, too, in itself.

"You weren't pinching your nuts," I said, "when you had this built."

"I'm the one builder here," he said. "Two ruins gave up their stones for this, and three years gave up their days, but the work is my own." He looked up at me then, and I came on down.

"Just the wood and glass in it," I said. "They'd be two years' wages, easy, in my world."

He laughed at that. "And you don't believe," he said, "that the mutton and wool from my Jacobs, with the sale of my paintings, would account for my affluence!"

"Mutton and wool it must be," I said, "for you gave the impression just now that you haven't exactly taken the art world by storm."

"You're speaking like Dunphy now," he said. "Besides, *they* gave the impression just now, that all that has changed."

"That's as maybe," I said, "and the future's another thing entirely. It's the past I'm wondering about here."

"One mystery more, then," said he, "to go with the rest." And he turned his back on me.

I envied him the place. Not the place so much, but the making of it for himself. But once I'd my back to the windows, it seemed pretty bare. It put me in mind, actually, of the cockpit we raided one time in Rathmines, at the old distillery.

Halloran was stood in front of a big frame easel, with his hands on his hips. I might not have been there at all. I went over to look.

"*There's* a nightmare," I said. "And a piece of shite, too."

It was grim enough, anyway. Dark. Two faces is how you'd describe it, the one speering out at the other's shoulder, whispering to him maybe, or sharing the bad news. It's in Evans' catalogue now as "*The Boar Hunt*, unfinished." Dermot and Finn, by their account. I didn't think much of it, anyhow. The mist or the water, whatever it was, was good. It's the eyes you remember, though, grey and yellow like a crane's, and one with a droop to it.

"I'd be in trouble," he said, "if you admired it."

"You're in trouble enough, " I said. It was grating on me to see him so confident, as if he'd escaped me. And he didn't reply. He went over to a trestle by the wall and came back with a putty knife in his hand. "You've scared me now," I said. "Do you know how to use that thing?" He ignored that too, he was back at his picture. The little blade hovered for a moment, and then he dug some paint off the canvas, and smeared it on his hand.

"You're a lefty," I said.

"And what of it?" he said. "So was Leonardo, and Corot, and Schiele."

"I'm thinking of the room where my father died," I said, "and the angle of that doorway off the landing. I'm seeing it different."

He drew in a breath, and let it out slow and quiet. His shoulders went down. He made himself turn and look at me. He'd his glasses back on, but he removed them as he spoke. "You remember, then, do you?"

"I was two years old," I said. "What I remember is my mother's cries, and her silences after, and the way my brother was changed, and the life that we led."

"I am sorry for that," he said. "Indeed I am. They were confused times, you must know, and fearful things done on both sides." He looked down at the floor. "I was young, we all were, and we meant for the best."

"Easy words for a man still breathing," I said, "after fifty years."

"I know," he said, "and devil the good it did either party. Half the countryside on the dole, and we've English troops now, landing again in the North."

"I've no interest in politics," I said. I couldn't stand to look at him. I went over to his work table, where his brushes and paints and stuff were laid out. Very neat and clean they were. I get a charge always from any tools of the trade.

"Would it be politics, though," he called out, "if you took my life, and this son or grandson of mine came after you in twenty years' time?"

There was a painting, a sketch really, pinned up to the beam that supported the staircase. It might have been done in ink or charcoal, with a wash of colours across it, on a yellowish paper. A pig with great tusks on it, charging at you from the forest. "Now this," I said, "I'd take one like this over twenty of those concoctions you have on the easel."

"Would you so?" he said, and he gave a thin laugh. "You're a queer, deliberate man," he said. "There's no keeping up with you. But you're right, it is good. Else it wouldn't be up." He stepped over to a big cupboard set under the stairs. "If it's the studies you prefer," he said, "try those shelves next the door there. It's the truth that I keep all my sketches, though I burn three paintings out of four."

He was rummaging in the cupboard while I went to the shelves. There was sheet after sheet of thick paper, hundreds at least. The man was a worker. I pulled out a handful, and laid them on top to see.

"Turn around now," he said.

I'd had guns levelled at me twice in my life before – the first time I'd been cold as a stone, and the other I found myself flying into a rage. But I sensed, maybe, that he didn't mean to fire it.

"That's a nice class of weapon," I said.

"You're right," he said, "it's a Greener. And will do the job."

It was a queer thing to have those tapered barrels squinting at my chest, with a little shake to them. "Now I don't imagine," I said, "you'd be wanting to spoil this studio of yours with a mess of blood." And I turned again to his sketches.

"That might be," he said, "but I could drop you under my trees just outside, and you'd never be found."

I shuffled the sketches. They were wonderful, effortless things – the look on a face, the mood in a room, a girl singing.

"That's where I should park *you* then, is it?" I said.

"It's me has the gun," he whispered. "And the difference is, they'd come looking for me, but no one would give you a thought."

"For all you know," I told him, "I've left a trail like Carberry's bull."

"No killer would do that," he said.

"See here," I said. "In this country, and under the circumstances, I'd get two years at the most, and no shame in it. My children are grown, my wife has the pension. What would I sneak around for?"

"Boys, oh boys," he said.

I pulled out another sketch. "Look at this now," I said. "You're a wonder at middle distances."

"Ah, is that what I am?" he said, but his pleasure in it overtook him. He dipped the gun barrels a fraction. "The geniuses for that," he said, "were Sisley and Courbet. Sisley for a snow scene, or the thither side of a pond, but Courbet . . . . It was *his* opinion you should be able to paint an object that was a half-mile off, even if you couldn't tell what it was."

"I'm getting a schooling, anyhow," I said. Which, from where I stand now, was the truth.

"You're a cool one," he said. "There's something cold-blooded about you."

I touched my finger to the page. "It's that break, there, in the line, that does it," I said. "Where the paint takes over."

"You've an eye for the details."

"I was trained to it," I said.

"What are you at all?" he asked. "Not police, surely?"

"I was until Thursday," I said.

"Sweet Jesus," he said, "a *garda siochanta*." And he laughed. "A guardian of the peace!"

"For thirty years," I said. "To the day."

The shotgun came back up, right at my face. I thought again of the cockpit, and the two of us, after a fashion, circling each other, making feints, taking aim.

"We'll go out, then," he said, and tilted his head at the door.

There was a spent artillery shell by the jamb. An umbrella in it, and a good stick, and a black cane with silver bands at the hilt. I handled it – "The gentleman gunman," I said.

"That came after the fighting," he said. "Leave it be."

"You call that fighting?" I said.

"More than you'll know," he said. "Outside with you, now."

If I'd left at the trot, I'd have found myself airborne. There was wind on my face, and a wonderful view, straight down. There were sea birds drying their wings on a low black reef, and the water around them, chopping and crawling. I took a step back, and Halloran moved away, with the gun trained on me still.

"I'll show you my orchard," he said.

The dog came round to meet us beside the house, and fell in at his heel as we started up the bankside. Through a narrow gate in the wall there, the grass was uncropped, it was like a young forest, an acre and a half maybe.

You could see, though, the paths he had worn. He settled himself on a flat grey rock, with the gun on his knees. There were bird songs here, little flirts of wings in the branches. They came and went, unafraid, as we talked.

"The most damage a man could do me," he said, of a sudden, "would be to ruin this place. If you understand that, you'll understand me."

I was filling my pipe. "He could burn your pictures," I said.

"Was that your plan?" he asked.

"Not at all," I said. I lit up my pipe. I've never enjoyed a first draw as I did that one. "I'm a simpler person than you think," I told him.

"Well," he said, "you paint for the dead, for God, for yourself, who knows? Just the thing itself. The rest doesn't matter. The world never gets it right, anyways."

The sun had gone in. His old face, and the skin of the rock he was sat on, and the bark of the trees around, were the same grey shade. His eyes were a snake's. For that moment only, I really believed he would shoot me. And do it right there.

"Well, to lower the tone," I said, "you need cash to support such purity. And I'd certainly like to know how you came to be living so free and easy while my family knew only want, and my mother worked herself to an early grave."

"No, no," he protested, and I felt the danger pass. "It wasn't so." He rested the gun on his boot, holding it by the barrels. His hand had left paint, I saw, on the pistol grip.

"I'll tell you the whole of it," he said, and he took me into his story.

"It goes back to the time you know about," he said. "There'd been an affair in King's County, as it was then, and we'd lost two men. And the day after that three of us were in a car, out on a bog road, to an old gravel pit near the Lacey estate. Myself, another youngster, Phil Kent, and Pat Flemming, the sergeant in charge.

"We parked in the pit just at dusk, and climbed up behind with shovels, and dug a trench in the floor of a ruin there. Pat opened the boot of the car, and there were three ammunition boxes, tin ones and heavy as sin. We buried them, and went on.

"The week after, Pat got himself shot to pieces. Young Phil was locked up for a spell, and I visited him, just before the Peace. He mentioned those boxes. 'I wonder,' he said, 'was there more than grenades in there?' But I forgot it and he, I believe, went off to America.

"I took over this place from my uncle, and kept alive somehow, with the few sheep he left, and what I could plant here, in this old garden, and working with the surface crew when they'd take me. Some days my evening meal was a pot of winkles off the rocks. And all the time I was learning to draw, and scrounging old brushes and paint off the nuns, and spending the wool money, when it came, on materials. I wanted to be Jack Yeats. I wanted to be great."

He eased himself on his seat, and laughed like a young man.

"Well, I got my show in Dublin. After twenty years working. And I was crucified. And I went off and sulked, as I see it now, and turned my back on the whole idea. Just the framing of those damned paintings had me sunk in debt. And the war came then and work was scarcer than ever.

"But one morning, in the spring of 19 and 45, I woke up with the thought of those boxes in my head. After 25 years! And I walked, I *walked* across Ireland, knowing the madness of it, but feeling at least a small bit alive. And I found that place. The pit had been worked at since, but the ruin above was there yet, and so were the boxes."

He stopped for a minute, I suppose for the effect of it. It was easy to see the younger man in those features, now, as he took himself back.

"It wasn't grenades," he said. "It wasn't money, even. It was better than that. Heavy as sin is right." And he laughed aloud. "The devil of it was, finding a way to change the first bit of it into cash, and then lugging those boxes down without being spied on, and getting them clear.

"But I came home in style," he said. "And I straightway put a new roof on this house, and I spent two hundred pounds upon paint and canvas."

"That was when you went travelling," I said. "1946, the hard winter. I kept track of you."

A blackbird dropped to the grass from the tree above me. It hopped almost to the nose of his dog, lying there at his feet. We watched it pick at a worm, and strain to pull it clear of the earth, stretched like a rubber band. The dog didn't move. The bird went off with its beakful.

"Yes," he said. "I educated myself all over Europe, and then I came home."

"And you changed your name," I said. "That wasn't to hide yourself, surely?"

"Ah no," he shrugged. "The town's name was changed, we had the Republic, which seemed like a deal at the time – I was starting over."

"You've been touched by luck all the way," I said.

"If I have," he said, "I've treated her with respect." He gave a little groan, and rubbed at his thigh, the clench of his fingers striping paint on his corduroys. He used the gun as support, then, getting to his feet, but he had me covered straight after.

What plan had he now, I wondered. He shut the gate behind us, leaving the dog within. "You stay, now," he said, when it offered to clamber the wall.

We went down past the house, with no word spoken, around the tight corner, and onto the strip of turf at the cliff top. The sun kept dodging in and out of the clouds, and most of the time the windows behind him were mirrors. I could see myself, at his back as it were, and the wide bay beyond. Every time there was light, though, the mirrors vanished. I could see the room within, and the easel there, with the two queer faces staring out.

"Were you never afraid," he asked, "that I just might die, before you were ready?" The sea wind was blowing his hair around his face. He looked almost crazy then, gaunt and wild, with that gun between us.

"I thought of it," I told him, "but I left that up to chance. The truth is, I thought with two lives to live for, you'd still be around."

"Two lives, is it?" he said. "Well, you've lost me now."

"Your own and my father's," I said. "That's how a boy's mind works."

He stared at me as if I was totally mad. "Dear God," he said, "do you think you're the only one I've been watching for all these years?"

"You're joking, surely," I said.

He looked down past my feet, at the water below. You could tell he was seeing in his mind a body broken and awash on that black reef. Then, "Is it you, *a cara*?" he called out, with a smile, it might be, of welcome and relief.

I looked round, expecting a boat, I suppose. In a while I spotted the head of a seal, out past the rocks, bobbing in the waves with its dog face regarding us.

"He comes every day," said Halloran. "I choose to believe he's the man who first built on this spot."

Well, then.

"You're a great old boy, really," I told him. "You made a life for yourself."

"Well I thank you for that," he said softly. He looked off past my shoulder, and down at the ground between us. Then his eyes blazed up at my face. "Go shag yourself," he said.

The light and energy seemed to go out of him then. He looked only tired.

I took the gun out of his hands.

THREE

THE SCREAM OF
THE BUTTERFLY

I told this story once too often, and the moment I realized that, I knew I should write it down, tell it properly, fix it and let it go.

It had become part of a repertoire, like a favourite joke, and after twenty years I was *telling* it like a joke, when it wasn't funny at all. It may be the strangest and saddest thing I have ever witnessed.

It happened at Long Beach, on the west coast of Vancouver Island, upon one of those grey and white strands, wide and hard packed, which stretch almost unbroken the thirty miles between the fish ports and native villages of Tofino and Ucluelet. Where the trundle and energy of the Pacific surf never falters, where half of the jetsam is Japanese, where the Grey Whales and Sea Lions, the Killer Whales and Sea Otters animate the grey and green swells, where Ravens and Eagles, Crows and Sandpipers patrol the exposed sands.

Its natural face is grey, with mist and a slanting, light, almost perpetual rain blowing in at the forests. But when the sky does clear the light is radiant, the sun plays through the emerald caves of the surf, the stars cluster and multiply through the night.

But all that is true still, despite the paved roads, the camp grounds and the new resorts. And as I say that, I realize that when this story happened is as important as where.

There was no paved road to the west coast in 1969 and you didn't take those logging roads over two mountain ranges without carrying two or three spare tires. We went up three times a year – to escape the city, to walk, to beachcomb, to write, and to take mescaline.

There is a folklore among people who have used hallucinogenic drugs, or fasted for extended periods, or been mentally ill; and a vital part of that folklore involves close, and mutually uncomprehending, encounters with 'normality.' *"Forty days and forty nights Thou wast fasting in the wild . . . ."* I wonder what a Roman scouting party would have made of the emaciated carpenter at the desert's edge, with his "flashing eyes and floating hair," and his mind in thrall to the gorgeous visions and temptations of his Adversary. Or what he would have made of the Romans. It's irresistible, of course, to cast John Cleese as the officer in charge.

This isn't to trivialize the occasion, or the subject matter. The challenge of the ludicrous may be the only thing that will purge true seriousness of its inert parasite, solemnity.

The sacraments *can* be trivialized, though. Some people back then took peyote or mescaline or LSD as casual, social 'trips'; and some paid a ghastly price. For myself, the mountain crossing was a stage in a long preparation: I approached mescaline as an initiation, and when we went up to Long Beach (and Susan was the only human being I could ever have shared the ritual with) we waited for the occasion. That meant when the sun, untypically, came out for the day. Every time, after two days of walking, gathering, relearning the beach's rhythms, we were rewarded.

We rented a tiny cabin, down among the spruce trees and salal thickets, just a few feet in from the strand. It was built of driftwood planks, scarcely big enough for a bed and the wood-burning cookstove. Salal roots groped at its sodden foundations, salmonberry leaves drank the light of the narrow window.

We would swallow the mescaline in late morning, on empty stomachs, and go out of the hut, along the beach, till the sand began to writhe before our feet into snakes and shimmering lozenges, and then the weight of the force that had entered us would lead us up to the ramparts of driftwood logs at the storm-line, against the forest, and there, hidden from the outside world, we would make our nest.

Peyote and mescaline are desert drugs, born of a cactus, and that's why the beach was the exquisite place to experience them. Because sand exemplifies the first insight of the drug – that the universe is, as Leucippus surmised 2500 years ago, composed of atoms. That is the secret of matter, and the starting point for the visions. For the atoms themselves are worlds, and combine with each other to form richer, more luminous systems.

But there are preliminaries. Using the drug is, as I've hinted, a short cut to making yourself ill or – if you wish – mad. It isn't comfortable. You sweat, your legs jig like a hungry male adolescent's; and I felt every time an eagle's claws tightening under my ribs, a sort of uncadenced labour pain – as though my being were about to be squeezed out through the top of my head. It is a state of helplessness and often, naturally, terrifying.

Aldous Huxley called one of his studies *Heaven and Hell*, because some of the visions and transports that ecstatics endure are such nightmares. I don't think he quite realized that the terror precedes the joy, that Hell is the anteroom to Heaven, and that the pain or fear or confusion are a purifying stage, without which the Vision would be meaningless.

We are so cluttered with personal and cultural baggage. And in the eyes of Mescalito, the genius of peyote, as in the eyes of Christ, and the Buddha and Lao Tse, it is not just baggage, it is garbage. As my legs started to jig, I always saw a wall, a cliff face of figures and letters and images, shivering to the beat of a tinny, foxtrotting orchestra – all the plastic flash and offal of my culture and my life, the great whoredom of material distraction, looming there like a totalitarian monument, like the lettered cliffs in the posters for Hollywood epics – *Ben Hur* or *Spartacus* or, for that matter, *The Life Of Brian*.

As my legs twitched in time to that meretricious dance beat, my heels dug at the sand against the eagle fist choking my heart and guts, and I watched the cliff wall crumbling. First the plastic, then all the useless knowledge, then vanity; till the music stopped, and at last only personal guilt stood between me and the visions.

Guilt may be the last handhold that our reality has on "the doors of perception." But it's a dead hand, tugging you back from the threshold, its fingers upon your wrist, waking dim terrors in your heart, summoning the anguished faces of children at your shoulder.

As an Irish Catholic, I inherit guilt, I suppose. It seems to belong with melancholia, a taste for lost causes, and blithe superstition; but in 1969 I had specific things to dread in myself. My marriage had failed, and I faced the prospect of separating my daughters, with my own uncertainties and my wife's sad courage about that choice.

It was against the innocence of children and the betrayal of dreams that I fought to get through the slumping wreck of that cliff, and into the light.

Small wonder that my struggles in the anteroom were always more desperate than Susan's. I think she had learned to sit by, invisibly, and choose the moment to share something with me. She'd just point or nod at a patch of sand which for her was already bejewelled and transforming, and as I saw what was there (for the other reality is a telepathic state) we would collapse into each other's arms with the strained, exhausted laughter of lifeboat survivors. And then we would settle back, a few feet apart, to pursue the visions, the images, and sometimes, much later, the words.

But I've talked glibly about "the other reality," as if there were only one. The border I'm describing is a fearful place, the no man's land where schizophrenics, I believe, are helplessly suspended: immobilized – despite their best intelligence or will – by choice. I've mentioned the folklore – the freemasonry of close encounters, of leaks through that borderline. Most, in the end, become hilarious stories – because they are told by survivors. It's a demonology, all the same. When Charles Manson's zombies broke into that house in California and butchered Roman Polanski's pregnant wife, and scrawled *PIG* in her and her foetus's blood on the walls, she – Sharon Tate – was "high" on MDA. So, presumably, was her unborn child. That is horror. Not just squalor, not evil even, but horror.

One truth that we're even further from facing today than we were in the skeltering 60's, is that other, heightened worlds run parallel to "normality" all the time. We have glamorized serial killers and discovered child abuse. But the "quiet desperation" which Emerson ascribed to "the greater mass of humanity" can breed even stranger visions, as you will see, for that is what this story is really about.

And I must get back to that threshold above the beach. Guilt *does* get shaken off, and in its exhausting aftermath – which may last for six or seven hours – you are blessed with Vision, static and ecstatic: lambent, astonishing, harmonious. The Creation is so ineffably *lovely*, and even when the sand-atom gems by your feet combine in a pageant of ruined empires or human decay, your perspective is that of Time, which is to say, of God. You are a saint, or so you are lead to believe – a holy fool; and in your eyes Time is never linear. What will become, has already been, and so makes sense. Lovely, inevitable, affirmative sense.

"And Cancer blooms," wrote Carl Shapiro, "as simple as a flower." Across the threshold you accept that as truth, with no human irony.

You lie there, as the sand dances for you and through you: a guest in that boundless, miniature world; while outside, if you lift your eyes, the actual, physical world is enchanted too – a luminous, choreographed inscape of logs, sand, forest, clouds and waves.

This is where my story, in fact, begins. For onto the beach, from the North end, drove a white panel van. And that ludicrous, enamelled, chrome-trimmed, ungainly creature, with its headlight-and-grill cartoon face smirking, drove to within thirty yards of us, swung round to face the sea, and stopped.

It offended, but could not destroy. It blocked our view, but only one view. Even the sound of its motor could scarcely be heard through the surf. Yet there it stood, and wouldn't go away; its trembling exhaust merged with the sun-shaken glare of the sand in our staring, stoned eyes.

Scientifically explained, the world is enclosed by the screen of your eyeball, the sky vault is only the curve of your eye, the dancing currents of reality that the drug conjures up are just spasms and lapses of the optic nerve. We couldn't dispel the van, and there was nothing we could make of it but cartoon comedy. For Saints and Holy Fools do not give way to anger or irritation. And the van, of course, could not see us – two faces peering through the barricade of sun-bleached logs – besides, it had its back to us.

If it *had* seen us it would probably have moved considerately along: there were twenty more miles of good, empty beach for it. But if we'd got up and shouted (actually, standing up is physically close to impossible across that threshold), if we *had* made it aware of our presence, why it might have come booming up the strand, with its great, grinning face, and wanted to shoot the breeze.

So we lay low, pretended it wasn't there, and hoped it would go away.

The next thing I knew, as they say, the van doors opened. From the passenger side stepped down a lean, middle-aged woman in a green shirt and black jacket, and a scarf which seemed to combine both colours and whose loose end nagged at her face in the sea breeze. The driver was about the same age, and not much taller – stocky, in a cream-coloured anorak and grey pants. His hair, it seems to me, was sandy.

They walked to the back of the van, and the man opened the double rear doors. The engine was still running. He gestured towards the van's interior, and said something. His voice did not carry. The woman moved next to him, and craned forward, beckoning. A coaxing arm-movement.

After a moment, they both leaned into the back of the van, and helped someone climb out and down. The someone stood stiffly between them.

I don't know who or what we were looking at. Or what kind of mind was trapped inside that awkward, stolid body. I don't know if that someone had Down's Syndrome, I don't know if it was a boy or a girl. I would guess it was in its late teens or early twenties. It wore a cream anorak like the man's, and baggy grey trousers. A green tuque rode up high on its head, as if merely perched there.

Both of us were watching, despite ourselves, trying to filter out the dancing light and colours, the curtain-rippling of the pale clear sky, the trembling margins of the sea.

The man had his hand on the someone's shoulder. The woman had her hand on its arm. Both were chattering to it, animatedly, and gesturing past the idling van towards the ocean.

They led the someone along the passenger side of the van, and performed those gestures again. Then they stepped back, and stood by their respective doors. Their someone was immobile, staring out towards the offshore islands behind which, in a few more hours, the sun would go down.

The man and the woman waved their arms again, and shouted, gaily. Their voices just reached us, but not the words. But what they were saying was clear enough: "Go on," they were calling. "Walk, walk – it's lovely, enjoy yourself. You must."

Their someone squared its shoulders. I could sense it taking a deep breath, and releasing it like a sigh. It stood. And they waved, and called again. Another deep breath. And then it set out.

It didn't walk. It marched. That stiff, ungainly body, those uncoordinated arms, marching like a clumsy toy soldier, bravely towards the sea.

It *seemed* brave.

And the man and the woman climbed back into the van, and closed the doors.

Our eyes met – this was the bizzarest piece of theatre. Neither of us could laugh, but we couldn't turn back, either, to the illuminated scrolls at our feet. Something in the air, across the divide of the beach and the drug, insisted that we watch.

That world became suddenly two-dimensional to me. So that the clumsy marcher on the sand was moving diagonally upwards on a flat screen, across a three-toned painting of sky, sea, sand. I swear that I couldn't hear a single sound. My breath was held; I watched. And as the green tuque rose out of the grey sand-section of the painting, I realized that the figure, the toy soldier, the someone, was only thirty feet from the water, and that he was still going: innocent or not of what was unfolding, he was marching doggedly towards the sea.

I leaned forward and put my hands on a log. "Oh sweet Jesus," I thought, "I'm going to have to *do* something." I was racked with fear and responsibility; I had to get involved; adrenaline was at war in my cells with the cactus detachment of Mescalito.

Susan had hold of my arm. Our eyes met again. Her irises were flecked with yellow terrors. And then, as I braced myself to leap out onto the beach and run, shout, intervene, at the very moment those stiff, marching feet reached the water, the doors of the van flew open, the man and the woman rushed shouting down to the sea's edge, and there they embraced and hugged their someone, and stroked its face, and hugged again, and waved their arms, and laughed, and perhaps cried.

They led it back to the van, helped it up through the rear doors, and closed it in. They walked round, and climbed into their seats. Their doors shut. We subsided into our nest. And the van drove away.

The beach was empty. We turned to each other. In 1969 there was only one word that could compass a scene like that:

"Wow!"

Susan's fingers pushed into the sand and came up again coated with glimmering atom-flesh, snapping and spilling from her knuckles. "Did we just see what we just saw?" she murmured.

And that is my story, really – all of it; except that now, in the context I've given, it's become a story within a story, down twenty-five years of unpaved recollection, and I should close it out, and retrace that road to the present.

The truth is that Paradise had been tainted for me. Everything round me still pulsed and shivered with light and colour, but it was all scenery now. I was back at Long Beach, and the magic sand-carpet had dissolved.

So I got up and left, walking slowly, being very gentle with my body, while the beach, as the sun sank to my right, became a wide lunar landscape, where the shadows of pebbles were longer than trees, where tide ripples were mountain ranges, and where the sky and the sea glowed behind me like a soft and enormous butterfly wing.

Eventually I found my way back to the trail through the salal, and stood in the cabin's darkness, listening to my heart beat. I struck a match and stared at my face in the single pane window, and then lit the oil lamp. The flame was as shy as an eyelid, opening at last into a fishtail fringed with cobalt, vitriol and amber. I fell in love with fire, and knelt to light the woodstove. Each stick I chose was pregnant in my hands with an indwelling beauty and lineage.

But before I could light the kindling, I was struck with remorse. For Susan, back there on the beach, might feel deserted, betrayed.

I took an orange from the shelf, went down through the salal, and placed it, like a beacon, on a driftwood spar jutting out from the storm-line of logs, four feet above the sand.

I was "coming down." The stove was hot, I had a pot of tea made when she came in, laughing, holding up the orange like a trophy. She told me it had blazed at her across the mile of beach, calling her home.

She sat at the end of the bed, by the window, her hair the last silhouette on the darkening sky, with that glowing, segmented live jewel of an orange unfolding on her lap. As she peeled and opened it, she began to sing, quietly, a Jefferson Air-plane tune:

> *Lather was 30 years old today*
> *They took away all of his toys*
> *His mother sent newspaper clippings to him*
> *Of his friends who had stopped being boys*

I moved over to the bed – she handed me a section of the fruit, like a benediction, then another, with fond mockery, as a prize:

> *Lather was 30 years old today*
> *And Lather came home from the fun*
> *He looked at me eyes wide and plainly said*
> *Is it true that I'm no longer young*

We shared the warm godflesh of the orange and then, almost insubstantially, made love, guiding and intermingling the radiant molecules of ourselves.

Then we ate, and slept, and woke, and were gentle with ourselves as we walked, and gathered, and sat, and wrote in our notebooks through the next day.

And then we drove back, over two mountain ranges, to the world of paved roads and policemen and hospitals.

In that world, in *this* world, we keep ourselves sane and together, you and I, by sharing laughter and stories. All stories are fiction, but some tell the truth, all the same.

I found myself telling a true story like a lie. It was becoming a lie. I have told it again, by searching it out for myself, and this was it, and perhaps I have let it go.

"A TRAVELLER
CAME BY..."

About five days after he'd died, out on the Coast, Freddy came
knocking at my door. He was standing there in the darkness,
with the screen held open, and it took me a moment to know
him. "I don't believe it," I said, and I found his name on my
tongue. "How in Hell did you track me down here?"

I hadn't seen him for fifteen years maybe, though I'd heard
the stories, and I'd spent that time in two countries, three
provinces, more homes than I'd care to count.

He put his finger to his lips and slipped past me into the
house, shimmying away from my hesitant impulse to hug him.
"Don't tell anyone I was here," he murmured, and then stepped
into my living room. He looked about him and nodded slowly,
folding his arms. "You always find a home," he said, more to the
room than to me.

And it's true – if that's what he meant – that I've learned to
turn a new space into mine very quickly. A roof, four walls, hot
running water: bare, luxurious necessity, decked out with my
touchstones and tokens of memory, with the pictures and masks
and statuettes, the prayer-rugs and hangings, which this nomad
has gathered and hung onto. In the two months I'd been here the
little house had taken on the blend of lair and study which makes
me at home.

And now, like the breathing past, his name and features distilled from the misty Pacific islands where I had come to know
him, this thick-shouldered figure stood in my living room, a

thousand miles from the Coast, and seemed to take stock of my life.

I was surprised, and touched I guess, that he had remembered me. But there it is – I remember people, why should I expect them to forget me? And I do confess, I was wondering, too, *What does he want?* Why would he be here, down near the border, at the edge of the Cypress Hills? I'd never had trouble with Freddy, but his name spelled trouble to everybody who knew him.

He might want money; he might need somewhere to hide.

"So where are you heading?" I said. "Which way are you going?" Whatever the case, he'd made a detour fifty miles south of the Trans-Canada, on dirt roads mostly, to find this small town in its river-snake valley. Or had he come up from the States?

He turned, and his forefinger rose to his lips again: "Don't tell anyone I was here."

"You said that already," I laughed. "There's no one to tell, around here."

But he still didn't answer. There was something about his manner, something melodramatic and smug, as if he might twirl a cloak around him: *But soft, we are observed!* Yes, smug, as though he were fondling a secret.

"You want a drink?" I asked. "—or tea, coffee?"

"Tea's always good," and he filled his strong chest with air, breathing deliberately in through his nose, as I always remember him doing. He looked me up and down, with that knowing, nodding assessment of his, and his eyes passed over my shoulder to a mask that hung at the doorway. A Kwakiutl dance mask, *Bukwus* the Wild Man, one of my real treasures. He gave a small, soundless laugh, and stepped past me again, settling himself at the kitchen table, one leg thrusting out from his chair.

He didn't look different at all, I realize, which should have surprised me perhaps, but the surprise was all in his arrival. I was too busy reading his *tone*, his mood, I think, to focus much on his appearance. It was always the mood you watched for with Freddy. People felt he was dangerous.

Here he was anyway, in my kitchen; barefoot, at ease and smiling to himself. Nine-tenths, at least, of the time we had spent together had been at a kitchen table – as I warmed the teapot, I was back again in my narrow house-by-the-swamp, twenty-five years away across the straits of Hecate.

The first time, unannounced, he'd come visiting I knew nothing about him, yet I'd found myself wondering as he sat looking around, with one arm looped over his chair back, if what I sensed behind that compelling mask of a face was an incredulity – at himself, in this home; like a mountain bandit, lounging under safe-conduct in a residence, a tame fox scratching its ear in a henhouse. Mishka, my fey grey cat, jumped up on his knee as she did on each subsequent visit, and drowsed, while we talked, against the massive brown forearm with its faded jailcraft tattoo.

I looked now, as I had back then, for the con man at work. He seemed far less concerned with the impression he was making. And a quirk of amusement kept tightening his lips as though a private joke were unfolding.

I brought the tea things to the table and started to pour for us both. "Things going okay for you these days?"

"Oh, I've been through the changes," he said, eyes darting to mine for a moment. "Changing back, changing forth . . ."

He turned his cup slowly around with his finger.

"I've got some travelling to do," he said, with that half-surfaced smile at his lips again. "Got some connections to make, some debts to pay off, before I head home.

"Got something for you here," he said.

He leaned back and eased something out of his pocket. It was one of those fine-woven spruce-root pokes that some of the old Haida ladies still make. There was a design painted on it, a wolf perhaps, I'm not sure; garish blue as though it had been done in felt marker. Typical Freddy, I thought, and at once he looked straight up at me, into that moment we had long ago learned to laugh at, once we had named it, early in every visit – the ricochet, the skate between his black Haida eyes and my Celtic blues. No escaping the challenge, whatever the good will.

And the little spruce-root sack wasn't for me. He pulled out a plastic bag from it, and some blue zigzg papers, and started crumbling a golden bud onto the table.

He hadn't touched his tea. I sipped mine and watched his fingers in silence as he constructed a joint with the squinting concentration he'd have given to a carving. "You laid some hash on me that time," he said, "that I didn't get round to paying you for."

"C'mon, Freddy," I said, "that must have been twenty years ago," and I laughed. "There's a statute of limitations, you know."

"No such thing," he said. "Not now. Never was."

"Well, there is in my memory," I told him. I didn't want to smoke dope with Freddy; maybe I suspected a ploy to catch me off guard in some way.

He just held up the joint, a fat, humpbacked one, as if for my admiration. There was a book of matches beside a candle on the table. He lit the joint, took a quick triple-draw at it, and sat back while the smoke eddied down from his nostrils. His hand came towards me, proffering the smoke. "No, you go ahead," I said.

He leaned forward, took another deep draw, and held out the joint, daring me. Holding the smoke in, "Pelée," he said, or it sounded like "Pelée."

I thought of the killer volcano of Martinique, of the soccer star, of the weeping woman of Hawaii. I took the joint from his fingers. Maybe it was "Maui Wowie," the legendary weed of the seventies.

But you never knew with Freddy: sometimes he'd say things you couldn't work out at all; you'd wonder if you'd heard him aright, if maybe he'd just said something in Haida that sounded like gnomic English. Once, he turned to my daughter and said, "There's a hand inside your head," and she said, "I know," whether out of politeness or not, and he said "Room for two," and then went back to talking about the comet Cahoutec and the girl he knew in Vancouver who'd taken her grandfather's spyglass up Grouse Mountain to get a closer look, and got lost for three weeks.

I didn't really know – I still don't – what troubles Freddy had been in back then; people just hinted at things, for some reason. There was blood on his hands, no doubt, but whose blood? It does make a difference. I handed the joint back. "I'll pass now," I said. "I've got work to do."

"We all got work to do." He stood up, and held out the joint till I had to take it. "Another night gone to pot," he said.

If I'd made that old joke, I'd have felt white and foolish. I never will fathom how that works. Just the fact of self-consciousness, maybe. Meanwhile I was left holding the joint while he strolled off through my living room.

He stood in front of the bookcase in the corner, staring at my things. Arosi, Ashante and Sepik – the particular treasures on the top shelf are part of the medley that is, I suppose, my mind; I can only guess what secrets and memories they share with each other from their times before me, what whispery pidgin or macaronic they've evolved in the corners I've housed them in, what the carved faces see . . . .

But hanging on the wall above them is a necklace of eagle claws, the bird washed up on the sands below Tlell, the deerskin thongs and sachets sewed up by my friend Yvonne who shared that house-by-the-swamp with me then. A medley again: the thongs adorned with fragments of baltic amber, the pendant a bone harpoon point I had found near a long-dead village. And her patient work through the evenings at this love-gift for me, another power and memory.

Hung from the same nail, at the necklace's heart, is an argillite pendant, a sleeping raven, its beak tucked down upon its breast. Eagle and Raven, the great matrilineal clans of Haida Gwaii.

"Remember?" I said from the doorway. "The Sleeping Raven you gave me?"

He didn't look round. "You bought it," he said. "I sold it to you. Seventy-five bucks."

"I remember it as a gift, " I said.

"I couldn't sleep that night," he said, and his hand went out towards the carving, but did not touch it. "I got up before light and went out on the beach, and I watched a raven asleep on a hemlock branch. I went back to the house and sat on the steps and started to carve him. And after the people got up, I went back down the shore, and sat on a log with the tide running in, and got him finished."

It's a tiny thing, about the size of a thumb-joint, the feathers a pattern of scallops, the feet hooked around an invisible branch. Only the eyes, somehow open and closed at once, belong in the formal traditions of Freddy's people.

I went over and stood beside him. Through the reefer's aroma he smelled of the islands: the moss and the rain and the salt-barbed currents of cedar smoke. We stood, with our separate memories and the small finger-brush intimacies that come with sharing a joint.

He turned away. "Wish I had time to check out all the things I've made."

He crossed the room behind me and I whirled round, suspicious again, though of what I'm not sure. He sat down again, by the table; his casual way seemed to challenge me.

"Why no shoes?" I asked, as much as anything for something to say.

"My feet been in prison too long – look." He folded one leg across his knee, gripping the ankle in both hands to show me the sole. Unexpectedly slender, it was fissured with cracks and plateaus like an aerial photo. He flared and wriggled his toes, laughing at them. "Building some good calluses there," he said, putting his foot down again. "Like the Old People, eh?"

I wish I could remember more of what we talked about. What he talked about, that is. I wish I'd paid more attention.

I can blame the drug partly, I guess. The way my thoughts began, and then slipped out of sight, like carousel horses which I hoped would come round again if I waited long enough.

But I was also too taken up with *watching* Freddy. His face was ancestral, that's the only way I can express it: like a portrait that after two hundred years still offers the living features of the dead. A face you might see, too, in an Edward Curtis photograph. And he was more interesting to watch – or so I assumed from past experience – than to listen to: for he'd always spoken essentially to himself, though he wanted response and approval, and the criminal optimism of his plans was depressing after a while.

Oh, he talked about finding "a better handle on life," I know that. And he was going home with things to accomplish. Which I'd heard before.

But he said a lot more than that, and the subject kept changing. He was excited, intent, and I was just listening in.

"I can't keep up with you," I told him at last. "You're way ahead of me." He stopped, with that up-tilted chin that is part of the Haida language, a basic challenge, and I reached across the table to grab his hand, to say, *Hey, no offence: I'm just drifting.* His eyes were suddenly dangerous: *Don't touch me,* they said.

But then he laughed, as though the joke I'd been sensing throughout had at last broken through. He rubbed his hands along his thighs, "This is easy," he said. And looked up again, carefree and almost shy. "I gotta go."

It was so sudden. And I was totally relieved. I followed him to the door and held out my hand, expecting the centurion shake they'd all used in my time on the Queen Charlottes, but his palm merely glided across mine before he stepped outside.

I called out, *"Howah!"* thank you, the only Haida word from my tiny vocabulary that came to mind, as he jogged across my lawn into the box-elder shadows. I saw him jump onto the low retaining wall of my yard, up to street level, and he was gone.

I listened for a car, but heard nothing for five minutes before I went inside.

I was definitely stoned. I sat back down in my kitchen. He hadn't touched the tea I'd made him. I drank it for him; the drug was drying out my mouth.

I was reaching that state of lassitude where three, at least, of the Seven Sins become, if not friends exactly, no longer adversaries, when the phone rang on the wall just beside me.

I grabbed it without thinking, and at once regretted it. It had been a long time since I'd spoken on the phone under the influence, and if this wasn't a close friend I'd probably sound incoherent.

It was a woman whose first novel I was editing at the time, and I didn't yet know her well enough to discard my professional half-mask. But what was the point? My laboured efforts to concentrate and respond made me sound doleful, if not stupid. After two attempts to discuss structure and voice, I gave up.

"Look," I said, "this is a little hard to explain. Someone I haven't seen for years has just this minute left my house. He was here and gone so fast I can hardly believe he was here. He came in, sat down, smoked a joint and took off. But the point is, I'm completely roofed and I'm not going to make any sense tonight. I'll call you tomorrow, okay?"

She seemed merely amused. I hung up.

All I really wanted to do was turn off the lights, go and lie on my bed with the window wide open, and listen to the coyotes.

And doing that, I began to think about Freddy. It was easier to do now that he wasn't there in person, talking, insisting.

He was so potent, yet so lost.

Freddy could have been a wonderful carver if he'd worked on it. He'd get crazy, original notions and go at it like a fiend for a day or two till he was done. But then he'd slacken right off, for some reason or other: maybe he'd made enough cash, maybe people didn't respond to his work as he expected. And then he'd leave the islands.

A few generations back he might have been an innovator, a man with respect or an outlaw like the legendary K'uundong'a.

Who knows, given the Haida cosmology, he may have been all of those. But in this life anyway, he relied upon inspiration, on being in the mood, or on the need to turn something out for quick money.

With the deadly escape hatch of heroin.

Yet I was exhilarated by his visit, and grateful. I loved the thought, as I replayed it in my mind, of an artist revisiting something he'd made years ago, and remembering its making and the man he had been then himself. I could hug the fact that that had happened in my living room. And the sleeping raven seemed a treasure twice over.

Sleep came towards me in the soft, soft darkness like an ecstasy. The coyotes were crying in the infinite distance as my bones rocked and settled in my flesh, drifting down into forgetfulness.

So I was late to wake, and moving pretty slowly.

It had rained in the night. Everywhere down the lane, as I walked to the post office, there were lilac petals: plastered to the wet earth, floating on the rain-filled wheel ruts. At one point I saw below me the roof of the United Church and the quick flock of waxwings that were even then whistling above my head.

> *As by some puddle I did play*
> *Another world within it lay.*

I love it when poetry surfaces to the occasion. My head was clearing already. Old Thomas Traherne, whose poems lay undiscovered for two hundred years, and whose sense of Grace was the simplicity of childhood.

> *That through a little watery chink*
> *Which one dry ox or horse might drink,*
> *We other worlds should see,*
> *Yet not admitted be . . .*

Spring had come to stay: you could tell somehow, from the rain-washed air and the green creeping into the hills, there'd be no more killing frosts. I bounded up the post office steps, greeting other citizens, though I'd forgotten my keys and had to ask the postmistress to empty my mailbox. And I walked back down the lane in the sunlight.

One of the letters was from Susan, my oldest friend and adoptive sister, who also shared that house-by-the-swamp and writes marvellous letters. I opened it as I walked; when the sun is out I can read without glasses. The envelope contained a nine of diamonds playing card and a poem, as well as the letter which I read as I weaved and splashed absent-mindedly through the puddles.

Most of it described the wake for our old friend Robin in Victoria the previous Saturday. It was wicked, ironic and heartfelt as her letters always are. Then, as I crossed over to my house: *"When I arrived home after the 'service' there was a message on our machine from Henry in Masset . . . ."*

The words were for Stephen, her husband: an intimate, cryptic message between more-than-friends, and not mine to repeat, except for two lines: *"Freddy Y. kicked the bucket. Died of an overdose in an alley."*

I walked down to my front door. Opened it, went inside, closed it and leaned back against it like a TV actor.

Fairy tales end with a token – the ring or the flower or fragrance left behind from the dream time. But I didn't examine the ashtray, or the cups unwashed in the sink. I looked at my empty room – at the table and chairs, the space of blank carpet before my bookshelf, the carved, watchful faces – and waited to be spelled out of memory, like the kids in *Rewards & Fairies*, as if the pages of Susan's letter were the oak, ash and thorn leaves which erase impossible things.

I was still holding her letter when I started to laugh.

I looked over at the raven, asleep in his wreath of eagle's claws, and I saw – as clearly as I saw the room where I stood – the beach at Masset, as the sun comes up across the wide inlet, and the carver who sits there making a bird into stone.

WINDFLOWERS

Does everybody, I wonder, who doesn't die young, reach the place where imagination turns back on itself? Where instead of seducing the present, or teasing the phantoms of thought into nervous life, it seeks out the past, and lingers, to reinvent memory?

I started to realize, a year or so back, just how many fantasies, daydreams, brown studies of mine, were making their home in late puberty; as though the world of my sixteenth and seventeenth summers were mine to explore again. I could not get to sleep without them; they'd accost me sometimes in mid-afternoon.

Was this common Temptation, which others shrugged off, or had brief sport with, or spurned absolutely? Were the girls in my reveries (as there so often were) really Succubi, clothed in the flesh of old sweethearts?

Young sweethearts.

I could banish them, with a censoring effort of will, but I was not too sure that I ought to. They might be a turning away from life, but they seemed just as much to be making life over again.

It begins with intense recollection, a sudden immersion, complete repossession of that time and place. Not through one of those luminous moments which transfixed you at once, even as they occurred, already pregnant with meaning (for *those* images are obsessive, they detach themselves from memory, they're our language to ourselves), but with the forgotten beginnings of something, whose offer and promise you were blind to.

The shy old soldier behind the wheel: "Don't stay out in this rain. I can drive you back up to the road in the morning."

The fairy face staring back through the hawthorn leaves, below the rath.

Ailsa, naked, slipping towards the bed in her darkened room. Her slim, inclined body, her fleeting breasts against the dim curtains.

The girl with frightened, sad eyes across the railway tearoom.

The book left unopened by an aunt on the bedside table.

Marian under the lilacs: "It's so nice, do you love me?"

The node of horror in the nettles by the broken wall, swarming out in pursuit through the hollow beech woods.

The whirlpool of faces at nightfall, swirling and calling under the tide bridge.

Pauline wrenching away, buttoning her blouse, turning her coat collar up: "Why did you wait until now?"

The path to the dairy.

The letter from Jean.

You are still who you were, but you can make new words come out of your mouth, change the things that you do. You can give, and take.

You can mend.

I imagine an afterlife would be exactly this state of mind: revisiting, and exploring, the world that you made, or endured, that belongs to you only. ("He who kills a man" – a Talmudic gloss on the sixth commandment – "destroys a world.")

This was Meister Eckhardt's vision and version of Hell – the treadmill of living your life again, over and over – except that where there's Remorse there is Conscience, and if there is conscience the Imagination's at work. And at play.

The idea of Eternal Recurrence is so mechanical, cynical, and therefore too easily grasped – a smug undergraduate tag. It outlaws imagination, or denies its existence; when imagination's the essence of personal being.

Damnation's waste defies the imagination, or rather, is defied by it. Goethe redeemed his Faust, there was no other way.

Yeats wrote his Purgatory. Christ harrowed Hell.

There's a passage in a Romantic poem which starts: "For never did two lovers kiss but they . . ." and though I've lost the words the meaning is that they know they are not alone. A third person watches. I thought it was Keats, but I cannot find it. Who knows – when I was 15 or 16 half of my poems were pastiches of Keats – it could have been me. Whoever the poet was, I don't believe that he sensed some divinity, or spirit of place: it was his own, later self, drawn back from the future, that he felt. Each of his lovers did.

If there *is* a rough symmetry to our lives, like an island's profile – two spiritual adolescences, as well as childhoods – then perhaps there's a question of scale involved. Scale, and a curious balance. Do we reach back to reclaim that first version of where we now find ourselves, and having claimed it, feel free to inhabit and change it?

In Heatherlands, when I was four or five, a mile down the lane from my grandmother's cottage a caravan stood on the lawn of the big house. It was maroon, and shiny, with bright yellow trim on its wheels and its turkish gables, and staring white flowers painted along the buckboard. The poem in my mind was, *"I wish I lived in a caravan With a horse to drive like a tinker man,"* for tinkers and gypsies were almost the same to us – they both had their secret languages, Shelta and Romany.

I'd go past every day, to stand and look up at the wheels, and the door with its curtained window, and envy the children who had it for a play house. And sometimes at bedtime I fetched it away, and was trundled to sleep in its warm rocking darkness, with the smell of pipes and horses and handkerchiefs as the world stole by.

We left for England, and when next I came back I was almost 11. We drove in at night, and when I walked down in the morning the caravan had shrunk on its lawn. I stood, disbelieving, faced with the theft of my childhood. Even the colours had faded out of my reach. It was all scaled down to my image of Mr Toad, sprawled in the roadside dust, in the wake of progress, grasping a make-believe wheel in his hands: *"Oh bliss! Oh poop-poop! Oh my! Oh my!"*

It happens so slowly, but then, overnight, you're an outcast.

Must I live to be eighty, to reclaim those colours?

Five summers ago, my daughter came crying that one of the barn cats was in with the baby chicks. I ran down to the coop, and when I grabbed him up carelessly, to throw him out, he convulsed upon my hand, biting and raking it almost to the bone. By evening the tell-tale blue line of poison had crept up my arm; and at daybreak, with my armpit bloated and my eyelids on fire, we were driving the twenty miles of back roads to the hospital in Kincardine.

As the dust flounced behind us and the gravel rapped at the car's underbelly, I was aware of surfing on an almost unreal veneer. By telephone, and now in an automobile, I was crossing the miles to a hospital where, I'd no doubt, they could cure me. The fields wheeled away, the barns and the trees stood and turned. My disease, which had just begun, was already in my mind a mere inconvenient interval, to be endured and planned around – when in my parents' childhood, or in any of hundreds of places in the world today, I'd be facing the brief accident of my own mortality.

Cat Scratch Fever held sway for a day and a night, and then retreated before the drugs and the blood-thinners that were dripping into my wrist. I shared my room with an old bachelor who came in two or three times a year when his blood-pressure got out of hand. Lean and twinkling, with a permanent 12-year-old cast to his mind, he gave me Kincardine's history, from the 1930's, with tale after tale in the three days we spent together. Not a single personal memory – all gossip, wonderful hearsay: the thefts, adulteries, frauds and scandals, a murder even, a crime of passion at a lakeside dance pavilion; an indelible, tabloid map of a world ten miles wide and sixty years in the past. A great lad to pass time in Purgatory with. Even the expatriate English matron loved him. He had no interest in radio or television: when he wasn't talking, or when I was out of the room, shunting my tripod i.v.

pole down to the smoking lounge, he would settle back on his bed into cat-nap contentment.

I came in once and found him on his side, his hands at prayer between his knees, chuckling away to himself, his eyebrows doing a two-step. "Ah Dan," I said, "you're up in the haymow with that young girl again."

I say things, sometimes, without meaning to. Erratically through my family, from my mother and before her from Catherine, my great-aunt, there moves this unbidden thing, like a muddled and willful vein of the sixth sense. It is not that I know, or see things, but the words speak themselves. They are out – and I hear and understand them not a second before my listener does, if even then. I have found myself doing it on the phone, and the small catch of amazement or fear down the line has told me to listen to what I've just said. Occasionally it has taken years for me to understand what I spoke at a certain moment. The memory, like any other, comes back, redefined, in its own good time.

That old man on the hospital bed looked up with an owlish wonder, and then turned back, laughing soundlessly, to his long-ago dalliance. Of course, I will never know what kind of memory he was reliving: was it factual, embroidered, invented, or something of each? Did he come to it often and then, if he did, did it change?

He seemed to me utterly content.

Maybe some of us die, or at least cease to live, when the weight of our memories crushes us. When we can grasp nothing more. If so, then forgetfulness must seem like nirvana, like the promise of sleep at dawn to a rigid insomniac; and Heaven will be reached by the path of elimination. As a miser at death's door might go out in the sunlight to count and recover once more his bright store of lust and conquest, touching and naming each coin before he casts it down into the well.

It's a conscious assembly and shedding of self: making one's memories entirely one's own, and then choosing to discard them – as a novelist can say goodbye to a book, never think of it again, when it's wholly accomplished. Louise Bourgeois, in her eighties, said, "I am a prisoner of my memories, and my aim is to get rid of them."

But *"things,"* I found out, in a poem long ago, *"are not forgotten, just because people forget them."*

And a novelist does remember – remembers things, even, that were not in the finished book: still breathing things that were axed in the second or third draft. Flawed deeds, and words, and cadences, too, come back out of nowhere, too late to rewrite – and betray one's trust in oneself. A novel can no more be "wholly accomplished" than a life can. Things return, as I've said, in their own good, or bad, time. We remember so much less than we own, and may stray into ambush wherever the mind goes. As for the lies that we tell to ourselves or the world, however much we may come to believe them, there's a grinning, malignant imp behind each of their shadows, biding its time. And when the time comes, the imagination is powerless; it can only live more intensely the things it denied.

We cannot be judges of anyone else's conscience. It is, after all, the luminosity of the image – of the event distilled to an image – that haunts its bearer, and it is the effect of this haunting which is so private and compelling; though to anyone else the compulsion may seem wonderfully trite or foolish, and though the image, if ever confessed – the event itself – might be "folly in the world's eyes."

Much has been made of Augustine's stolen apple: its triviality (for all of the biblical echoes), the morbid nicety of the man's conscience. While the drama of Saul, unhorsed and blinded in the dust of the Road to Damascus, the savage, articulate catastrophe, the voice from the darkness, the poetry of God's interpreters – the *"sparks flying upwards,"* the *"kicking against the pricks,"* the Caravaggio stage-light – all this gives conversion and conscience the glamour of flaming gesture.

But Augustine lived in the mind, as did Columcille, Francis, Ignatius, Theresa, and the poisoned side of the apple was lodged in his throat.

At the end of my grandmother's garden, set into the wall where the wild fuchsias tangled and arched, was a disused turf-shed, with rubble-stone walls and a rusty tin roof which moaned and rattled at night when the wind blew in off the bog. Or perhaps that sound was partly its door, which leaned on one hinge, half in and half out of the threshold. There were bottles and newspapers in it, and the smell of the generations of peat and scraw, whose litter spread over the floor, ankle deep, and soggy around the doorway. Old cloths and belts, and nooses of hairy-ned binder twine hung from nails in the low rafters, and one leg-hold trap, its teeth blunt with rust, red as scabs.

It didn't appeal to me, as you'd suppose that it might as a hideout for a boy. It scared me. The creatures that hid under my bed, or that chased me down the staircase at home, must come from a place like that. And why did it cry out and rattle only at night? There were thick rambling-rose vines, gone wild beyond the fuchsias, and my job was to snap briar thorns off, like giant cat claws, as needles for my sister's wind-up gramophone. The blackbirds – *lon dubh* was my grandmother's name for them – would scold me each time I went out, and I started to hear in their voices a warning: that the turf-shed was breathing, and crouching, and its door was a mouth, and something was watching, and waiting to get me.

One afternoon I came over the wall, with the blackbirds' cries at my back, and decided that in the courage of sunlight I was going to close up that shed. Nobody used it, anyway; the last third of the garden, after the lazybeds, was a wilderness of brambles, and stones, and weeds; I was the only one who went there. I laid my briar-thorns on an upturned tin pail, and looked up at the door. Its grey planks angled above me, and I braced myself for its weight. It was almost as wide as my arms. As I lifted, it offered to swing me off my feet, but all at once it went meekly into place. The latch was intact. I closed it. There was blood on my hand.

I'd done something forbidden. The birds were distraught at my folly. Their cries filled the garden – the brown mother flew so close to my face that her wing touched my ear, and I ran back in terror, forgetting my handful of thorns by the path, convinced that the beast of the shed had me marked as its enemy, and would find its way out. My friends, the blackbirds, were telling me *flee.*

I would not go back out. My sister had to retrieve the thorns, and the songs on her gramophone could scarcely shut out the bird voices in my ears. They clamoured till dusk, and I woke to the noise of them still. But they were gone after breakfast. I went down through the garden, and the door of the shed was still closely shut up. I did not trust it, but I felt that the danger had passed. I could straddle the wall, unafraid now to turn my back on the grey door.

Sometime later that week there were people at the house, talking about news and geography, drinking tea from my grand-mother's best china cups. I know that the sinking of the *Athenia* came up, as it often did, and that my Aunt Kitty asked for the *Picture Post*, with the lifeboat photographs in it. No one had seen it for a while; it must be out in the old shed, with the papers. And I found myself following a friend of my uncle's down the garden, to show him the way.

I'd no fear when he pulled the door open, as wide as it would, to let in the light. It did not occur to me that the beast would leap onto me, or even slip out. With that big adult figure beside me, the smell of a man, and the light breaking over the back wall, I knew that the beast would be cowed and powerless. I was saucy with it; I lounged against the door-jamb, with my hand in my pocket, defying it.

The man crouched over the stack of papers, sorting them out beside him, and I saw past his shoulder, on a little ledge in the wall, the nest with its slate-blue eggs, smudged with grey, perfect and cold.

I stepped back into the garden where the birds sang no more.

I could smell the whole air. My shame, which was a call on my imagination, cast me out of Eden at the very moment I discovered it. The burning sword would forever stand in my way. The leap beyond myself into the birds' helpless hearts left me marooned in the green, ghosted world where the animals and the dead were the only watchers.

Yet this memory, I am certain, has never come back until now.

It cannot be recast, or fleshed out, or explored as it might deserve to be explored. Simply, I must be there; not to see with my own eyes, but to repossess the eyes, and the mind, I had then.

I shall not forget it again, though. And the time may come when I see or feel more than I did as that child. Or I may reach the place where imagination takes over.

But why do these things come back out of limbo, as a line from a poem (one's own, or anyone else's) may surface and speak to the occasion, as if murmured by an unnoticed guest from a chair in the corner? Do they come back to remind us, *inform* us who we are?

For the strangest thing, we all know, is how often the luminous past – the moments which turned and define us – leaves no trace whatsoever for those whom we shared it with.

I remember England, as though it never was. A town in the Yorkshire Dales where the sky opened out, where the jackdaws nested in every chimney and cried on the moor wind over the slates and the grey, cobbled square. I spent two summers there with my Considine cousins, climbing through bracken up to the heather ridges of Arkendale, or wandering under the wooded scars which hung over the River Swale.

My cousins were adults. I'd go out every day, alone, with a little two-barrelled shotgun to bring in rabbits and wood doves for the pot. But mostly I wandered, and sat under hedges, or in the shelter of the cliffs. A jay perched once on the toe of my boot, and I saw my face staring back from his shining black eye. A stoat ran across my lap, a woodcock allowed me to stroke her upon her nest, I watched for an hour as a chick broke its way from a curlew's egg, the tiny, toothed beak feeling blindly for the world outside. The gun was my passport to solitude and reverie, as smoking had become my excuse for breaking the bounds of my boarding school, to sit under hedges again, or in hay barns, dreaming my dreams.

When the south wind blew in up the valley, the hanging woods became wild and subaqueous, and I'd sit with my back to a beech tree or ash, drowned in the ghost of the old, scouring river, and watch the high branches swaying under the clouds.

All that is mine now; it belongs to each one of my senses. I could enter and explore it for ever in my mind. Yet it's only the setting, and try as I may, I cannot recover her name.

She was my cousin Paul's wife's younger sister, visiting like me, but from a city in the south. She had her own record player, she played songs from *Kiss Me Kate* and *New Faces* and *Carmen Jones*, and was often bored, and wore powder-pink lipstick to match her new mohair sweater, and teased up her hair with the sharp tail of her comb.

She could be ugly at breakfast, and savage for her turn at the bathroom, but sometimes she'd call me in after supper to lie on her bedroom rug and listen to her music, while she painted her nails and told me about London, and her friends there, and what they would do when she got out of school, and how Richard Burton had smiled at her from his car.

I was barely fifteen; she could not have been very much older; but I was a child in her eyes, and my own. When I offered to go with her, the four-mile walk to the bus stop up on the high road, she gave me her suitcase to carry and scarcely spoke as we walked through the town. She dreaded, no doubt, that someone might think I was "with" her. But once we were out on the foot-path across the fields, taking the shortcut down to the back bridge, she let me walk closer, and talked like herself.

I was shy and excited. I wondered if she would let me hold her hand. I was beginning to love the idea of love. I wrote poems for every girl that I knew, but I was also, of course, a crude little boy, and the first time that I had really kissed a girl I'd been horrified to find that my prick stood up. I had tried to smother it; I was nowhere near ready to combine love and lust. If I'd been taught to be crude, I had not yet learned to be tender – though my instincts all pointed that way.

I counted to seven, then to seven times seven. It had always been ugly to me as a child, a malign, awkward goblin, the only two-syllable one of the ten, always at odds with the others. But when I turned fourteen, twice seven, it had suddenly revealed its true grace, and changed from taboo into my lucky number. Seven times seven; I promised myself I would reach for her hand at that point, but I dared not, and after some minutes of scowling silence, I gave up on the whole thing and became a clown.

I could not be a man for her, but, oh, I could make her laugh. I ran on ahead, and circled back, and babbled and capered and mimicked till she was crying with laughter. Then she started in too, and grew helpless, and at one point I dropped her suitcase and we rolled on the grass and kicked at the sky, and were screamingly lost in our innocence.

I was Horatio at the bridge, and the troll from the *Billy Goats Gruff,* and when we turned off into Hartswell Woods I was the puppy who bounded on, up through the trees, and leaped out in ambush, pulling outrageous faces, completely drunk on attention and the power to delight. The woods were open, with beech roots snaking across the earth, and none of that true-forest reservoir of patience and mold; and because they face north, the flowers came late – where the hangers were hazy already with long pools of bluebells, there were only small pockets of windflowers here: white drifts in the shadiest places.

Back home my Aunt Kitty would put a few drops of ink or cochineal in a glass of water, and settle a handful of windflowers there, and we'd watch as the veins of the petals turned blue, or

red. But you had to take the glass with you out to the woods –
the flowers were so wild and delicate that they'd wilt as soon as
you'd picked them. I made a small nosegay now, all the same, and
proffered them, with much bowing and scraping, to my princess
of the forest.

Then I ran on in my glory, and at a break in the trees I turned
and called out to her, "Show me your breasts!"

I think about that. Why did I say "breasts?" For though "tits"
was taboo in those days, it was what we all used, out of adult
earshot. I heard an old farmwife once, in the chemist's store, asking for "tits for the babby's bottle" and marvelled to hear the
rude word used so plainly. I thought her delightfully ignorant.
"Breasts," though, had a strange inverted taboo of their own:
they belonged to the world of mothers, and infants, and to adult
lovemaking, maybe – which we thought of as brutal, or ludicrous
or, when it came to our parents, unthinkable. Breasts were what
I had glimpsed of my mother, lying beside her in bed as a child;
the sudden, mulberry-coloured dugs on her white skin. There
was shame in the word, and discomfort at what we weren't ready
for yet.

And why "Show me," not "Let me see." Why not, in the natural idiom of our tribe, "Let's see your tits?"

I see myself now, in that moment of glory betrayed, simply
standing there.

I was scared and appalled. I could not believe what I'd said.
And I set things in train quite beyond me.

"Come here," she said, and took one more step. "You just
come here."

I expected her breakfast face, but it was something quite different. I guess outrage and shame and hilarity warred in her eyes,
but I could feel her reaching for a new voice and manner – as an
elder sister, at need, will take on a mother's face.

She was scolding me, but even as she spoke she seemed more
to be thinking aloud. "When you're old enough," she said, "you'll
learn what it feels like to kiss and be held in someone's arms, and

you'll know when you can touch her, because she'll let you know without saying anything – and you won't need to ask."

I couldn't look in her face. I could not understand what her words were saying.

She dropped the little posy of windflowers, their stalks and limp petals spilled on the dry ground. And, crossing her arms at her waist, she pulled up her pink sweater over her head, and bent, and laid it beside the flowers.

She was looking out somewhere beyond me. She reached behind her, and then pulled the straps of her slip from her shoulders. Her hands held each other across her stomach. "You can touch them," she said.

"But I don't want to touch them," I heard myself crying.

And I think that the sun came out at that moment, or found a gap in the branches, for, "Look at your shadow," I exclaimed, and she turned where her shade bent from tree trunk to earth, and I was spared the challenge of that nakedness, with its staring blind eyes.

I could supply a woodpecker knocking at this moment; a wood dove calling; a dog barking in the distance. But what I do remember is seeing all at once how young she was, and lean, and awkward; and understanding, with my eyes on her slip and the twisted brassiere, with its scuffed laces – so clearly misfitting and handed down from her sister – that she was poor, that we were all poor; and that her dreams were beyond her reach.

And as though I had just discovered that a peeping Tom was watching, and saw with his eyes, I *did* want to touch her; the ugly sexuality of my age flooded that place even as she pulled on her mohair sweater, and I reached for her suitcase.

We went out through the woods in silence, I think, and struck off across the fields.

And was there a peeping Tom, under those trees?

I believe there was.

I think it was me. Me now. Me almost ready to ransack this memory . . . .

I do not remember the rest of the afternoon (though how simply I could invent it) – it has vanished, along with her name.

But what of *her* memory? It must have been something to her, that moment: she must have been changed by it, learned something of herself, treasured or giggled or cringed – maybe told her friends – for a little while. Though no doubt it's forgotten now – wherever she is, and whoever she may have become – is its echo still there, a part of her sense of herself and her judgment of others? Or is it still lying in ambush?

In any case – *"things are not forgotten . . . ."* They have their own lives, independent, who knows? of those who once owned them.

Perhaps the dense air of the Old World, its soft, haunted texture, owes something to them – overburdened, maybe, with the long weight of memories, but reminding us, now and again, who we are.

As pansies from a dead woman's vanished garden revert and grow small and upright, and change to violas; and later still, as the seeds go out over the wayside, you find them in sprawling rosettes, on waste places and sandy soil, from which peer a dozen or more bright miniature faces, the loveliest of weeds, which some people know as Johnny-Jump-Up but which still, in the shires and the townlands, go by the name of Heartsease.

A note on *Ithaca*:

I am not a Greek scholar. When I was 14 I read *The Odyssey* in translation, obsessively. It was mostly, of course, the Return, the Revenge, the "Battle" in the Hall which bewitched me.

Twenty years later, with a little more knowledge of Greek, and life, I came back to the story. Apart from wincing at the Whitehall English of that Penguin translation, I realized that the Battle was a Massacre, and wondered if the vivid brilliance of the violence might actually be expressing horror, not triumph. Questions like that have nagged at me ever since.

The Odysseus legends have been a playground since before Homer's time, and I'm sure will continue to be; but Odysseus wears Homer's mask (as Richard III wears Shakespeare's) and most revisionists have accepted Homer's premises. I don't know why they should (most Ancient Greek writers didn't), nor do I understand why the marvellous Sinbadery of the voyages has been solemnly co-opted in our time as a "Quest" archetype.

Demodokos has always been seen as Homer's self-portrait, and he may be. But I think Phemios is more eloquent about being a poet; I'm suggesting that he was Homer before he lost his eyesight.

There is evidence, outside *The Odyssey*, that Penelope was doing what I suggest she was. Far more evidence, anyway, than that Sappho was – and Sappho's "Academy," though a nineteenth-century invention, is still widely believed in.

This story is not just about *The Odyssey* but, apart from two words, the translated dactylic fragments are all by (or rather, attributed to) Homeros the Hostage, whoever he may or may not have been.

Some of these stories have appeared in the magazines *Exile: The Literary Quarterly, Brick, Grain* and *Knjizevna Rijeka.*

Two have appeared as chapbooks: "Telegony," from Punch-penny Press, Winnipeg; and "The Scream of the Butterfly" from Hawthorne Press, Victoria.

"A Traveller Came By . . ." was the title piece in my book of "stories about dying" (Thistledown Press) which also included earlier versions of "Keepsakes" and "Guardians."

Versions of "The Boar Hunt" and "Delivered By Hand" can be heard on the CD, *Virgo Out Loud* (Cyclops Press).

"Telegony" is a sequel, privately commissioned, to the story "Interact," itself available in *White Lies and Other Fictions + 2* (Exile Editions).

I'm more than grateful to the Saskatchewan Arts Board for a grant which gave me the time to work on this collection.